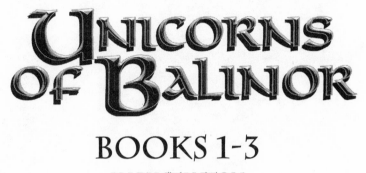

BOOKS 1-3

MARY STANTON

SCHOLASTIC INC.
New York Toronto London Auckland Sydney
Mexico City New Delhi Hong Kong Buenos Aires

ISBN 0-439-80843-X

The Road to Balinor, ISBN 0-439-06280-2, text copyright © 1999 by Mary Stanton. Illustrations copyright © 1999 by Scholastic Inc. *Sunchaser's Quest*, ISBN 0-439-06281-0, text copyright © 1999 by Mary Stanton. Illustrations copyright © 1999 by Scholastic Inc. *Valley of Fear*, ISBN 0-439-06282-9, text copyright © 1999 by Mary Stanton. Illustrations copyright © 1999 by Scholastic Inc. All rights reserved. Published by Scholastic Inc. SCHOLASTIC and associated logos are trademarks and/or registered trademarks of Scholastic Inc.

12 11 10 9 8 7 6 5 4 3 2 1   5 6 7 8 9 10/0

Printed in the U.S.A.   23

This edition first printing, August 2005

Cover illustration by D. Craig

CONTENTS

THE ROAD TO BALINOR

For Les Stanton,
A Hero All the Way.

1

It was dawn in the Celestial Valley. The sky over the Eastern Ridge slowly turned pink. Silver light spilled across the wooded hills, touching the waters of the river winding through meadows and flowering trees, then spreading over the herd of sleeping unicorns.

A few unicorns stirred in their sleep. All slept peacefully. The Celestial Valley was their home, and had been since time began. Above the valley, between the clouds that drifted across the sky, was the home of the gods and goddesses who had created them. Below the valley, by way of a rocky, treacherous path known only to a few, lay the world of humans. In this world, there was Balinor, the country guarded by the celestial unicorns, and then there was the land beyond the Gap. The Gap was haunted by mists and legends. A few chosen unicorns had been down to Balinor, fewer still had crossed over the Gap to Earth. But for thousands of years, after each sunrise in the Celestial Valley, all the unicorns had gathered shoulder to shoulder to form the rainbow. Then they would sing in the new day.

They wouldn't fully awaken until the sun itself peeked over the ridge. And for now, the sun was still out of sight behind the mountains. So they slept, curled horn-to-tail. Some lay back-to-back, others dozed peacefully alone under the sapphire willows that lined the banks of the Imperial River.

All of them slept but one.

Atalanta, the Dreamspeaker, was up early. She hadn't rested at all that night. Just before the sun came up, she gave up trying to rest. She trotted up the Eastern Ridge to the Watching Pool to wait for the visions she knew would come.

Atalanta was the color of the sky before moonrise, a soft blend of lavender, violet, and shadowy grays. Her mane, tail, and horn were of purest silver. She was the mate of Numinor, the Golden One, leader of the Celestial Valley herd. As the Dreamspeaker, Atalanta was the link between unicorns and the world of humans, just as twilight was the link between night and day. Atalanta, alone of all the celestial unicorns, could appear in the dreams of both humans and animals alike. And she was able to call up visions from the Watching Pool, where magic allowed Atalanta to watch events in the world of humans below.

The headwaters of the Imperial River formed

the Watching Pool. The Imperial River began as a small stream trickling from a curiously shaped stone spout in the side of the ridge. This stream flowed into a pond lined with amethyst rock, and from there into a waterfall that fed the Imperial River.

The jeweled rocks — found nowhere else in the Celestial Valley — formed a glittering violet circle, perfectly round and enormously deep. This was the Watching Pool. Atalanta stood there now, hock-deep in the velvety grass that lined the banks. Images formed there, one after the other. The visions remained for a few moments, then sank to the depths of the pool. They disappeared like snowflakes. Atalanta knew she didn't have much time to watch the visions.

She bent over the Watching Pool and touched her horn upon the water, saying, "I, Atalanta, Dreamspeaker, call forth the Princess of Balinor."

The silvery-blue water stirred clockwise, faster and faster. Small waves slapped against the amethyst rock. The waters dimpled, as if an invisible hand scattered raindrops on the surface. Then the whirlpool stilled, and an image formed in the water.

Atalanta saw a slender, bronze-haired girl twisted in pain on a hospital bed. Her legs were bandaged from knee to ankle. "Arianna!" Atalanta called. But the girl made no answer. She slept; a deep, unnatural sleep that Atalanta's dreams couldn't reach. So Atalanta had been right. Arianna had been gravely hurt.

3

Atalanta's purple eyes filled with grief.

The Dreamspeaker touched her horn twice more on the water. The girl in the hospital bed faded into the depths of the Watching Pool. A new vision formed.

A unicorn stallion knelt in a dark horse stall, head bowed so that his muzzle touched the ground. His coat was bronze, the same hair color as that of the girl on the hospital bed. Atalanta knew him: He was the Sunchaser, Lord of Animals in the world of humans, Bonded to Arianna, and kin to Atalanta herself. Not so long ago, Atalanta watched the Sunchaser, tall and proud down in Balinor. Now he lay wounded on the other side of the Gap. There was a bloody stump in the center of his forehead where his bronze horn once had been.

He groaned once, enduring a pain-filled sleep.

"Sunchaser!" Atalanta called.

The great unicorn raised his head. Atalanta quivered. His bronze horn was gone! A cruel white scar was the only reminder of his former glory. His dark brown eyes were dull. He dropped his head onto the stall floor and lay still. He had heard her Dreamspeaking, Atalanta was sure of it. But he no longer understood the Unicorn's language — he could no longer speak!

Two tears slid down Atalanta's cheeks and dropped into the water of the Watching Pool.

The image of the bronze unicorn sank. Atalanta held her breath, reluctant to see what she had to see next. She shook herself all over, scattering a flowery scent through the cool air. The Sunchaser, greatest of those unicorns who roamed the world of humans, lay broken beyond the reach of the Celestial Valley herd; Arianna, the lost Princess of Balinor, endured the pain of mangled legs, not knowing who she really was. Atalanta couldn't bear the horror of what would next appear in the Watching Pool.

But she had to know: Did Entia, the evil Shifter, know where the Princess and her wounded unicorn were hidden? And if he did, what terrible vengeance would the Shifter seek?

2

$\mathcal{A}$rianna Langley opened her eyes to the dull green of the hospital ceiling. As dim as it was, the light made her head hurt. Her stomach was empty and her throat was raw, as if she'd thrown up after being sick.

"Feelin' better, honey?"

Ari turned her head. This was a mistake. The room swayed, and her stomach lurched.

"The anesthetic made you sicker 'n a *dog*."

A fat woman sat in a chair next to her bed. Large. Large and familiar. Ari narrowed her eyes, trying to focus.

"It's Ann," the large lady said helpfully. "The doc said you might have a little trouble rememberin'." Ann was dressed in blue jeans, a red sweatshirt, and a tentlike denim jacket. A little embroidered horse galloped across the jacket's breast pocket. Ari's head swam. It wasn't a horse — it was a unicorn.

6

Ann chuckled nervously. "You recall anything at all, honey?"

"My name. I remember my name." She rested her head against the pillows. Her stomach was feeling better now. "Arianna Langley."

Ann didn't say anything for a moment. Then, "Right you are, sweetie."

"What happened to me?" She raised herself off the pillow, which was harder than it should have been. It was as if she was pushing a dead weight. She looked down at her legs. Both of them were wrapped in casts. "What happened to me!" she gasped.

Ann patted Ari's hand. "You just rest a little bit now. I'm goin' to find the doctor and she'll explain the whole thing. It's just lucky you weren't hurt worse, that's all."

Ari fell back onto her pillow. A confusion of memories hit her. A tunnel. The smell of dead and dying things. The sound of black flies buzzing. A great bronze four-legged creature plunging in front of her. "Chase!" she shouted suddenly. "Where's Chase?"

"Shush-shush-shush!" Ann's face was pale. She looked nervously over her shoulder. "Chase is fine," Ann said. "It's a miracle, really. I thought that poor . . . uh . . . horse was a goner. But he came out of the accident with a big ol' bump on his head, and that was about it."

"Chase is a horse?" Ari frowned. "That's

not . . ." She trailed off. Her head hurt. And she couldn't remember a thing about who she was or where she'd been. Just her name . . . and the tunnel. She turned her head so that Ann wouldn't see the tears. Her hair lay spread across the pillow, the bronze gleaming dully in the indirect light. There was something familiar about the color of her hair. That color was hers, but it also belonged to someone, something else. Chase! The Chaser! "Chase?" she asked. "Chase is my horse?"

"Horse," Ann said firmly. "He's right at home, in his stall at Glacier River Farm." Ann heaved herself to her feet. Her eyes were small and brown. She gave Ari a thoughtful look. "He's gonna be just fine except for that wound on his forehead. We had the vet take care of that."

"Good," Ari said doubtfully. "A vet is taking care of him."

"Best vet we've got!" Ann said cheerfully.

"What happened to him?" Ari asked.

"Oh, jeez." Ann ran a chubby palm through her scant brown hair. "Don't you fret. I'll go get the doc. Now that you're awake, we can talk about gettin' you back home, too."

But the doctor didn't hold out much hope for going home, at least not right away. She was a tall, neat woman with blond hair pulled into a tight bun at the back of her neck. Her hands were cool and sympathetic on Ari's aching head. She smiled at

Ari, took her pulse, and gazed intently into her eyes with a penlight. "Can you sleep a little now, Ari?" Her voice was kind.

"Yes," Ari said.

"Are you in a lot of pain?"

"No," Ari lied.

"Hmm." She bent over and examined the casts on both legs, one after the other. "I'm going to give you a mild painkiller, okay? Then sleep if you can. Sleep's the best thing for you right now." The doctor took a small syringe from a collection of instruments on the bedside table and slipped the shot into Ari's arm. The needle was so thin Ari hardly felt the sting at all. In a few moments, the terrible ache in her head and legs receded, and Ari sank gratefully back onto the pillows. She could sleep now. And suddenly, that's all she wanted to do. Sleep.

The doctor drew the curtains around the hospital bed and left Ari alone. Sleep began to drift around her. "Retrograde amnesia," Ari heard the doctor say to Ann. "I'm surprised she even remembers her name. She seems to recall a few things about her life before the accident. But it's bits and pieces, nothing more. It's going to take a while. And I have to tell you, Mrs. Langley, her entire memory may never come back."

"She's all right in other ways, though?" Ari heard Ann ask.

"Except for the two compound fractures of the lower legs." The doctor's voice was dry. "She's going to take a while to heal."

"Will she be able to walk?"

"I don't know." The doctor hesitated. "There'll be scars, of course. And perhaps a permanent limp. But your foster daughter's very fortunate, ma'am. She's not going to lose either leg. Not if I can help it."

Lose my legs! Ari thought. *No! NO!*

Sleep came like a wave of dark water. She sank beneath it gratefully. She didn't want to think. Not of the past, which she couldn't recall anyway, or of the future, which she feared.

Arianna woke up. The slant of the sun through the window told her it was late afternoon. The pain in her legs was dull, constant but bearable. She made herself calm and tried to think.

She was Ari Langley. She was thirteen. She'd been in the hospital for several days, maybe more. There'd been an operation on her legs.

She had a horse named Chase. She had a foster mother named Ann. And she must have a home, this place called Glacier River Farm that Ann had mentioned.

None of this seemed right. But Ann had said it was right. And Ann was her foster mother. That was what the doctor had said.

But who was Ari Langley? What had happened to her?

10

She didn't know. She couldn't recall. There had been some sort of tunnel, hadn't there? And an accident. But even those memories, fragmented as they were, didn't tell her who she was or why she was here. Or where she was going. Panic hit her. She was so alone! She didn't remember anyone!

"Calm down," she murmured to herself. "Keep calm." She clenched her hands and relaxed, deliberately. She would take things one at a time.

Okay. She was in a hospital bed. The sheets were clean and smelled of starch. A nightstand was on her left, a plastic chair on her right. The room was — how large was the room? And there was a window. So she could see out. Perhaps discover what this strange place was.

3

*talanta saw Arianna lie back in the hospital bed and drop into a deep sleep from the drug she had been given by the doctor. Then the image disappeared as fast as a candle blows out. Atalanta reared in distress. The princess didn't know who she was! She barely remembered the Sunchaser! And now the visions in the Watching Pool were failing. Was this the Shifter's work? His evil magic had never before worked in the haven of the Celestial Valley. Only in Balinor. And the celestial unicorns had helped send Arianna and her unicorn to safety on the other side of the Gap — where they should have been safe from the demon Shifter's work.

Driven by fear, Atalanta struck the water in the Watching Pool three times with her silver horn. She had to find out! She chanted the words to the water over and over again until finally she saw Ari, sitting upright in a wheelchair.

Atalanta wasn't sure how much time had passed on the other side of the Gap. It could have been minutes — it could have been days. Arianna was talking to Anale, one of the two servants Atalanta had commanded to attend Arianna on the other side of the Gap. She heard Arianna call her Ann.

Atalanta calmed down. Perhaps things were going to be all right after all.

Suddenly, unbidden, the waters of the Watching Pool darkened to black. A tiny whirlwind appeared at the bottom of the pool. It rose swiftly through the water and burst into the air. It was a vision of black flies! Thousands of them, spinning in a vicious vortex of spite and hate. Atalanta forced herself to stand. Black flies were terrifying to her and to her kind. There had been times — too many times! — when the evil made by the Shifter turned into swarms of stinging flies, filling the unicorns' ears and sensitive noses, blinding their eyes.

For now, the swarm was only an image. No actual harm could come to the herd through the Watching Pool. Just the terror of the visions.

The flies filled the water from edge to edge, then disappeared.

Atalanta took a deep breath and looked into the waters.

She saw an iron gate, spikes reaching to a black and threatening sky. An ominous smear of dark, dirty clouds drifted behind the gate. The

13

smear billowed and shrank, then shifted into a towering pillar of fire and darkness. Sickly yellow-green light wheeled in the center of the pillar. Gradually, the light resolved itself into a lidless eye. There was a face and form behind the Eye, but yellow-green clouds of smoke obscured them. All Atalanta could see was the lidless socket, the pupil blazing red.

The Eye of Entia, the Shifter!

The Shifter was enemy of all humans and animals in the worlds above and below the Celestial Valley. A demon — or worse! — whom no living being had ever seen. A ghastly presence that could shift, change shape, look like friend or foe, and no one could tell the difference. The only safety humans and unicorns had against the Shifter was that he couldn't hold a shape — any shape — for more than a few hours.

No one really knew the nature of the Shifter's Eye. Some said it was a part of the ghoul himself, split off in the time before animals could speak. Others said it was a grisly servant, created by the Shifter to spy on all those that he considered his enemies.

The area around the demon-red pupil was a wounded white, filled with red veins engorged with blood. The fiery pupil rolled in the socket, searching for prey.

And then the voice of the Shifter called for the Princess of Balinor. *"Arianna!"*

It was a huge, hollow voice, with the timbre of dull iron. It filled Atalanta with horror.

"Arianna!"

The Eye rolled as the voice called. Searching, while its Master distracted Atalanta with his calling.

The Shifter's voice echoed a third time, filled with a horrible coaxing.

"Arianna!"

Atalanta shivered. She struck the water sharply, one decisive blow that made the waters part and foam over the Shifter's terrible form. The dreadful Eye winked out. The Shifter's voice sounded farther and farther away, still calling for the bronze-haired girl. Finally, the voice was gone. The waters of the Watching Pool shone clear.

But now Atalanta knew why she hadn't slept last night. She had thought the Princess would be safe in the place where the unicorns had sent her. Instead, the Princess and the Sunchaser were in danger worse than they had been before. They were both wounded. They were separated. And the Shifter's Eye searched on. Atalanta knew that what the Shifter wanted, the Shifter got. He never gave up.

The events in the Pool meant sad news for Numinor, the Golden One, King of the Celestial Valley herd.

Atalanta left the banks of the Imperial River and walked through the meadow to the Crystal

Arch. This was the bridge between the Celestial Valley and the worlds above and below. This was where the rainbow was formed each morning, and where the unicorns sang in the new day.

Hooves whispering in the scented grass, the unicorns lined up under the Crystal Arch, ears alert, tails high, manes waving gently in the light breeze. Their horns shone and their glossy coats gleamed in the tender light of the fresh morning. There were hundreds of unicorns, one for each of all the colors of the Celestial Valley and all the worlds above and below it. Each unicorn made a separate part of the rainbow, from the violet Atalanta herself to the crimson Rednal of the Fiery Coals.

By custom, they faced the east. They waited for Numinor, the Golden One, lead stallion of the Celestial Valley herd. And as the sun's rim cleared the top of the Eastern Ridge, the stallion himself came down the mountain.

Numinor was the color of the sun at high noon. His shining mane fell to his knees. His tail floated like a golden banner. At the base of his golden horn, a diamond sparkled brighter than the sun itself. This jewel — like the jewels at the base of all the unicorns' horns in every part of the Celestial Valley — held a unicorn's personal magic.

Numinor trotted powerfully over the rocks and brush that lay on the side of his mountain. He halted in front of the rainbow ranks and arched his neck.

"I greet the rainbow," Numinor said, his voice like a great bronze bell.

"We welcome the sun," the unicorns said in response.

And then they all sang the first part of the Ceremony to Greet the Sun, as they had from the beginning of time:

"Red and yellow, orange and green
Purple, silver, and blue
The rainbow we make defends those we guard
In Balinor's cities and fields."

And Numinor asked, "When will we cross the Crystal Arch, to walk to the earth below?"

"When the dwellers of Balinor need us!" the unicorns responded.

Then they turned to the rising sun, toward the One Who Rules humans and animals alike. They pledged in a mighty chorus: *"We guard life! We guard freedom! We guard peace!"*

The Ceremony to Greet the Sun was over. Most of the unicorns dropped their heads abruptly to the grass and began to eat, which was their favorite occupation unless there was work to be done below. Numinor nodded to Atalanta and she approached. It was time to talk.

"Any news?" Numinor's eyes were wise and kind.

"It's very bad," Atalanta said. "With the help

of the resistance movement in Balinor, we sent the Princess through the Gap to live in safety at Glacier River Farm. The Sunchaser went with her, of course. But things went wrong. She's hurt. And there's worse."

Numinor's golden eyes widened. There was alarm in his deep voice. "Worse than the Princess's injury? How seriously is she wounded?"

"I can't tell. Not from here. She's alive. But her legs have been broken."

"And the Sunchaser? He is not . . . dead?"

"He has lost his horn, and the jewel that holds his magic. He has lost the ability to speak. I called to him, Numinor. I know he heard me. But he didn't understand me! What's worse, the two of them are separated. She is in a human place, with Anale and Franc to guard her, as we planned. "

"And Sunchaser?"

"He's at the farm. As we had hoped. But he is lost to us."

Numinor closed his eyes and breathed out hard, as a stallion will when he is angry. For a moment, he said nothing. Then he said, "The Sacred Bond between the Princess and Sunchaser? Does the loss of his horn and jewel mean he is deaf and dumb to the Princess, too?"

Atalanta sighed. "I don't know. A great deal depends upon Arianna herself. We've never sent a Bonded Pair through the Gap before, of course. And the Princess and the Sunchaser are more than just a

Bonded Pair, they are the source of bonds between all humans and animals in Balinor."

Numinor tapped his foreleg impatiently. He knew this. What he didn't know was what the consequences would be if the bond between the Sunchaser and the Princess was broken. For generations, the Royal Family of Balinor had dedicated the firstborn Princess to a unicorn from the Celestial Valley. The bond between the two was a unique magic, a magic that created the friendships between humans and animals in the world below.

"Atalanta? Do you know what may happen?"

She shook her head. "I'm worried, Numinor. The very nature of the Shifter's magic seems to be changing! He — or something — snatched the vision right from the waters of the pool! It took me many moments to get it back."

"But you did."

"I did. But I was *not* able to see what happened to Arianna for far too long a time."

"But when you were able to see again?"

"She seemed to be fine." A line of worry appeared between her eyes. "I think."

"Entia the Shifter? Our enemy?" Numinor half reared, his forelegs striking the air as if to strike at the Shifter himself. "Does he dare to attack our own?"

"He has sent his Eye to look for them. As far as I can see, he has not found them yet. I doubt he knows how to get through the Gap. But if we discov-

19

ered how to get Arianna and the Sunchaser to Glacier River Farm, it won't be long before he figures it out, too."

Atalanta's mane drifted in front of her face, obscuring her violet eyes for a moment. "Who knows what will happen then? Our magic is limited on the other side of the Gap. I thought his evil was, too. Now I am not so sure. The loss of visions from the Watching Pool is not natural. And I have no idea what happened to Arianna between the time I saw her fall asleep in the hospital and when I saw her in the wheelchair. But I do know this: Without Arianna and the Sunchaser, the animals in Balinor will begin to lose their ability to speak. And when that happens, there will be chaos. If the bullocks can't be asked to pull the plow, there will be no crops, and eventually no food. If the Balinor unicorns can't be told where to carry their riders, the army won't be able to fight! Balinor will be in the Shifter's power.

"And then . . ." Atalanta turned to face the sun. Her horn gleamed with a hot, pure light. "The waters of the Watching Pool will go dark. Humans and animals alike will be forced into slavery to serve the Shifter's will. Then, Numinor, the Imperial River will dry up, and the Celestial Valley will wither. The Shifter will attack us here. And if we lose . . ." Her voice trailed away.

Atalanta's deep purple gaze swept the lovely valley. The sapphire willow trees were in full flower.

The meadow was thick and green. Two unicorn colts skipped in the sunshine and sang. She said, so softly that Numinor could barely hear her, "All this will be lost."

The great stallion looked toward the sun. His voice was grim. "It's what the Shifter wants, Atalanta. Chaos. The animals of Balinor used as slaves and worse. So he can rule totally and without opposition. He has already kidnapped the King and Queen. Hidden the Princes. All this before we could act. We thought that sending Arianna and the Sunchaser through the Gap would at least ensure that the humans and animals of Balinor could still speak together. If they cannot, if the two races cannot communicate, there is no way the Shifter can be overthrown."

Atalanta stood close to Numinor. He smelled of fresh grass and clear water. The terrible Eye was gone, but it seemed to her that a faint scent of dead and dying things still drifted in the air. "You know the law, Numinor. I cannot cross into the Gap. Not unless Arianna and the Sunchaser summon me. I can only appear to her in dreams. That's all. If for some reason she cannot bond with the Sunchaser, we are in terrible trouble indeed."

"There must be something we can do, Atalanta."

The Dreamspeaker bowed her head in thought. "There may be one thing, at least. If I can find the Sunchaser's jewel and get it to him, it may help him, and Ari, too. The jewel is a crucial part of the bonding, Numinor."

"I know that," the stallion said testily. "But where is it? And how will you get to the Sunchaser? And how will he know what to do with it when he does have it?"

"Leave that to me."

"I have left it to you. I've left it to you and look what's happened!"

Atalanta looked at him, a long, level look. "Do you wish to quarrel, Numinor? After all these years together? It's to the Shifter's advantage to have us at each other's throats."

"You're right. I'm sorry. But this . . . our whole way of life! It could disappear in war!"

"I will do all I can do. But I have to act now. The Shifter may have thought of it himself. If he has . . ." She closed her eyes. "I won't think about it. Not now. Leave me, Numinor. I have work to do. I have to send someone to help them."

4

Ari jerked from her deep sleep. Was that a sound of bells? She blinked. Time had passed. She didn't know how much. Suddenly, she knew without a doubt there was someone else in the hospital room with her.

Instinctively, she grabbed for the heaviest weapon she could find — her water pitcher. She held her breath. Her hand tightened on the pitcher. Whatever this danger was, she was ready.

A dog trotted around the side of the hospital bed and thrust its cold nose under her hand. Ari breathed out in relief. The dog was friendly. She could tell that right away. It was a male collie with a magnificent gold-and-black coat. The ruff around his neck was creamy white. His head was elegantly narrow, and his ears were up. A white blaze ran down the middle of his tawny nose.

Ari ran her fingers gently over his head, then snuggled them deep in his ruff. If he had a collar, she might be able to find his owner. Yes, there it was, a thin chain wound deep in the fur. Was that what had made the chiming sound? She fumbled for a minute, then tugged it free.

A necklace, not a collar! She held it up. The chain was made of a fine silver and gold metal. Each link in the chain was a curiously twisted spiral. A ruby-colored jewel hung at the end, as large as her thumb. The late afternoon sun struck crimson lights from the jewel. "Well!" Ari said. "Your owner must miss this!"

The dog barked and pawed urgently at her hand.

"Shall I keep it for you? It might get lost if you have it. And we'll give it back when we find your master."

He panted happily at her, then licked her wrist with his pink tongue. Ari slipped the chain over her neck. The ruby nestled against her chest. It was warm, perhaps from being snuggled in the dog's fur.

"Who are you?" Ari asked softly. "And what are you doing here?"

The dog nudged her hand with his head. Suddenly, he turned to face the door to her room. A low rumbling began in his throat. It rose to a growl, then a snarl. The door swung inward, and a nurse Ari didn't know walked into the room. He was pushing a wheelchair. He stopped at the sight of the menacing dog.

"Wow," he said. "Hey." He lifted both hands,

24

either to keep the dog away, or to show that he didn't mean any harm. "Don't make any sudden moves, Miss Langley. You just keep calm." He edged sideways into the room. The dog swung his head as the nurse came closer. The snarls increased. "Now look, Miss Langley. I know you can't get out of bed, but you can cover your head and chest with the pillows, okay? I'm gonna have to call Security. I can't handle a dog this big by myself. But you're going to be all right. Just stay calm."

"I am calm," Ari said. "I'm just fine." She tapped the dog lightly on the head. "Easy, boy. Easy."

The growls stopped. The collie turned and looked up at her, as if to say, *Are you sure this is okay?*

"I'm sure," Ari said. "Lie down, boy."

The big dog lay down with a thump.

"It's *your* dog?" the nurse said in astonishment. His face turned red with embarrassment and anger. "You can't keep a dog in here!"

The door behind him banged open. Two uniformed men rushed in. Behind them were Ann and a thin man with a worried face and a long brown mustache. The collie leaped to his feet, then backed protectively against the bed, staying between Ari and the others.

"Linc! Lincoln!" Ann said. "There he is! Come here, boy. Come *here*! Frank! Do something!"

The worried-looking man dropped to one knee and began to chirp, "Here, Lincoln. Good doggie. Good doggie."

The dog turned to Ari, ignoring them all. There was a question in his deep brown eyes. Ari twined one hand deep in his ruff.

"He jumped in the car when we left the farm," Ann explained to the security guard. "Then he jumped out when we got to the hospital and ran off. I don't know how he knew Ari was here. He's always been her dog, and none of us can do a thing with him. Lincoln!" she added despairingly. "Come HERE!"

"Lincoln," Ari said. "Is that your name?"

He barked. Ari's hand went to the neck of her hospital gown. The ruby lay warm beneath her hand. If the necklace belonged to the collie's owner — then the jewel was hers?

"You don't remember Lincoln?" Ann burst into tears. Frank patted her awkwardly on the back. "Oh, Ari. Oh, Ari!" Ann sobbed.

"I don't care if it belongs to the President of the United States, that dog has got to go," the nurse said. "Here, you two guys are with Security, right? Take him out of here."

Lincoln growled. He rolled his upper lip back, showing his sharp white teeth. The two security men exchanged a nervous look. One of them cleared his throat. "Ah," he said, "I don't think this-here is in my job description. I don't think it is. No-sir."

"It doesn't matter," Ann said impatiently. She wiped her nose with the back of her hand and

26

sniffed. "Ari's coming home with us now, anyway, and the dog goes wherever she goes."

"You know the doctors don't think she's ready to go home," the nurse said in a fussy way. "If you two were responsible foster parents, you'd keep her right here. Where she belongs."

"Responsible foster parents don't run up hospital bills they can't pay," Ann said tartly. "And we've made some arrangements. A friend of ours suddenly showed up this afternoon, and she's going to stay with Ari as long as we need her. She's a medical person, a veterinarian. Her name is Dr. Bohnes. You remember Dr. Bohnes, Ari?"

Ari didn't. She shook her head. All at once, an image of a short, stocky old lady with bright blue eyes and white hair popped into her head. As if someone or something had sent the image to her!

"Well, you will," Ann said in a positive way. "She's a very old friend of yours, milady, I mean Ari." She turned back to the nurse. "So you see? We can take Ari home now. Dr. Bohnes has been given all the instructions needed for her therapy. She'll get the best care we can give her. Come on, Ari. Let's get you *home.*"

Ari allowed herself to be helped into the wheelchair. Ann draped a light jacket over her shoulders and a cotton throw over her knees. Then the nurse pushed the wheelchair down the long corridor and out into the sunshine. Lincoln walked gravely by her side.

27

Free of the hospital at last! Ari blinked in the bright light, at the cars in the parking lot, a plane flying overhead, the smell of gasoline, the crowds of people. Ann explained everything Ari saw. Each time Ari asked and asked again, she felt more desperate. None of this was familiar. None of this was *home*. But she had no idea of what *would* be home. Ann and Frank helped her into the van. They were on their way to Glacier River Farm.

Ari kept a tight hand on Lincoln's ruff and tried to fight her fear.

Frank lifted Ari onto the backseat and folded the wheelchair down to store it. Ari held on to the overhead strap and gazed out the window all the way to the farm. They passed quickly through the city and out onto a huge road that seemed to end at the sky. "The Thruway," Ann explained. "The farm is only twenty minutes from here. Do you remember yet?"

Ari remembered nothing. She held on to the collie as the van went down an exit ramp and turned onto a small deserted road. They passed fields of corn and purple-green alfalfa. Finally, they came to a long stretch of white three-board fence. A sign read GLACIER RIVER FARM, with an arrow pointing away from them toward the east.

Frank turned into a winding driveway made of gravel and stone, and they bumped along toward a large gray farmhouse standing on the crest of the hill. Long gray barns with green roofs spilled down the hillside. Ari could see horses in the pastures, grazing quietly under the sun.

"You'll want to see Chase first, I expect." Ann turned and looked at Ari over the passenger headrest.

CHASE! Ari's heart leaped at the name. Her hand tightened on Linc's ruff. He whined in sympathy. The van bumped to a stop in front of the largest barn. Ari waited patiently while Frank carefully set the wheelchair up on the gravel drive. Then he reached into the van and hoisted Ari into the chair with a grunt of effort.

"Watch her legs, Frank," Ann fussed. "Take it easy, now. And don't push her too fast!"

Frank rolled the chair into the barn. Ari took a deep breath: She loved the barn at once. There was the scent of horses, straw, and the spicy odor of sun-cured hay. Stalls lined the broad gravel aisle. Most of them were empty, but a few curious horses poked their heads over the half doors and watched the little procession roll past. Lincoln trotted beside Ari, his head up, ears tuliped forward in eager attention. His eyes brightened. And as they came to the end of the long aisle, to a large box stall in the corner, he gave a welcoming bark.

Frank rolled the wheelchair to a stop and stepped back. Ari couldn't see anything in the gloom at first. Her heart beating fast, she rolled herself forward, then pushed the half door to the stall aside. It rolled back and daylight flooded in. A great shape lay curled in the corner. The head turned as

29

she rolled farther into the stall, and then the animal got to his feet.

It was a stallion. The light gleamed on his bronze coat. His chest and quarters were heavily muscled, his withers well-shaped. But it was his head and eyes that were the most beautiful to Ari. His forehead was broad, the muzzle well-shaped, with delicately flared nostrils. As he stepped forward, she looked deep into his eyes, large, brown, and full of sorrow.

"Chase," she whispered. "You are Chase. I . . . Ann!" She gasped and bit short a scream. The light hit a great wound in his forehead. She could see the stitches holding the gouge shut.

"The accident," Ann said gloomily. "Hadn't been for Dr. Bohnes, we might have lost him."

"Might have lost Ari as well," a tart voice snapped.

"Oh, Dr. Bohnes." Frank gave his mustache a nervous tug and backed away respectfully. The vet marched into the stall and put her hand on Ari's shoulder. She was small, but sturdily built, with snow-white hair and bright blue eyes. She was wearing high rubber boots, a stethoscope swinging from her neck.

Ari half turned in her wheelchair, reluctant to take her eyes from the stallion. If she gazed at him long enough, if she could touch him . . .

"Do you remember anything?" Dr. Bohnes asked softly.

30

"I know his name," Ari said sadly. "And that's all. He is mine, isn't he?"

"Till the end of time." Dr. Bohnes clapped her hands together with a competent air. Her sharp blue eyes traveled over Ari's face. "Humph! They didn't feed you too well in that place, I see."

"Please!" Ari said. She stretched her hands out to the stallion. He stepped forward delicately, as if treading on fragile ground. He bent his head and breathed into her hair. "Chase!" Ari cried. She wound her arms around his neck, as far as she could reach. She laid her cheek against his warm chest. She could feel the mighty heart, slow and steady, and his even breathing.

"Do you remember . . . anything?" Dr. Bohnes asked softly.

"I've lost something!" Ari cried. "That's all I know. But I don't know what it is!"

Dr. Bohnes patted her back in brisk sympathy. "I'll tell you what, young lady. We'll get to work on those legs of yours. And I know just what will help strengthen them."

"Riding?" Ann said, her voice alight with satisfaction.

"Riding," Dr. Bohnes confirmed. "As soon as we get you on your feet, my dear, we'll get you on your horse. And as soon as we get you on your horse . . ." The three adults exchanged glances.

"Yes?" Ari prompted. She kept her hand on

31

the stallion's side, as if to make sure they wouldn't be parted again.

"Well. We'll see."

"How soon?" Ari asked. Her eyes met the stallion's, and she smiled. "How soon before I ride?"

Dr. Bohnes screwed up her face. It looked like a potato. "How soon? That, my dear, depends on you. And on how much pain you want to put up with."

Ari set her jaw. "As much as I have to," she said. "I used to ride him? Every day?"

"Never apart," Frank said sadly. He chewed his mustache with a melancholy air. "Well, you slept in the palace, I mean — in the house, of course. Not in his stall. But still!"

"We won't be apart for long," Ari promised. She raised her hands to his face. He bent his head further so that she could examine the wound on his forehead. Whatever had happened, it had been a terrible blow. The stitches had healed well, but the skin was soft over a depression right in the middle of his forehead. She remembered something: Scars like this one healed white. She closed her eyes so that the others wouldn't see the tears. Why could she remember things like this, and nothing about her own past? She felt his breath on her cheek. It was warm and smelled of grass. She looked into his eyes, and he gazed back, his own eyes searching hers.

Horses didn't look directly at humans. No an-

32

imal did. Ari knew that, just the way she knew how to pull on a pair of jeans or wear a T-shirt. "Dr. Bohnes," Ari said after a moment. "The accident . . . both of us were in it?"

"That's right," Dr. Bohnes said.

"It was a car accident?"

"We don't talk about it," Ann said. "It doesn't do to talk about it. It was terrible. Terrible."

"I just wanted to know — did Chase forget, as I did? Has he lost his memory?" She rubbed her eyes. She was tired. So tired! Not much was making sense right now. "I know that's a silly question, in a way. How would you know if a horse lost his memory? But I can't help feeling that — I don't know. That he's trying to tell me something."

"Perhaps he is," Dr. Bohnes agreed. "The coming weeks will tell, won't they?" She put her hand on Ari's shoulder. "This one needs sleep, Anale. She's practically falling out of her chair. Let's get her up to bed."

"Anale," Ari said drowsily. "Anale. I knew someone by that name, once."

"You will again, milady," Ann said, tucking the blanket around her knees. Frank began to push the wheelchair down the barn aisle.

Ari could barely keep her eyes open. "Chase," she whispered. "Chase."

The stallion whinnied, a loud, trumpeting call that jerked her back from the shores of sleep. "I'll be back soon, Chase," she said. "I promise."

5

The sun sank below the Western Ridge of the Celestial Valley. A few stars shone at the edge of the twilight sky. Atalanta backed away from the Watching Pool. She was disturbed by what she'd seen. No. She was afraid. Arianna had no memory of who she was. Chase was deaf to his Bonded Mistress. And there was the dog. What was she going to do about the dog?

The Imperial River reflected the stars and the line of rainbow-shower trees that grew at the north side of the Watching Pool, but tonight the waters would not reflect the moon. This was the first night of the Shifter's Moon, when the Silver Traveler's Dark Side faced the Celestial Valley. For four nights in a row, no magic would work at all.

The Dreamspeaker cantered up the hillside. There would be no sleep again for her tonight, nor for any of the Celestial Valley herd. On Dark Side

34

nights, the unicorns stayed awake. Mares with colts and fillies took shelter on the lee side of the valley, out of the evening wind. The others, mares and stallions alike, were supposed to pace the valley in a guardian circle, alert for sights or sounds of the Shifter's forces. There had never been an invasion of the Celestial Valley, not within Atalanta's memory. So the Ritual of the Shifter's Moon had become an excuse for staying up all night, singing, dancing, and telling stories and tales unicorns loved to hear.

It was different tonight. Because of what Atalanta had just seen, the Ritual of the Shifter's Moon was a grim necessity.

Atalanta jumped gracefully over a log, then picked her way through a fall of rocks to the place where the brood mares stood with their young. She came to a halt on an outcrop of rock. Just below her, the unicorns cropped grass and exchanged gossip. The colts and fillies jumped and rolled, excited to be up this late. Nobody, Atalanta thought sadly, had a thought of war. Only Ash, a silver-gray unicorn close to Atalanta's own color, and a leader in the Rainbow Army, knew anything at all about fighting. Ash was practicing attack. But then, Ash spent all of his free time practicing fighting, because he liked the exercise. He dove forward, forelegs extended, head down, ears flattened against his skull. His steel-gray horn pierced the night air. This movement was called the "Otter," after the sleek river creature. Then Ash darted sideways, head moving back and forth, back and forth, snapping his teeth. This was called the "Snake." Atalanta watched him for a few moments. Then she tapped her foreleg on the rock shelf.

"Friends!" she called. Her voice was low and sweet. But somehow, the call attracted the attention of the entire herd. In silence, they gathered in front of her, the rainbow colors of their coats invisible in the dim light thrown by the stars. "Friends! You must guard in pairs tonight. And tell me if you find any of these things in our valley:

"A smell of dead and dying things. This is an odor like none you've encountered before. Once you smell it, you will not mistake it.

"The sight of a black unicorn, or one with eyes of fire.

"Any human or animal unknown to us." She paused for a long moment. "Especially a dog."

"A dog, Dreamspeaker?" Rednal, the crimson unicorn, spoke. "But I thought . . . we had heard that the Princess has the Sunchaser's jewel, and that the jewel was brought to her by —"

"Be quiet!" Atalanta said, not quite angry, but close. "There are ears and eyes abroad tonight that are no friends of ours. You will not speak, or guess at what events are occurring in the world below, in Balinor, or on the other side of the Gap. We can't take the chance that it will give the enemy information that he could use. Just remember that the

Shifter can take the form of anything. Anything at all."

"We know that, Dreamspeaker," Rednal said cheerfully. "But even Entia himself can't hold the shape of another for very long. So if we, say, stare at a tree for more than a few minutes, and it turns into, um . . . alfalfa, we'll know immediately . . ."

"To eat it!" another unicorn called out. "Alfalfa's my favorite food!"

There were some giggles from the herd. Atalanta frowned to herself. How would they react to what she had just learned? "The nature of magic changes," she said. "We no longer know how long the Shifter can maintain a shape that is not his own. Now, I'd like three or four of you to take the colts and fillies below. Down to the windbreak by the river."

"But, Dreamspeaker." A portly mare with a very young colt by her side spoke up in protest. The colt's horn was barely the length of Atalanta's hoof, which meant he wasn't more than a few days old. "We were all going to tell stories tonight. It will be the first time for my young one here."

"Please," Atalanta said. The word was mild, but her tone wasn't. Several of the unicorns exchanged significant looks. They were a little afraid of the Dreamspeaker. There had been rumors that she went beyond the usual use of magic to . . . what, no one really knew.

There wasn't any more discussion. Two

mares herded the colts and fillies into a small circle and led them out of the grove. Atalanta waited until she was sure they couldn't hear her. Then, since there was no way to soften her news, she said it straight out.

"I did not send the dog to Arianna. I did not find the jewel."A soft breeze picked up her forelock and stirred her mane. "I don't know who did. There is other magic abroad in Balinor and beyond the Gap. I don't know where this magic is from."

"But what shall we do?" Rednal was bewildered.

"We wait. She will heal, in time. And as she does, I will send her dreams. I can do no more. Except one thing. I can hope. I shall hope. I hope that Arianna remembers who and what she is. And that she puts the Sunchaser's jewel to its proper use."

6

The first month at Glacier River Farm, Ari was confined to her room. She slept a lot, her dreams frequent and puzzling. She had no idea what they meant.

She lived for the mornings. Each morning, Frank brought Chase out to pasture and stopped beneath her window. She waved and called to him, fighting the intense longing to be up and with him. Her legs wouldn't heal fast enough. It seemed to take forever.

"You're coming along quite nicely," Dr. Bohnes said. It was a fresh summer morning. Ari's window was open. The smell of new-mown grass drifted into her room. Six weeks before, she had come home from the hospital. Her days had been an endless round of doctor's visits, and X rays, and casts.

She was tired of it all. And even the memory of the tunnel had faded.

Dr. Bohnes picked up another gob of salve from the jar and dug her fingers into Ari's right calf.

Ari winced, but she didn't cry out. The massage therapy worked. She'd walked outside on the lawn every day this week, hardly using the crutches at all. "But when can I ride Chase?"

Dr. Bohnes's old fingers were strong. She worked the salve all the way down to Ari's ankle, then took an elastic bandage and wrapped her leg all the way to the knee. "Get up," she said.

Ari swung her legs over the side of the bed. Linc was asleep on the floor and she nudged him gently with her toe. He opened one eye and yawned, then rolled out of the way. She stood up, determined not to use the cane. Pain slammed her right leg like a hot iron brand. She bit her lip and shifted her weight to her left side. That at least was only an ache. "It's fine," she said with a gasp. "Just fine."

"Hmph." Dr. Bohnes drew her eyebrows together in a skeptical way. "You're going down to dinner tonight? With Frank and Ann?"

"Yes."

"You ask your foster parents about riding Chase."

"They'll want to know if it's okay with you."

"It's okay with me."

"Then is there a problem? Chase is mine, isn't he." She didn't say this as a question. She'd asked questions for two months. Where are my real parents? How long have I lived here? Where did I live before? Why are my dreams so weird? And Dr. Bohnes didn't have any answers. None that Ari believed, at any rate. But Ari didn't have to ask who owned Chase, she *knew* it: Chase was hers. Forever.

Dr. Bohnes narrowed her eyes. They were a sharp, clear blue. Ari thought they saw everything. "Your memory any better?"

Ari shook her head.

"Well. You'll remember how to ride. It's like breathing, to somebody like you, anyhow."

"I rode? Was I . . ." Ari was shy of this particular question, but she had to ask. "Was I any good?"

"You were very good." Dr. Bohnes sniffed disapprovingly. Ari blushed. Being conceited was the worst crime ever in Dr. Bohnes's mind. Um . . . no, Ari thought. The second worst crime. Abusing an animal was worse. Dr. Bohnes rapped her knuckles with the stethoscope. "Are you listening to me? I'm giving you your riding program. Don't blink those big blue eyes at me, miss. I know how excited you are. Now. You ride twenty minutes *once* a day for a week. Hot baths every day and more massage. Then you can ride twenty minutes *twice* a day for a week. All at the walk. Then divide the time in the saddle between the walk and the trot. We'll extend the time, twenty minutes at a time, until you're up to an hour. Once you're up to an hour, you can try cantering. No jumping for a month."

41

"No jumping for a month," Ari concluded at dinner. She was so excited, she hardly noticed what she was eating. "So if it's fine with Dr. Bohnes, it's fine with you?"

Ann poked her fork into her mashed potatoes. "You tell her, Frank."

"Me!" Frank twisted his mustache. Then he ran his hands through his hair. He'd been eating peas, and one of them was stuck in his thin, wispy beard. "Why me?"

Ann put her fork down and glared at him. "Because *I'm* not gonna do it."

"Tell me what?" Ari asked.

"There's a problem with Chase."

Ari's heart went cold in her chest. "He's not sick. If he were sick, I'd know about it. I can almost feel him think. And that wound in his forehead is almost healed. Isn't it?"

"He's just fine, honey." Frank patted her hand. "But we have these bills from the hospital . . ."

Ari ignored this. "If Chase is healthy, it's okay. You can tell me anything."

Ann cleared her throat. "You know the Carmichaels."

"That rich guy and his daughter? You've told me about them."

"We — she's taken a shine to Chase."

"Anyone would," Ari said lovingly.

42

"And they've offered us a lot of money to lease him for a year."

"What?" Ari was aware that her voice was soft and her tone mild. "You said no, of course."

"We're not selling him, or anything like that, of course!" Frank said in a shocked way. "This lease is just like rent. He'll be right here at Glacier River Farm. They won't own him, or anything like that. I mean, he's not ours to sell."

"He's *mine*!" Ari burst out.

"He's not yours to sell, either, milady," Ann said gently. "But we need the cash bad, Ari."

"Lease her another horse," Ari said.

"She doesn't want another horse," Frank said. He wriggled in his chair. He was very upset, Ari could see. She could also see that no one would want another horse if Chase were around.

"Well, she can't have him," Ari said flatly. "He's special. He's *mine*!"

Frank shrugged. "He's just another horse now, Ari, without his . . ."

"Frank!" Ann said warningly. "You know Dr. Bohnes said she has to remember all by herself. Or it won't stick." She leaned over and patted Ari's hand. "I'm sorry. I'm real sorry. But we don't know what else to do. We gotta eat, Ari. And this is the only way we know how to make money. Please, honey. Please. You've got a month more. Then they take him."

The bills. The hospital bills. They were her fault. But she had a month. Four weeks when she didn't have to think about it. And, holding back hot tears, Ari said, "All right."

She thought the words would choke her.

7

The sun rose over Glacier River Farm, washing pale color over the green pastures and turning the white fences to butter-yellow. Linc walked down the gravel path to the stream that bordered the woods surrounding the barns and old gray house.

"Linc! Lincoln!" Ari's voice had wisdom and a warm authority in it. The dog turned eagerly. The call came from a thick stand of pines that stood just beyond the small waterfall that fed Glacier Brook. He cocked his head, and his ears tuliped forward.

"L-i-i-incoln!" Ari and Chase cantered out of the trees and into the sunlight. She drew in the reins, stopped, and smiled at the collie. "Where have you been?" she teased him. "Chase and I have been out for miles. And you missed it all, Linc."

The dog raised his muzzle and barked happily. Ari snapped her fingers lightly, and the dog pranced to her side.

Ari wore breeches, high black boots, and a faded T-shirt. The sun glanced off the ruby jewel suspended from a gold chain at her throat. She had left her hair unbound this morning, and it swept past her waist and just touched the back of her saddle. The great horse she rode bent his neck and danced as the collie approached. Ari swayed gracefully in the saddle and flexed the reins. "Easy now, Chase," she said. Amusement colored her tones. "You know Linc."

The horse snorted and pawed the ground, arrogance in the set of his head and neck. *Ah, yes, I know him,* he seemed to say. *But will he obey the Great Me?*

Ari settled into the saddle and quieted Chase to a full halt. She patted her left thigh. Linc rose on his hindquarters, resting his front paws against thickly padded girth. Chase shook his head irritably but stayed quiet under her hands. Ari scratched the collie's nose affectionately. "I want you both to be good today," she said softly. "I know neither of you is going to understand what will happen. But you have to bear it. You have to bear it for my sake." Linc dropped to the ground and cocked his head to one side. His forehead wrinkled with a question. "Our month is up. And we've got a problem. It's a girl who takes riding lessons here. Her name is Lori Carmichael."

Linc growled a little. Chase shifted on his hooves.

"She met Chase while I was laid up with these stupid legs of mine. She really . . . likes him." Ari took a deep breath and fought back tears. She had to act normally, for her animals' sake. "Her parents have taken out a lease on you, Chase. They're paying a lot of money so that she can ride you for a year. And the farm needs the money. This . . ." She swallowed hard, the tears she'd sworn she'd never shed now rising in her throat. She stroked the horse's neck. "This is our last ride, Chase. Just for a while, that is. This morning, Lori's coming over and I'm going to give her a lesson, to show her how to ride you." She sat a little straighter in the saddle. "So. I still own you, Chase. I've just had to lend you out a bit. Frank and Ann need the money for my medical bills, and there's no other way for me to raise it. I'm so sorry. I'm so dreadfully sorry. But there's no other way around it. Now, both of you are going to behave, aren't you? Linc? Chase?"

The collie barked. Chase flicked one ear back. Ari waited a moment for her voice to come under control. "We'll be late for morning chores," Ari said to the both of them. "Let's ride!" She touched her heels lightly to Chase's side, and they cantered toward the big barn that formed the heart of Glacier River Farm. Chase jumped the three-board fence that bordered the south pasture with careless ease, but the fence was too high for Linc. The collie grumbled softly under his breath, then wriggled through between the two lowest boards. Ari glanced over her shoulder and grinned to herself. The big dog was fastidious, and he hated to get his coat rumpled. She'd brush him after she cooled Chase out.

As horse and girl swept through the pasture, Ari kept a keen eye on the ground ahead. Here, the grass was knee-high, due to be mowed for hay. The heavy growth disguised the earth and would conceal any woodchuck holes that might trip the great chestnut stallion up. But more than that, there was something about this spot that suddenly disturbed her. She didn't know why, just that this place, a mile or more from the safety of the farm itself, was eerily quiet. No birds sang here, and the wildflowers were scarce.

She flexed Chase to a walk. She wasn't anxious to get back on this, her last free morning on her stallion.

At first, the sound was no more than a breath on the wind sailing past her ears:

Arianna, Arianna, Arianna.

She drove her back lightly into the saddle and flexed the reins to check Chase's forward stride. Yes, there it was again. Her name, sailing the breeze.

Arianna!

"Yes?" she said. She came to a full halt and turned in the saddle. The pasture was quiet under the morning sun. Unnaturally quiet for this already spooky place. Even the breeze was stilled. It was as if the world held its breath.

Chase curvetted under her hand. She sat easily erect as he turned in a circle.

Nothing stirred. Nothing at all. Then, to her astonishment, she heard a quarrel: two voices — one low, angry, and hissing, the other high and panicked. Ari's throat tightened. The grass here was high, but not high enough to conceal a person, not even a small child. Where were the voices coming from? And what was the quarrel about? She couldn't distinguish the words, just the pitch of the two speakers. She guessed the fight was over something that the high-voiced one had, which the hisser wanted badly.

Suddenly, Lincoln dashed forward, barking furiously. He leaped into a stand of taller grass that grew just in front of them. The high-pitched voice shrieked. Lincoln's deep barks turned to angry growls.

"Lincoln!" Ari swung out of the saddle, wincing a little as her bad leg hit the ground. She held Chase's reins in one hand and walked forward. Her heart was hammering in her chest, but she said calmly, "Hello? Is anyone there?"

Lincoln's barks stopped abruptly, as if a brutal hand had closed around his throat. Fear for her pet drove Ari forward. "Lincoln," she called firmly. "Here, boy."

There was no movement in the clump of grass, just a flash of Lincoln's gold-and-black coat.

And something else. A shadow slipped through the grass. Quietly. Slyly.

She took a deep breath. A terrible odor hit her like a blow. Dark, fetid, and bloody. Chase shrilled a high, warning whinny. He threw his great bronze body in front of hers and she reeled backward, landing on the ground with a painful thud.

"Whoa, Chase," she said, in an I-really-mean-it voice. "You *stand*."

The horse flung his head up and down, up and down, the odd white scar on his forehead catching the sunlight like a prism. But he obeyed her and stood trembling as she dropped the reins and walked forward to the brush that concealed her dog.

She knelt and parted the grass with both hands. Lincoln bolted out of the grass, his jaws speckled with a dark, oily liquid that gave off that hideous smell, his barks splitting the air like a hammer. Behind him, the hissing voice rose in a frustrated wail: *Give it back!*

The dog snarled, almost if he were saying, *No!*

Ari grabbed Linc's ruff with both hands. "You *sit*," she told him.

He sat, his brown eyes desperate. He raised one white forepaw and clawed urgently at her knees.

"It's okay," she soothed him. "It's *okay*." Gently, she pushed him aside and bent forward. She parted the long grass. Whatever it was lay coiled in a stinking puddle just beneath her searching hand. She held back a scream and took a deep breath. She narrowed her eyes, trying to bring whatever it was into focus, but the black and oily substance shifted, twisted, and coiled like a snake. Impossible to make out the shape.

She bent lower, her hair falling around her cheeks. The blackness spun in a whirlpool that burrowed deep into the earth. And at the bottom of the pool was a red-rimmed, fiery eye. The eye turned, rolled, searched the air above her. Saw her. And fastened its hideous gaze on her face.

Fear hit Ari like a tidal wave. It engulfed her: cold, relentless, unimaginable. She struggled with the fear like a rabbit in the jaws of a snake. She forced her hands over her own eyes, to shut out that terrible searching gaze.

Then a whisper came out of the air over her shoulder, from the first speaker. An older man, perhaps? *Come back, Arianna. Come back.*

Ari straightened her shoulders and took her hands from her face. Whatever was going on, it was better to face it than to hide. She spun around. Her dog and her horse looked back at her. There was nothing else in the meadow. She forced herself to turn to the terrible pool and the red-rimmed eye in its depths. Ari swallowed the sickness rising in her throat and said, too loudly, "Get out of here. Go on. GET! Both of you!"

The eye blinked and disappeared. Nothing

remained of the oily pool. No scent. No sound. And the voice on the breeze was gone. Her fear receded. Just like a wave at the beach, it ebbed and flowed away.

Ari sat back on her heels, frowning. Her heartbeats slowed to normal. She got up and ran swift hands over Chase's back and legs: He was okay at least. She turned to Linc, who waited patiently as she explored his fur with quick fingers. No cuts. No bruises. If that *thing* had been trapped somehow, it hadn't hurt the dog. Then she felt something deep in the fur at Linc's throat. She tugged it carefully free and turned it over in her palm.

"What's this?!" she said. "Look at this!" She held it up so that the sun struck white light from it. A twisted shell of silver, the size of charms on a necklace. The charm was about an inch and a half long and no more than an eighth of an inch wide. It was the long, pointy sort of shell that might have held a very thin snail. Ari held it up and admired it.

Chase whinnied. Ari jumped a little at the sound. Chase whinnied again, more urgently. Ari looked at her watch. "Uh-oh. You're right, Chase. We *are* going to be late!" She tucked the tiny shell in her shirt pocket and scrambled to her feet. If she was very late, poor Ann would be as mad as fire. Ari knew how hard it was, making a living on a horse farm, even one as beautiful and big as Glacier River.

Ari remounted, and the three of them headed home.

8

Just a few minutes later, Ari and Chase leaped the five-bar gate in the fence that bordered the farmyard. Ann came out of the barn at the sound of hooves on the driveway.

"You were gone awhile," she said. Ari noticed that Ann had patched her jeans with duct tape. No wonder Ann and Frank hadn't been able to resist the huge amount of money Lori's parents were willing to pay the farm to lease Chase for Lori's private use.

Ari closed her eyes briefly against the familiar stab of pain: Chase being leased, *used*, by a stranger. She shoved the thoughts out of her head and smiled down at Ann.

"Thought you might have fallen off." Ann's eyes were bright and curious.

"Off Chase?" Ari kept her voice warm. "Never." She hesitated. Should she tell Ann about the strange incident in the pasture?

Ann shot a swift, secretive glance toward Ari's legs in their breeches and high black boots. "A person never knows what you're up to," she said. Her mouth thinned in affectionate annoyance. "And I worry about you." Then Ann asked, "How are your legs? The hospital called about getting a new set of X rays."

Oh, my, Ari thought. X rays were expensive. It's a bad day for her already. She doesn't need to hear about that creepy eye. "My legs feel fine this morning," Ari lied. "I don't need any more X rays." She swung out of the saddle and dropped to the ground. It was an effort, but she kept the pain out of her face. "A few more weeks of riding, and you'll never know that I've been in an accident."

That strange, flickering glance at her legs again. Ann ducked her head. Ari knew Ann didn't believe her. "Well," she said with a brave smile, "I'm sure we all hope so. But you must be careful, my . . ." She stopped herself. "Ari," she added.

Ari wished for the thousandth time that she could remember her life before the accident that broke her legs and gave her a concussion. That she could recall her mother and her father. That she knew why, out of all the foster parents that the county social services department could have chosen, she'd been placed here with Ann and Frank, who never seemed to know how to deal with her. Who had treated her with a weird mixture of love and respect in the three slow, painful months of recovery she had spent here already.

"I think the orthopedist will be pleased when he sees me next week, Ann. We managed to jump five fences this morning, Chase and I. And we galloped for a good twenty minutes."

"Cool him out really well before the Carmichaels get here," Ann suggested. Then she said with mock bossiness, "And you get to cleaning those stalls quick, you hear?"

"You bet," Ari said cheerfully. She looped Chase's reins into one hand and walked him into the barn.

She took Chase down the aisle to the wash racks, past the stalls lining either side. She didn't remember anything about her life before the accident, but she knew she must have loved this place. Each stall was made of varnished oak, with black iron hayracks and black barred doors. Most of the horses were turned out to pasture. They'd been in their stalls all night. Ari had volunteered to clean out the manure and put fresh bedding in for them before they came in from pasture. Their names were on brass plates over the doors: MAX, SCOOTER, SHY-NO-MORE, BEECHER, and CINNAMON — the names went on and on.

She led Chase to the cool-water wash rack and took off his saddle and bridle. She hooked him into the cross ties and turned the shower on. Lincoln curled into the corner with a heavy sigh. Ari suppressed a giggle. Lincoln was resigned to what the rest of the morning would bring: the routine that went on day after day, cooling down, mucking out, training the young horses on the longe line. It'd be hours before she'd have time to brush Linc and clean his white forepaws. And Lori Carmichael would be coming this morning for her first lesson on Chase.

Ari frowned at that and stroked the great horse's neck. She was going to do her best to talk Lori out of using a harsh bit on Chase. Frank had admitted Lori wasn't a very good rider. Lori would want to use the harshest bit she could, since that was an easy way for a bad rider to get control of a horse that knew more than the rider did.

Chase turned and looked at her, a question in his deep brown eyes.

"It'll be a short lesson, Chase. I promise." He was a huge horse, close to seventeen hands high, and she had to stand on tiptoe to whisper in his ear. She ignored the spray of water down her back. "And I'll make sure she uses a snaffle today. You know that if it were up to me, I'd throw all the Carmichaels off the farm, don't you?"

He nodded, as if he understood. Ari ran her hands down his satiny neck, then over the white scar in the center of his forehead. That was the thing about Chase. He always understood.

In the months she'd spent recovering, Ari

had relearned Glacier River Farm and how it worked. Ann and Frank boarded and trained more than forty horses at the farm. Frank said that the farm had everything a horse owner could want, and more. The pastures were green and smooth, with triple-barred white fences all around. The buildings — barns, house, and indoor arena — were built of a warm red brick that glowed in the sun and was softened by rain. The farm veterinarian, Dr. Bohnes, had her own special office with a little clinic for injured horses in the boarder barn. There was even a small restaurant that was open for lunch and dinner for horse shows.

And, of course, there were trails. Miles and miles of trails. Ari and Dr. Bohnes had explored the strange, twisting roads that wound through the woods and valleys of the farm one afternoon. Dr. Bohnes had pushed Ari in a wheelchair. Some of the trails seemed to lead nowhere. At other times they seemed to lead everywhere. Ari had asked Dr. Bohnes about the unexpected caves and tunnels that filled the woods. She told the vet how they pulled at her — especially the cave in the south pasture.

Remembering now, she paused, one hand on Chase's neck. The south pasture. Where she'd seen that awful eye.

The old vet hadn't seemed surprised. But she'd warned Ari away from the tunnels. Millions of years ago, the glaciers moved through the land here

57

like titanic ghost ships. As they moved, the land swelled under the glaciers like ocean waves, rising, falling, and folding itself to help smooth the glaciers' path to the sea beyond. The huge icebergs had long gone, but they'd left caves and tunnels under the softly swelling hills.

Ari was drawn to them in a way she couldn't explain. She'd told Frank about her need to explore, to find her way through them, and he'd given her an alarmed look. He was a mild-mannered man, and anxious. Worry lines creased his forehead, drew deep grooves on either side of his mouth. They got even more prominent when she'd told him about the way the caves seem to draw her in, beckoning.

"You can't!" he'd said, leaning forward, so close she could feel his breath. "You *stay away from them!*"

"Lincoln wouldn't let me get lost," she'd replied, frowning at the strangeness of his reaction. "He'd lead me home. And so would Chase."

Except that Chase wasn't hers anymore. You've got to remember that, she told herself.

"I remember that," Ari said aloud, softly. "I may not remember anything else, but I remember that." She wiped the water away from Chase's neck. His mane was long and gleaming. "How could I forget you belong to someone else now?" She touched the silver shell in her pocket. It lay there, warm under her hand. "Oh, Chase," she said sadly. "How can I remember if I belong anywhere? Or to anyone?"

She rolled the shell in her hand. It felt warm, almost hot.

"There's something," she murmured aloud. "There's something I'm supposed to do! Somewhere I'm supposed to go! Chase. Help me!"

The big horse rested his muzzle on her shoulder and breathed softly into her hair. But he didn't have an answer.

9

"Just take it easy, Princess," Mr. Carmichael shouted across the arena. "And if the horse gives you any trouble, give him the whip."

Lori Carmichael scowled and said, "For goodness *sake*, Dad," and bent to brush her spotless riding boots with a towel. She was shorter than Ari, and sturdily built. Her hair was white-blond and drawn back in a tight bun low on her neck. "Aren't you ready yet?" she snapped at Ari.

Ari hated her on sight.

The three of them, Chase, Ari, and Lori, were in the middle of the huge indoor arena, the center of all the riding activities at Glacier River Farm. Six inches of sand covered the floor. This made a cushioned footing for the horses. The building itself was huge. The rafters soared thirty feet high at the peak. They dropped to twenty feet at the walls to meet the bleachers that surrounded the arena on three sides. Mr. Carmichael, his wife, and Lori's older brother sat in the judge's box, where celebrities gathered at official horse shows when the prizes were given out.

"Let's *go*," Lori demanded. "Give me a leg up, will you?"

"You'll remember not to pull at his mouth," Ari said quietly. "And keep your weight off his back unless you want him to turn or stop."

"Excuse me?" Lori said. She lifted one eyebrow. Her eyes narrowed in sarcasm. "My father turned the check over to Frank five minutes ago. Which means this horse is *mine*."

Ari couldn't stop herself. All her good resolutions about accepting the lease agreement with courage went flying. "It's just for a year," she said. "And the agreement was that he's yours only when you come to the farm." She was angry, but she kept her gestures calm and her expression unexcited. "Could you wait a second, please? I'll just check the length of the stirrup leathers." Ari gave Lori a polite smile and moved closer to Chase. She slid one hand over his sleek withers and murmured so that only the horse could hear. "Please, Chase. Listen to me when she gets on. Listen to *me*."

She stepped back, handed the reins to Lori, and cupped her hands together to give Lori a leg up. The girl planted one black-booted foot in Ari's palm and heaved herself onto Chase's back. A short whip dangled from one wrist. She dropped into the saddle with a thump. She clutched the reins and pulled. Chase tossed his head and backed up.

"Whoa, now," Ari said. "Walk on, Chase."

The bronze horse shook his head from side to side, the harsh bit Lori's father had insisted on jingling in his mouth. Lori gave a small shriek and clapped both heels against his sides. Chase raised his muzzle and rolled his eye back so that the whites showed.

"Just sit still," Ari said, more loudly than she'd meant to. "He's never had anyone on his back but me. And he's not used to . . ."

"He'll just have to *get* used to it," Lori snarled. She sawed the reins back and forth, back and forth, a technique good riders use in only the most extreme circumstances. Ari had never used it on Chase. Even with the mild snaffle bit in his mouth, it would have hurt to have cold iron drawn harshly over his teeth. This cruel copper bit was much, much worse. If Lori kept it up, his mouth would bleed.

"Easy," Ari said. "Please, Chase."

Sweat patched the great animal's shoulders. He shuddered, his ears turned to Ari's voice. He danced on the tips of his hooves.

"What's *wrong* with him?" Lori yelled. "You've done something to him!" She jounced uncomfortably, her legs banging against Chase's side. Ari saw she was beginning to panic. In the stands, Linc began to bark.

"You keep that blasted animal under control," Mr. Carmichael shouted. "Give him the whip, Princess. Give him the whip!"

Chase whinnied, a low, urgent, what's-happening-here sort of noise.

Ari bit her lip and walked toward them, hand outstretched. "Why don't you slide off, and we'll try again tomorrow, Lori?" she suggested. "It might be a good idea if you helped groom him and saddle him, for instance. It'll give him a chance to get to know you bet —" She stopped in midsentence. Chase gathered himself together. His muscled haunches bulged. His chest expanded with the effort of keeping his forelegs safely on the ground. Ari knew what those signs meant. "Easy. Please, Chase. Listen to me."

Lori raised her right arm, the crop in her hand. Ari stiffened and shouted out, "NO!"

The whip descended onto Chase's back.

Chase went berserk. He put his nose to the ground. His hind legs flew out and up. Lori slid forward over his neck, screaming. He reared back, forelegs reaching to the roof. Lori slid back in the saddle, both hands clutching his mane, her feet dangling free from the stirrups. Ari heard the *thump* of running feet from the stands, Linc's deep barks, and Mr. Carmichael shouting, "Lori. *Lori*. LORI!"

Lori sawed frantically at the reins. Chase's jaws were wide open, blood-flecked foam spraying over his neck, spotting the strange white scar on his forehead. He pitched up and down, eyes furious, the breath exploding from his nostrils. His ears lay flat against his skull.

Ari moved fast. She came to a stop directly in front of the giant horse. She raised both hands, ignoring the pain in her legs, her voice level. "Whoa, boy. You *stand*!"

Chase's ears flicked forward.

"You hear me, don't you?" Ari commanded. "Stand, please!"

Chase stood. He dropped his head, sighing. A little blood trickled over his muzzle.

Lori slumped over his neck, crying in a loud way. Ari stepped up to Chase, looped the reins in one hand, and stroked his chest with the other. She could feel him trembling. She soothed him gently as Frank and Mr. Carmichael ran across the arena and up to them.

"Outta the way, girl!" Mr. Carmichael shoved Ari aside and grabbed Lori. "Lori! Lori, baby! Are you all right?" He pulled his daughter from the saddle and set her on the ground. Then he hugged her, his back to Ari. Lori glared at Ari over her father's shoulder.

"Well!" Frank said. One thin hand tugged nervously at his long brown mustache. The other twisted the top button of his denim shirt. "Doesn't seem as though anyone was hurt. Does it?"

Mr. Carmichael whirled, holding Lori tight to his side. "How dare you put my daughter on that horse! It's unsafe! He could have killed her!" His fat face grew dark with rage. "I want him shot!"

Ari clutched the reins. Chase's head went up. His ears went forward. He stared straight at Mr. Carmichael.

And a voice bellowed angrily in Ari's mind: *Little man!*

She looked at Chase, hardly believing what the voice in her head must mean.

The horse pawed at the arena floor. Again, Ari heard his voice inside her head:

You shall be dirt beneath my hooves, little man.

"Chase?" she wondered aloud. "Chase?!"

He turned to her, his gaze direct and angry. His nostrils flared red. He reared, pulling the reins from Ari's hands. Then he dropped his head low to the ground and swung his head from side to side, the way a stallion will when he is ready to strike at an enemy. He pawed at the ground with his iron hooves. *I will crush his bones with the Snake!*

"But they'll shoot you!" she said. And then to herself, *I can't believe this. I won't believe this. Is Chase talking to me?* She put her hands over her eyes, to quiet her thoughts. She dropped them abruptly when Mr. Carmichael stormed, "I'm getting the gun. Where's the gun, Frank? I want the darn *gun.*"

Lori shrieked, "Shoot him, Daddy. Shoot him!"

"No one is going to shoot anyone here," Ari said with quiet authority. "Chase. You stand, please. Please, boy. For my sake!"

For a long, agonizing moment, she didn't think the command would work. Then the great stallion took a shuddering breath and stood still.

Ari kept her eyes on his every move. Moving slowly, she picked up the reins and walked toward him. "Are you all right now?"

Chase looked down, his eyes calm, his flanks moving in and out with regular, easy breaths.

"Chase?"

No answer in her mind. Perhaps she had been dreaming. Ari shook her head briefly to clear it. She'd been nuts to think that he had spoken to her. She ran her hand down Chase's neck, then turned to walk him back to his stall.

"Just a minute there, young lady." Mr. Carmichael folded his arms across his chest and glared at her. Lori leaned against him, her cheek pushed into the shoulder of his sport coat. She gave Ari a measuring kind of look.

"Oh. Of course. The check. You'll want that back." Ari fumbled in her jeans pocket, then remembered Mr. Carmichael had given the check to Frank. She looked at him. "I'm sorry the lease didn't work out."

Lori pushed herself away from her father and whined, "But I want to ride Chase, Daddy. And I *can* ride him. That horse isn't going to listen to me with her around." She jerked her chin at Ari. "She made Chase throw me off."

"He didn't throw you off," Ari said. "You fell off. There's a big difference."

"She did it on purpose, Daddy. I know she did. She wouldn't let me ride him with the right kind of bit. He can't stand that copper bit. Look how his mouth is bleeding."

"*You* made me put that bit in his mouth!" Ari said, astonished. "Why are you lying?"

"I'm not lying. You're the one who's lying. You're the one that trained that horse to make me look like a jerk. It's because you don't want me to have him! You want to have him all to yourself."

"That's not true," Ari said.

"Now, Ari. Now, Ari." Frank put his hand on her shoulder. "I know you're unhappy with this leasing agreement, but we've talked about it. Remember? With your legs so busted up right now, it isn't really possible for you to ride the horse as much as he needs to be ridden to keep fit. If you look at it one way, the Carmichaels are doing us a big favor."

Ari stared at him. She knew Frank was embarrassed by needing the money from the lease to keep Glacier River Farm up and running. But to blame Lori's bad riding on her!

"Here." Mr. Carmichael shoved Frank with one finger. "We'll keep the horse. But my little girl here is right. The horse hasn't been trained properly. Give him here." He snatched the reins from Ari's hand before she could move. "We'll call around, Princess. And we'll find a real trainer to knock some sense into this animal." He jerked hard on the reins. "Come on, you."

Chase dug both front hooves into the sand and pulled his head back. He wasn't upset, Ari saw, just wondering what the heck was going on.

"Make him come with you, Daddy," Lori whined. "Wait! I'll get back on. You hold him!" She remounted, smiling angelically at her father.

"Move, darn you!" Mr. Carmichael jerked again. Chase didn't budge. He stood looking down at all of them, splendid head held high. Mr. Carmichael took the lower part of the reins in one hand then swung them around. The loose reins came down hard. The blow raised a thin welt on Chase's glossy neck and he jumped back, snorting. He was still puzzled, Ari saw.

And she knew why he was confused.

Ari didn't remember anything about her life before the accident that crippled her legs. Not her mother; not her father. Not even if she had any brothers or sisters. But she did know that she had always owned Chase. He was as much a part of her as her heart, or her lungs, or her hands. And she knew that she had never, ever laid a hand or a whip on him. Which was why he was calm now. He didn't believe anyone would hurt him deliberately. She could almost hear his thoughts — not in the way she had heard his voice a few moments ago, but because

68

she loved him. And that love let her understand him the way she could understand no one else. His expression told her: *The pain from the slashing reins was an accident. Wasn't it?*

Mr. Carmichael jerked on the reins to make Chase come forward. Obediently, the big horse stepped closer. With the horse directly in front of him now, Mr. Carmichael swung the reins and struck. Blood welled against Chase's golden neck in a thin trickle. It was only a matter of seconds before he lost his temper. Mr. Carmichael was a fool to think he could control an angry fourteen-hundred-pound stallion with anything but a gun. What might happen after Chase exploded was unthinkable. Lori, her face pale, jumped off.

Ari thought fast. There was only one thing she could do.

Suddenly, Ari shouted, "Linc!" Lincoln bounded down from the bleachers in three giant leaps and flew toward her, a gold-and-black blur. She pointed at Mr. Carmichael. Linc laid his ears back and growled. Mr. Carmichael dropped the reins with a yelp. Ari sprang forward, scooped up Chase's reins, and leaped into the saddle. She urged Chase into a hand gallop. With Lincoln streaking beside them, Ari guided the horse to the south end of the arena, which was open to the soft summer air.

Ari galloped to the clinic. Then she pulled Chase up and sat quietly. Lincoln settled gravely on the gravel drive, forepaws extended. He cocked his head and looked at her. She sighed and ran one hand through her long hair. "I hated to do that, Chase."

Chase shifted underneath her. Lincoln lifted his head to look at her.

"I know. I know. It's a terrible thing I did. Ann and Frank are going to be really upset. But what else could I do? You saw how Mr. Carmichael was beating Chase."

Lincoln rumbled — a cross between a growl and a low bark. He curled his upper lip a little so that she could see the point of one ivory-colored eyetooth.

Ari added hopefully, "Maybe Lori and her father will be so upset they'll forget all about the lease."

The collie sneezed. It was more of a snort than a sneeze, the kind of snort that meant *yeah, right!* in a very sarcastic way. Ari slipped out of the saddle and knelt beside her dog. She ran her hands lovingly through his creamy ruff. "Are you talking to me, too, now?" She laughed a little sadly. "I don't know, guys. The both of you talking to me? Phooey. Maybe I'm just going flat-out crazy." She bent and kissed the tawny spot right in the middle of Linc's forehead. Chase nudged her shoulder with his nose. Behind her, she could hear loud, angry voices: Mr. Carmichael shouting at Frank, Lori shouting at her father.

Ari stood up a little straighter and looped

Chase's reins over her arm. She'd have to take Chase back into the arena and face them all. But not now. The scars on her legs throbbed with a fierce pain. She closed her eyes and bit her lip to keep from crying out.

Everything was going totally wrong.

10

"Just stand there a bit," a fussy voice said at her elbow. "I've told you before. Those are just muscle spasms. It hurts now, but it shows your legs are healing."

Ari opened her eyes and smiled. Dr. Bohnes had come out of the clinic, attracted by the noise and the shouting. "Hi, Dr. Bohnes."

The little vet jigged back and forth from one foot to the other. Ari would never say it aloud, but the way Dr. Bohnes dressed made her want to laugh. She liked bright-colored shirts, leather sandals, and long, baggy skirts. Her hair was pure, brilliant white, cut short. It curled over her pink skull like a wispy cloud. Ari hadn't seen Dr. Bohnes yet today, what with one thing and another. This morning's shirt was a bright, tie-dyed orange, yellow, and red. Ari didn't know how old she was. But she would be Ari's grandmother's age, at least. Ari blinked back tears.

She couldn't even remember if she had a grand-mother.

"Older than that, milady," Dr. Bohnes said cheerfully.

"That makes three of you today," Ari said with surprise. She smiled. She didn't mind Dr. Bohnes calling her milady. She always did. And it made her feel less alone somehow.

"Three of us what?" Dr. Bohnes demanded.

"Reading my thoughts."

"Oh?" Her bright blue eyes sharpened. She looked at Lincoln and then at Chase. "And what kind of thoughts were you having, that the animals could read them?"

"Never mind." Ari nodded toward the arena. Ann had joined the quarrel, and the voices were even louder. "There's been kind of an upset this morning. Maybe I just imagined it."

"Hah! I told Frank and Ann not to lease Chase out. Especially to those dratted Carmichaels." She snorted, with far more gruffness than Lincoln had. "That horse never tolerated anyone on his back but you. And he never will."

"I thought he would if I asked him," Ari said simply. "And we need the money, Dr. Bohnes."

"We wouldn't if —" She bit off what she was going to say.

"If what?"

"Never mind. Come along. It's past time to massage your legs."

"But . . ." Ari looked toward the arena building. The argument had drifted outside. Mr. Carmichael and Lori were gathered around Frank. Mr. Carmichael was waving his arms and yelling about how dangerous Chase was. "I should . . ."

"Nothing you can do there," Dr. Bohnes said briskly. "And if you ask me, it's better to get Chase out of sight."

This made sense. Dr. Bohnes almost always made sense. Ari took Chase and followed her colorful, tiny figure past the round pen and to the back of the big barn, where the elderly vet kept her little clinic.

Although Dr. Bohnes was a horse vet, injured or sick animals from miles around eventually found their way to the bright blue door of her clinic. There was a short line there today: the little boy from the Peterson farm up the road with a fat calico cat; a sorry-looking yellow dog with a sore paw; a motherly lady with a parakeet perched on her shoulder. The parakeet squawked angrily at the cat, who opened its golden eyes once, snarled, then went back to sleep in its owner's arms.

"Huh!" Dr. Bohnes grumbled. This meant she was irritated at all the work in front of her. "Sponge Chase down, Ari, and put some of that sticky salve on the cuts in his mouth. You know, it's the same stuff I use on your legs. Then turn him out, won't you? By the time you've finished with that, I'll get through this lot here."

Ari gave her a quick hug, smiled at the little Peterson boy, and took Chase to the small paddock where Dr. Bohnes treated the larger animals. She removed his bridle and haltered him, then asked him to stand while she fetched warm water and the sticky salve. Ari didn't know of any other horse that would obey the "stand" command as well as Chase did. She'd never known him once to break it.

Lincoln followed Ari into the storeroom, where the vet kept her medicines. Ari loved the scents of the storeroom. Dr. Bohnes mixed many of her own salves and poultices from herbs, nuts, and berries that she grew in a special garden. The air was filled with the sharp scent of arrowroot, a lingering odor of lavender, and something roselike.

Ari inhaled with delight. Linc took a breath and sneezed. Ari grinned to herself and searched the shelves for the midnight-colored cream that Dr. Bohnes used to heal her scars from the accident. Her hands were quick, sorting through the jars and herb bags on the shelves. She picked up a small ceramic pot so that she could reach for the large canister of salve against the back wall.

A horrible smell hit her like a fist. Her hand loosened and the pot fell. Ari made a hasty grab to catch it before it smashed onto the flagstone floor. Behind her, the dog growled, then barked. Ari caught the jar just in time and looked at it, puzzled. She'd never seen anything like it on the vet's shelves before. The closer she looked at it, the harder it was

75

to see just what color the pot was: flame-red? Sickly yellow-green? And was that where the terrible stink came from? Curious, Ari tugged at the cork stopper.

Lincoln leaped to her side and pushed his nose against her wrist. His snarls twisted like snakes, if snakes had been sounds.

"Just a minute, Linc," she said. "Easy, now." She hesitated. She was pretty sure that the vet had nothing truly dangerous out in the open. But maybe she'd had this curious thing locked up somewhere and forgotten to put it back.

The urge to open the pot was powerful. Something, *something* twisted her fingers around the top, as if . . . as if a huge, clawed hand — invisible, powerful, mean — were forcing her to open it.

Ari pulled off the stopper and looked in.

At first, she saw nothing but dark. Then a thin coil of acid smoke rose from the depths of the jar. There were shapes in the smoke. Ari was sure of it. She held the jar up and watched the shapes spiral toward the low ceiling. Lincoln barked and barked. The smoke curled around her face, slid past her nose, poured into her eyes.

And she saw . . . she heard . . .

She was in the center of nighttime, in a place she'd never been before. The sky was dark and starless. At her feet was a humped mound, blacker than the black night sky. The mound shifted, moved, then screamed with the sound of a million hornets. Ari jumped and shouted with surprise. The mound at

76

her feet swelled, grew, unfolded like an evil flower. And an eye formed in the center of the hooded blackness, a green-and-yellow eye, multifaceted, like some grotesque and terrible insect. The same terrible vision she'd seen in the meadow!

Where are you? a thousand voices whispered. The eye rolled in its bloodied socket, searching, searching. . . .

It was all Ari could do to hold onto the pot. She was dimly aware of Linc's excited barking, the dashes he was making to get out of the range of that terrible eye. The rest of her world faded, leaving her to this terrifying encounter. She took a deep breath, then another . . .

And fainted.

11

"Tell me what you saw," Dr. Bohnes demanded. "Everything." She peered into Ari's face. Ari was lying on the old leather couch in the vet's office.

"Chase?" she said aloud. Her voice was foggy. She cleared her throat.

"He's fine," Dr. Bohnes said impatiently. Her strong old hand closed around Ari's wrist. Her grip was warm.

Ari focused on the fierce blue eyes. "What happened? It wasn't —" She forced the words out. "I haven't been in another accident?"

Were there tears in those wise eyes? Dr. Bohnes blinked hard. "Nonsense," she said briskly. "You're as fit as a fiddle." She pointed at the collie, sitting anxiously next to the couch. "Lincoln here was barking fit to raise the . . . that is, fit to bust. When I came into the storeroom, I found you on the floor."

78

"The pot," Ari said.

"What about the pot?"

"Did it break? There was something awful in it, and something terrible was after me. . . ." Ari trailed off. She tried to concentrate. She remembered the eye. The yellow-green eye that was searching, searching. The feeling that if it saw her, it would pierce her to the heart. And the buzzing of angry hornets. She shivered. "I opened the ceramic pot. The one with the funny smell. It was an awful smell, to tell you the truth. I can't imagine what that kind of medicine would be for."

"There was no ceramic pot." The vet's voice was firm. "Nothing like that at all on my shelves. Ari, *you must tell me* what you saw."

Ari ran her hands through her hair. The back of her neck was sweaty. "Insects," she said in a small voice. "Hornets, or maybe wasps. It was dark. Really dark. And this horrible yellow-green . . ."

"Yellow-green what?" Dr. Bohnes commanded.

Ari opened her mouth to tell her. She couldn't get the words out. It was as if they were stuck in molasses. She knew — somehow she knew — that if she could tell Dr. Bohnes about the hideous eye, she would be safe, safe from it, because . . .

"It . . ." she struggled. "It was . . . looking . . ." Her brain felt as if it were wading through hip-deep mud. Suddenly, she broke free of the strange lock on her tongue and gasped, "Look . . . looking FOR ME!"

Dr. Bohnes turned pale and started to speak.

"Ari!" Ann opened the clinic door with a bang and thudded into the room. She wore green rubber boots plastered with manure. Her hair was sticking to her skull with sweat. "There you are! It's past time for four o'clock chores, so I started without you. Have you been here all this time?"

Ari struggled to sit up. The whole afternoon gone? Fear clutched her heart. In the days after the accident, there had been many days like that, when she had drifted in and out of consciousness, not knowing where the time had gone. She buried one hand in Lincoln's soft fur. He whined and licked her wrist with his warm pink tongue. She couldn't, wouldn't tell either Ann or Dr. Bohnes that she'd lost all that time. She couldn't face going back to more doctors. They would question her, probe her, ask her things she couldn't answer. "I'm sorry," she said, a little surprised to find her voice so normal. "I guess I got wrapped up in taking care of Chase."

The thought of her great stallion alone in the paddock drove her to get off the couch. She sighed with relief; she was steady on her feet. She wasn't dizzy. And the dark thoughts of the eye drifted away from her like a leaf on Glacier River Brook.

"He's okay, isn't he?" Ann was anxious, Ari

could tell. "His, um, mouth is okay?" Her glance shifted nervously away from Ari's.

"Yes," Ari said. "Lori's not all that strong, thank goodness. He has two scrapes on each corner of his mouth, but they should heal."

"That's all right, then." Ann twisted her hands together. "She'll do better next time, I'm sure. With the . . . ah . . . new trainer, I mean."

Ari stared at Ann, astonished. "What?"

"Now, it's not that you aren't a wonderful trainer, but Mr. Carmichael's right. You're only thirteen, and you and the . . . um . . . horse have spent just too much time together. Far too much time. He said it isn't natural . . ." She paused, a peculiar look on her face. ". . . Not natural for that kind of bond to exist between horse and rider. And you know, he may be right. So, it will be good for both of you to have Chase handled by someone else for a change. Just for the year's lease."

Ari swallowed hard. Lincoln pressed against her knees, growling softly.

"You do understand, Ari. Don't you?"

Ari kept her eyes steadily on Ann's face. She controlled her rage with a terrific effort of will. She could feel the red in her cheeks, and her heart pound. After a long moment she said, "Do we really need the money that badly, Ann?"

Ann's eyes shifted. A long look passed between her and Dr. Bohnes. The vet said, "Pah!"

and stamped angrily to her desk. She sat down, slammed open a drawer, took out some papers, and pretended to read. Then she shouted, "I am NOT taking part in this discussion!"

Ari tried again. "Maybe I could work on the Peterson Farm, after school starts. I could earn money there. They need a stable hand."

"You have your duties here."

"I can do two jobs," Ari said stubbornly.

Neither woman looked at her legs, but Ari knew what they were thinking. She pressed on, "The healing's coming along really well, isn't it, Dr. Bohnes?"

"It is," the vet said shortly. She peered at Ann over the rim of her spectacles.

"I don't think it's a good idea for you to go off the farm just yet, Ari." Ann rubbed her neck. Her hand was muddy; it left a streak of mud between the folds of fat. "And as for school —"

"Of course I'll go to school," Ari said, astonished. "Why ever wouldn't I?"

Ann gestured vaguely. "The farm . . . the work. We were thinking of Dr. Bohnes home-schooling you."

Lincoln's growls deepened. "You make it sound as if I'm a prisoner here," she said quietly. "I haven't been off the farm since the accident except to go to the hospital. Not to the mall, not to the movies. Nowhere."

"Don't be silly!" Ann said. She chewed her lip

82

nervously. "Of course you can leave the farm. Not just now, of course. But soon."

"It's for your own safety," Dr. Bohnes said at the same time.

Ari looked from one to the other. Something was going on here. Something weird, and a little scary. "I'm going to check on Chase," she said. "And then I'll be in for dinner. Sorry I missed afternoon chores, Ann. I'll make it up to you tomorrow."

"That'll be fine," Ann mumbled. "I didn't mind. I didn't mind doing them at all."

Outside the clinic, Chase was standing with his muzzle to the air, ears up, his deep chocolate eyes gazing far into the distance. The sun was setting over Glacier River Farm. Streaks of red, pink, and gold flowed from the setting sun like water from a fountain. The green of the fields was shadowed almost to black. A few stars poked white light through the oncoming night. The white scar on Chase's forehead glowed briefly, like a firefly, and then dimmed as the sun sank in the pink ocean of light. Something . . . an animal perhaps, scrabbled briefly in the bushes planted against the grain shed at the rear of the paddock.

Ari held her breath and listened hard. She heard the slight scrape of something — feet? — on gravel. Then silence.

"Rabbit?" Ari said to Linc.

He brought his head up at that, ears tuliped forward. He grinned and wagged his tail.

"No rabbits, huh?" Ari asked.

Linc dropped his head with a disappointed sigh. Ari chuckled and let herself into the paddock. She stood beside Chase, one hand on his mighty side. Lincoln panted softly as he stood next to them. For a minute, she stood there and thought of absolutely nothing

"It's been a strange day, Chase," she said.

He whinnied.

"You seem to agree." She paused, then sent him an urgent thought with all the force of her mind. *Do you remember today? How you spoke to me in the arena?*

Chase shook himself, then dropped his muzzle to the earth and began to graze. Ari gazed at him a long moment. He seemed larger than usual, as he stood in the half dark. The twilight shadowed his haunches, traced the muscles in his broad chest. He fed quietly.

So she'd dreamed it, imagined it, maybe even had a delusion. Maybe Ann was right, and it wasn't safe for her to go away from the farm. No, that was stupid. Stupid. She wouldn't let them — any of them — talk her into questioning her own mind. She was as sane as she'd ever been. She knew it. She was as sure of that as she was of her love for her horse and her dog.

"Would you like to stay here for the night, Chase?" she asked aloud. There was a tank of clean water in the corner of the paddock, and she could bring him his hay and grain. It was pleasant here, in the evening air. And, if she had to do what she *thought* she had to do, it would be easier with him here, instead of in the big barn.

She took two flakes of hay from the stack Dr. Bohnes kept for the clinic animals and scattered them on the ground. It was good hay, timothy and clover, with a little alfalfa mixed in for flavor. Chase examined the hay with a pleased air. Ari knew he was happy because his lower lip softened, and the wrinkles above his eyes deepened. He snorted happily and stuck his nose in the pile, searching for the purple-green alfalfa blossoms before the others. Alfalfa to horses was like chocolate to people; a little was delicious, but too much meant a stomachache.

"Now, how did I know that, Linc?" she said to the collie. Perhaps her memory was coming back, in bits and pieces. Her heart lightened, and she hummed to herself as she went in search of grain for Chase's dinner.

Dr. Bohnes kept the grain locked in the shed at the back of the paddock. Ari remembered something else that she must have known before her accident: Too much grain could colic a horse. And colic could be a killer. She was careful to measure three scoops of oats and a half scoop of corn into the feed bucket. She liked the warm, cereal smell of the grain, and she ran both hands through the kernels, partly to mix the corn and oats together and

85

partly because she liked the feel of it between her palms.

Except that grain was soft and giving. What she'd found in the middle of the oats was not. Curious, Ari stepped under the light over the back door.

Another spiraled stone. This one was creamy violet, much thicker and heavier. It was twice as long and wide as Ari's thumb. She patted her shirt pocket. Yes, there was the other stone. She took it out and laid the two together in her hand. They appeared to be made of the same stuff, but the colors of each stone were totally different: one rose, one violet. A wisp of a melody came to her and without thinking, she sang:

> "*Yellow, silver, blue*
> *The rainbow we make . . .*

— and something-something something," she muttered. Darn! She'd almost had it. The song chimed softly in the back of her mind, like a car radio set too low. She shook her head impatiently. Don't push it, Dr. Bohnes had said. Memory's like a spiderweb; push too hard and it will break. Breathe softly, and the web will hold.

A wind rose and died again, chilling the back of her neck. Suddenly, she desperately wanted the warmth and light in the farmhouse. She didn't want her memory to come back if it brought her horrible-looking eyes and strange spiraled stones and bits of songs that she couldn't complete.

She ran her hands through Chase's grain again, to make sure that no more mysterious stones lay in the bucket, and set it down for him. He looked up from the hay and hurried to the bucket, plunging his nose into the bottom. She watched him for a long moment, wrapping her arms around her body to shake off that sudden chill. She whistled to Linc, then climbed over the paddock fence and set off at a jog across the graveled drive to the house. The lights were on, and she could see Ann through the kitchen window, moving between the stove and the table. She slid her boots off by the back door, checked Linc's coat and paws for burrs, and let herself in. Frank sat in the rocking chair by the fireplace. He held a large red book in his lap, and he was frowning. Ari knew that this was the account book for the farm. It recorded all the money that Glacier River Farm took in and paid out. It was a bad sign when Frank scowled.

Ari smiled at Ann and washed her hands at the tap. "Shall I set the table?" Ann nodded abruptly. Ari had no idea why it embarrassed Ann to have her set the table, but it did. The dinner table sat in the center of the kitchen. It was made of a shiny wood that was chipped in places to reveal spongy orange wood beneath. Ari set out the cornflower blue table-cloth and the plates with the blue ladies on the rims.

She liked these plates. The center was white, but the figures circling the center were blue. Each lady was different, some slim and lovely, with long dresses and windblown hair, some curvy and smiling, with violets, roses, and silver wands in their hands. Each woman danced beneath a delicately carved arch. Above the arch was a soft drift of clouds. . . .

Ari stopped and stared at the plates, the knives, forks, and spoons for the table clutched in one hand. Crystal arch. Violet, rose, and . . . it was the song.

Had she made the song up?

She frowned. She'd seen these plates every day of her life. At least, every day of her life that she could remember. Which was the last three months. So she could imagine that she had made up a song to go with the images she'd seen.

But the melody?

The melody was like nothing she'd ever heard before.

"Ari?"

She was dimly aware that Ann was speaking to her. Lincoln nudged her urgently with his nose.

"Ari!"

She focused on Ann with a start of surprise. "Yes, Ann. Sorry. I was daydreaming, I guess."

"Are you sure you're all right?" Ann came closer and reached one hand out to smooth Ari's hair. "Dr. Bohnes didn't know how long you'd been asleep on the floor in the storeroom, but she didn't think it was too long."

Just all afternoon, Ari thought. *She'd go wild if I told her I fell asleep for hours and that I had nightmares every minute and then I heard this strange song. Not to mention the eye. What's happening to me? Did the accident scramble my brains and my legs, both?* Aloud, she merely said, "I'm fine, Ann." She set the knives, forks, and spoons in place and sat down at the table.

"Well, we're not." Frank closed the red book with a thump. There were deep purple smudges beneath his tired eyes. He rubbed the back of his hand over his mouth. "We're broke."

Ari looked down at her plate. Ann put a ladle full of macaroni and cheese in the center. The yellow cheese oozed onto a blue lady with a sweet, sad expression. Frank thumped heavily across the wooden floor and sat at Ari's right. Ann took her place across from her. Ari said, "We have to lease Chase, then. There's no way out."

"I'm sorry, Ari, I really am. But the money we can get from Mr. Carmichael is money to feed the other animals." He smiled, a tired, sad smile. "And us, of course." He reached over and touched her sleeve lightly. "I know you mind. I know you mind a lot."

"They're going to take him away? To another trainer?"

Neither Ann nor Frank said anything. It was,

Ari thought with a sudden spurt of rage, because they were too cowardly.

"Don't look like that," Frank said nervously. "If there was any other way, you know we'd take it."

"You could sell that necklace Lincoln had around his neck." Ari set her fork carefully across her plate. Then she drew the fine chain over her head and held the ruby up. It caught the firelight. Its glow was like the heart of the fire itself.

Ann looked away, as if the sight of the jewel were too much to bear. Frank put his hands before his eyes.

"No!" Ann's voice was hoarse. "You must never, ever let that out of your sight. Do you understand?" She leaned forward. Her breath smelled of peppermint.

"We could sell it," Ari said. "Where's it from, anyway? And what was a valuable thing like this doing around Linc's neck?"

"We don't know," Frank said uneasily. He cast a sidelong glance at Lincoln, curled as usual at Ari's feet. "But we can't sell it. You can't sell it."

"If it's mine, I can." Ari twirled the necklace carelessly around one finger.

Horror spread over Frank's face slowly like a stain spreading in water. "Put it away," he said in the grimmest voice she had ever heard from him. "And we'll have no more talk of that, Ari. Do you understand?"

"Frank," Ann said in a low voice. "Maybe

she's right. Maybe here, it doesn't matter. After all, here he's a horse. He doesn't look anything like . . ."

"What doesn't matter?" Ari asked. "And he doesn't look like what?"

"Nothing." Frank sighed. "Nothing. It's safer for you not to know. Eat your dinner, Ari. Please. And don't think about it anymore."

"You won't change your mind? About Chase?"

"I can't, Ari. I'm sorry."

Ari drew the necklace back over her head. She tucked the ruby inside her shirt next to her heart.

Ari helped with the dishes and went up to bed early. She kissed Ann and Frank good night and smiled when Ann drew back in surprise at the intensity of her hug. She whistled lightly at Lincoln. The big dog uncurled himself from the corner and padded up the stairs after her.

She went into her room and snapped on the light. It was strange, she thought. She only remembered three months of being in this room. She had no memory of what her bedroom had been like before. But she felt so cozy here; her room "before" (as she thought of the time when she had two whole legs) must have been a lot like this one. Pale green walls, and a flowered bedspread to match. White wicker dresser and nightstand. The desk where she'd thought she'd do homework when she started school in the fall. Except, according to Ann and Dr.

Bohnes, she wouldn't be starting school at all. Well, she could have done the homework Dr. Bohnes would have given her here. If she was going to stay.

"I can't, Linc. I can't stay here and let Chase go to someone else." The horse wouldn't stand for it. And when Chase didn't want to do something — the only person to stop him was Ari herself. If she didn't take him away in the morning, terrible things would happen. Mr. Carmichael meant his threat. If Chase did hurt Lori — and the way Lori rode, he would hurt Lori, even if he didn't mean to — Ari had heard Mr. Carmichael say it:

Chase would be shot.

Ari stripped off her breeches and T-shirt, then grabbed her pajamas. She put one bare leg into the bottoms and stopped, looking at the twisted muscle, the scars that the accident had left. She finished putting her nightclothes on and got into bed. She switched the bedside lamp off, then heard Linc settle heavily onto the rug at the side of the bed. She slept.

And as she slept, she dreamed.

12

The moon sailed high and white over Glacier River Farm. It shone through Ari's open window and turned the patchwork on her quilt to pale shadows. To Linc, who lay beside Ari's bed, the moon was known as the Silver Traveler. He watched it now, head on forepaws, dark eyes shining, as it bobbed along the river of sky until it reached the giant pines that guarded the forest. Then the Silver Traveler floated there, as if caught in the net of the trees.

Lincoln raised his head, eyes suddenly alert. A ray of moonlight passed through the window and touched Ari's sleeping form. She stirred in her sleep and sighed.

The moonlight grew stronger, harder, turning from heavenly light to earthly substance, until a solid arch appeared. One end rested at the foot of Ari's bed. The other rose to the Silver Traveler at the top of the pines. There was a distant sound of bells,

93

as if some celestial harness jingled. A light brighter than the moon appeared at the top of the arch and moved swiftly down the path. The jingling of the harness bells grew sweeter, not louder.

Lincoln whined, deep in his throat.

The bright light stopped at the window's ledge, as if hesitating to enter or considering where to go. Then it passed into Ari's bedroom and stopped at the arch's end.

Lincoln rose to his feet. The light dimmed for a second, or perhaps less, then flowered to a brilliant rose. A unicorn stood in the center, her horn a crystal spear, her coat a burnished violet. Her white mane flowed like spun silver, reaching her knees, covering her withers, so that she appeared to be wrapped in moonlight.

Atalanta. Goddess to All the Animals. Atalanta, the Bearer of Legends and the Keeper of Stories. The Dreamspeaker! She had come! Lincoln lowered his head and sighed, contented.

"And, you," she said to the dog, a steely note in her silvery voice. "Who are you, dog?"

Linc raised his eyes at her and thumped his tail.

"What? You cannot speak? Or will not?"

Linc whined, then rolled over on his back, white belly exposed to the unicorn's sharp horn.

Atalanta tilted her head to one side, considering the collie. Whatever had sent him seemed to bear the Princess no ill will. And there were limits to what she would be allowed to do. She, too, sighed deeply. She gazed at the sleeping Ari, her eyes a tender purple. She moved nearer, hovering over the bed, carried by the arch of moonlight. Gently, she lowered her crystal horn until the very tip touched the ruby at Ari's throat. The jewel warmed slowly to a deep red flame.

"I will tell you the Story, little one," Atalanta said in her gentle voice. "But you must come to me to hear it."

Ari stirred and murmured in her sleep. The ruby necklace shimmered as she turned.

"If you come to me, Ari, I may tell you everything."

"Mother?" Ari said sleepily. "No. Where are you? Who are you?"

"Ah, Ari, I live where the Arch meets the Imperial River. That is my home. But I will meet you elsewhere, if you will come."

"It isn't you, Mother, is it?" Ari's eyes fluttered. She yawned. Atalanta raised her head. As soon as her horn left the jewel, the fiery light in it died away. The silver Arch beneath her hooves began to dim.

"Remember, Ari. Come to me. Because you love the Sunchaser. Because you love me. Ari, the most important thing of all? You must use the jewel to save the Sunchaser. It is his, and his alone. Help him! He cannot be who he is without it!" She turned

95

and began to walk the arch to go back to the Silver Traveler in the sky. She left the scent of flowers behind her.

When Ari came fully awake, the only memento of Atalanta's visit was a faint silver shimmer in the air and a smell of roses. But that could have been only the moonlight and the air from the open window.

"Linc!" Ari sat up in bed. She rubbed her eyes and yawned again. She reached over the side of the bed to the floor, her hand fumbling for the dog. She felt the silken triangle of his head and then his warm tongue on her fingers. She scratched his ears a little, the way he liked best, then swung her feet onto the floor and switched on the bedside light. "I had the strangest dream," she said. He looked back at her, tongue hanging out, a grin on his face.

"You silly dog." She bent over and hugged him. "It was a nice dream," she said quietly into his ear. "A beautiful dream." She inhaled happily. "I believe I can still smell the flowers from that dream, Linc. Do you know what I saw?"

I do, his eyes seemed to say.

"Of course you don't, silly. So I'll tell you. But we have to tell Chase first. Okay?"

Lincoln cocked his head. Ari pulled on a heavy sweater and prepared to tiptoe as quietly as possible down the stairs and out to the barn. "But first," she whispered to the dog, "I'm going to put this in a really safe place." She tucked the ruby necklace carefully into her top drawer, under a pile of riding socks. "Just imagine what would happen if I lost it now!"

Linc followed her out of the house and to the back of the clinic, where Chase was stabled with Max the buckskin for company. Max stirred as she approached, and nickered. Ari smiled to herself. Hoping for a handout. She slipped through the fence rails and walked to her horse. Chase stood dreaming his own dreams. She slid her hand along his satiny sides. He turned to her with a look of surprise.

Ari wrapped her arms around his neck and whispered in his ear. "I dreamed of a magical creature. A unicorn. And it was so funny, Chase. I just know I've had this dream before." She frowned to herself. "Or maybe it wasn't a dream. Maybe it was from my time before the accident." She laughed. "Except there aren't any unicorns, are there, Chase?"

He blew out once.

Ari rubbed his ears tenderly, her expression thoughtful. "You know, Chase, I was getting just a little bit scared to take you and Linc away from here. I was thinking we could leave the farm here and find another farm, where they don't know us. I could work for our room and board, cleaning stalls and grooming the horses, and maybe we could sleep in the hayloft. It would be warm there, even in winter."

Chase whinnied. Ari knew what that whinny meant. "You think that's a bad idea? It has its disadvantages. Frank would plaster my photograph all over the television stations, and whoever took us in would take us right back. That is, if we didn't get hurt by some horrible person first. But you know — that dream gave me a fabulous idea."

Chase's eyes were mysterious in the dark of the barn. Ari rubbed his muzzle affectionately. "I'm going to start by talking nicely to Lori and her father in the morning. She can't possibly want a horse that doesn't want her. Once she sees that he'll never listen to another trainer, she's got to give it up." She hugged Chase hard. "I know. You think that she and her father are so selfish, they'll never let you go. I've thought about how to fix that, too." She frowned. "I've been thinking about money. Lori and her father like money more than anything, I think. Well, I've had an absolute brainstorm. I'm going to use the jewel to save you! That's what came to me in the dream. I think. Anyway, I'm going to get Dr. Bohnes to sell the ruby necklace for me! She's the only one who will really understand about you and me. And she knows that the necklace is mine to sell. She won't feel as *responsible* as Ann does." She laughed. "And that necklace has to be worth a huge amount. I'll give part of the cash to Lori and her father in return for breaking that lease agreement. The other part of the cash will pay off the debts we've got. This is going to work, Chase. I just know it will."

Ari fed him a handful of sweet feed, then limped barefooted through the damp grass and back into her room. She fell asleep and dreamed no more dreams.

13

ri was up with the sun. She dressed quickly. There is always more work than time to do it in on a horse farm. Ari felt guilty about missing her assigned chores from the day before. So she was determined to do twice as much work this morning. She owed it to Ann and Frank. She'd tried to thank Frank once. He'd given her the warmest smile she'd ever seen. "It's nothing, mila . . . my dear. We'd spend twice as much if we had to."

"But it doesn't mean they should," she said to Linc. The jewel was still in her sock drawer. She drew it out and held it tight for a moment. How much was it worth? A hundred thousand dollars? She didn't know. But Dr. Bohnes would. She tucked it carefully away again. She wore her blue denim shirt and her breeches and patted her breast pocket to make sure that the stones she'd found the day before were still safely there. Maybe she'd find more of them

100

today. And maybe, like the ruby necklace, they'd be worth some money. Heck! She could be rich and not even know it!

The morning air was fresh, the sun a narrow orange slice above the eastern horizon. Ari was happy. Her legs were achy this morning, but not too cramped. With luck, she'd have all her problems solved by lunchtime. Dr. Bohnes would sell the ruby necklace for a pile of money. Lori and her father would want the money instead of Chase. And all the bills would be paid off. She was sure of it.

Maybe she and the great stallion could take a long ride this afternoon!

She fed and watered all the horses — taking care of Chase first. Then she turned all the horses in the big barn out to pasture and began to clean the stalls. Lincoln helped her by staying out of the way.

Mucking out was hard work, but Ari enjoyed it. She worked hard this morning. She wanted to get every chore finished before breakfast. Lori had scheduled a lesson on Chase at nine o'clock, and so far she hadn't canceled it.

Ari used a large plastic manure fork that let her lift the piles neatly into the manure wagon. After the piles were dumped, she turned the fork over, pointy side down, and raked the sawdust bedding away from the damp spots. The air dried out the dirt floor.

Then she raked all the sawdust neatly to the sides of all the stalls and put the manure fork away.

She surveyed her work with satisfaction. She was a heck of a good barn rat, if she said so herself. She'd be employable anywhere. "Because," she reminded Linc, "you just never know when you're going to need a good job. You know? I can see it all. I'll have a job, a little money in the bank, and life will be wonderful. And all because of that necklace."

She checked the large clock over the barn office door. It was seven-forty-five. She had just enough time before breakfast to drive the tractor and wagon out to the manure pile and dump it.

She settled into the tractor seat, shifted the gear into drive, and drove slowly out of the barn. She put on the brake when she saw the Carmichaels' big red Cadillac pull into the parking lot. A pickup truck pulling a horse trailer came into the lot right behind them.

She took a deep breath. They were early. Way too early.

Mr. Carmichael got out of the car. He looked fatter and angrier than ever. Lori jumped out of the passenger side. She was wearing a new pair of breeches and shiny new paddock boots. The Cadillac had turned up dust when Mr. Carmichael pulled in. It settled on Lori's boots. She scowled, bent over, and fussily wiped them off. The driver of the pickup truck got out, too. Ari knew him. She'd seen him with his students at a farm horse show just two weeks ago. David Greer Smith. So that was the trainer the Carmichaels had hired with all their money. And he was a good trainer, too.

Mr. Carmichael waved his arms and jabbered at Mr. Smith. Lori stood next to her father, arms folded, the scowl still on her face. Suddenly, the three of them turned and walked off to the clinic, where Chase still stood in the paddock. Ari's heart quickened. How did the Carmichaels know where to find Chase? His usual stall was in the front of the barn. Who told them where Chase was?

"Morning, Ari."

Ari jumped. "Frank! Sorry. I didn't hear you come up."

He put his hand on her shoulder. "You did a lot of work this morning."

"Frank, what are they doing here so early?"

"The Carmichaels?" He turned and looked after them. The trainer walked in front of the other two. He was swinging a long lead line in one hand. "Smith called about half an hour ago. You were just starting to muck out. Said they wanted to take Chase bright and early. It's a long ride to his new stable, I guess."

"But you *can't!*" Ari burst out.

"He said they'd sue us if we didn't let him take Chase to a new stable! We'd lose everything, Ari. And our first duty is to you. Ann and I talked and talked about it this morning. We have no choice! This guy's backed us into a corner."

Ari remained calm. "I have this plan. We'll get lots of money, Frank. Truly we will. You have to stop them."

His hand lightened on her shoulder. "Honey, I just ca —"

"Won't, you mean," Ari said furiously. She ran to the clinic, Lincoln barking at her heels. She could hear Frank shout, "Stop! Stop!" She didn't care.

By the time she reached the paddock, she was out of breath. David Greer Smith was a tall man in cowboy boots, jeans, and a denim jacket. He was already inside the fence. Chase was backed into one corner. The stallion looked at the trainer out of the corner of his eye. Ari couldn't read Chase's expression. But she didn't think he was happy. Not upset, yet, she thought. Just curious. And a little annoyed.

"Sir!" she called out.

The trainer turned around. He had a nice face, Ari thought. But nice or not, he wasn't going to get her horse.

"What are you doing here?" Lori demanded.

"What are you doing here?" Ari shot back. "I've come to tell you the deal's off."

The door to the clinic opened and Dr. Bohnes came out. She was wearing a plastic rain hat and rubber boots over a screaming-loud green shirt and black pants. She looked ridiculous, but Ari was happy to see her. "Well," Dr. Bohnes said. She raised her scraggly white eyebrows to her hairline. "What's going on here?"

"We've come to get the horse, as agreed," Mr. Carmichael said in a curt way. "Get this kid out of the way, Frank. She could get hurt."

Ari bit her lip. She didn't have much time. She had to get to Dr. Bohnes alone — with no one else around. She knew Dr. Bohnes would help her sell the necklace. But how could she get all these people out of here?

She looked at Chase. The trainer was advancing on him, the lead line held behind his back. Chase snorted and flung his head up. Then he backed away. The trainer made soft clucking noises with his tongue. Chase danced a little on the tips of his hooves. When the trainer got close, the horse jumped away, just out of reach.

"Good," Ari said under her breath. Then aloud, "Dr. Bohnes?"

"What is it, my dear?"

"Could I talk to you? For just a second?"

"Whoa!" The trainer roared.

Everybody jumped. Except for Chase, who danced away again, just out of reach. The trainer's face was getting red.

"Maybe now's not the time, dear." Dr. Bohnes tied the plastic rain hat more firmly on her white hair. Frank looked up at the sky, which was clear and cloudless, but he didn't say anything. Ari ignored them both. Fine. So the little vet wouldn't help her. She'd just have to help herself. Get Chase away from here, just for a few hours, while she tried to settle things. Quietly, she moved away from the Carmichaels and the others and up to the paddock fence. Chase rolled his eye at her. She lifted her hand to make him whoa.

He stopped obediently at her signal.

"Jeez," said the trainer. He spat on the ground in a disgusted way. Then he grabbed Chase's halter and snapped the lead line onto the ring under his chin.

Ari moved her hand sideways, in a swift, abrupt motion. Chase jerked sharply to the left. The lead line tore out of the surprised trainer's hands. Ari raised her palm. Chase reared, forelegs pawing the air. He was having a good time.

The trainer swore angrily, leaped in the air, and grabbed the lead line. He gave one powerful tug on the line and jerked the horse forward. Then he grabbed the free end of the line and swung it viciously at the stallion's face. The horse roared in anger.

"NO!" Ari said.

I will trample you, little man!

Ari gasped. There it was again. Chase's voice. In her head. As though he was speaking to her. She jumped onto the fence and clung to the top board, her fingers digging into the rough wood. Chase was furious at the insult of the blow. He pawed at the ground, clouds of dirt flying from beneath his iron hooves. The trainer backed up, his face a mask of fear. Chase whinnied, a high, trumpeting challenge.

Get him out of here, milady. Or he will die!

"Sir!" Ari called. "Please! Sir! Just back up. Please just back up. Don't make him any madder."

OUT! shouted the voice in her head.

"You stop, Chase," she ordered aloud.

For a breathless moment, she wasn't sure it would work. It was crazy anyway, a part of her brain whispered. Talking to your horse?

Chase reared once more, black against the bright blue sky and the brilliant sun. Then he came to earth with a crash and stood still.

"You made him do that!" Lori shrieked. "You made him run away from the trainer. Daddy, I'm *telling* you, if we can just get him away from her, that horse will be just fine. She's just jealous, Daddy, because he likes me better or he would if he got half a chance!" Furious, she shoved her elbow into Ari's stomach. Ari fell backward with a gasp. There was a swirl of coffee-colored fur, a snarl, a scream. Linc jumped across her and barreled full tilt into Lori. He knocked her facedown, then settled all his eighty pounds right onto her back. Lori drummed her heels and yelled, but the big dog didn't turn a hair.

"That's enough out of everyone," Dr. Bohnes said briskly. To the trainer she said, "You, come out of that paddock and talk to me like a sensible man. And you," she turned to Mr. Carmichael, "pick up that spoiled little brat of yours and come into my office. All of you. You, too, Frank. We're going to settle this once and for all." She turned her back, marched into the clinic, and left the door wide open.

The trainer picked up his hat, dusted it off, and settled it firmly on his head. "I'll tell you what that horse needs," he said to no one in particular. "He needs a good whipping." He followed Dr. Bohnes into her office.

"Ari!" Frank tugged her arm. "Ari? Can you get that darn dog off of Ms. Carmichael?"

Ari turned around and bit her lip to keep from laughing. Mr. Carmichael was tugging like anything at the big collie's thick ruff. Linc wasn't budging. He sat on Lori's backside with a grin on his face, completely ignoring the infuriated man. Ari whistled. Linc pricked up his ears, hopped off Lori, and walked over to Ari, his tail wagging happily.

Lori picked herself up. Her new boots were smudged and her perfect blond hair didn't look anywhere near perfect anymore. Her face was redder than her father's.

"You two stay here," Mr. Carmichael ordered. "Come on, Frank. We'll settle this with the old bat inside."

"She is not," Ari said clearly, "an old bat."

"Just shut up," Lori muttered.

"Both of you keep quiet. Please?" Frank said. "I'll be with you in a minute, Mr. Carmichael." He waited until the other man had disappeared into Dr.

Bohnes's office. Then he came over to Ari and crouched in front of her. "Ari," he said.

"Yes, Frank?"

"You've got to let the horse go."

Ari shook her head. "I'm going to sell that necklace. Dr. Bohnes will do it for me."

"No, she won't. She can't."

"It's mine, isn't it?"

He hesitated. "Well, yes."

"Then I can sell it."

"Even if you do sell it, Ari, the Carmichaels don't have to take the money back. We have a contract." His thin face was lined with worry and distress. "Do you know what that means?"

"It means you signed my horse away."

"I signed your horse away. But it's just for a year. And then he'll be home, I promise." He stood up and ran his hands through his hair. Ari suddenly felt very sorry for him. "My gosh, this sure got mixed up," he said under his breath. "You two wait right here. I'll be back in a few minutes."

Ari watched as he went into the clinic and shut the door. Lori stood a little apart from her, arms folded defiantly over her chest. Finally she said, "That stupid dog of yours should be shot, too."

Ari decided not to respond to this. Lori was a horrible mess of a human being, and that was that. There wasn't a thing she could say to her. The best thing was to totally ignore her.

She gathered her long hair up into a knot,

fished a rubber band out of her jeans pocket, and wound it into a ponytail. Then she went into the paddock.

"Where are you going?"

"None of your business," Ari said shortly. She took the lead line the trainer had left in the dust and clipped it on the left ring of Chase's halter. Then she tied the free end to the ring on the other side. She looked up at her horse. Her legs were still too mangled to jump on him from the ground. She'd have to get a box. "You stand," she said softly. She left him there, still as a statue and as good as gold.

"I'm getting a step stool from the shed!" she said loudly.

Lori shrugged: *Who cares?*

Once in the shed, Ari peeked out. Lori was staring after her, but she was pretty sure she couldn't see what she was doing. She just hoped that Dr. Bohnes hadn't gotten a sudden (and rare) cleaning fit. The old vet hadn't. The windows were still as filthy as ever. Ari wrote on the dirty pane with one finger:

Sell the "DOG LEASH" in my sock drawer!

PLEASE!

Love, Ari.

"And I hope," Ari said fiercely to herself, "she remembers how the necklace came here. Linc was wearing it around his neck."

Then she picked up the step stool and marched out of the shed. She set it on the ground next to Chase.

"What are you *doing*?" Lori demanded.

"Leaving," Ari said briefly. She leaped neatly onto the stallion's back and settled her long legs just behind his withers. His chest and barrel were so powerful that the spot between them made a perfect place to keep a good grip. She squeezed her left leg, and he responded by turning in a circle. Max, the buckskin gave a startled squeal and jumped out of the way.

Ari spread the makeshift reins wide, tapped both heels lightly against his sides, and he backed up a few steps. Then she gathered the lead line in, tapped more firmly, and he sprang forward. They flew up and over the fence.

"You can't do that!" Lori screamed. "You come back here!"

"Linc!" Ari called. "Come on, boy!"

But Lori moved with astonishing speed. She grabbed the dog's ruff with both hands and held on. Linc wriggled in her grip. He looked at her. Ari looked back. Lori wasn't about to let go, unless Linc bit her. And Linc would bite only if she gave him permission. "Linc!" she called. "You find me when you can. Got that? Find me."

He barked. Ari prayed that he did understand. That, like Chase, when emotions were high he could somehow figure out what she needed.

She raised a hand in farewell and galloped Chase into the woods.

14

Atalanta splashed one cloven hoof in the water and watched the ripples drift away. She stood under a sapphire willow tree at the edge of the Imperial River, watching the world of Glacier River Farm in the magic waters of the Watching Pool. The vision was of Arianna and the Sunchaser fleeing the only security they had.

The willow branches dropped gracefully into the crystal-clear stream. Whenever a breeze came up, blossoms fell, blurring the images of Arianna and the Sunchaser. Then the flowers swirled away like little blue boats carried on the current. Sapphire willows grew only in the Valley of the Unicorns, as far as Atalanta knew. And Atalanta was the wisest unicorn in the Celestial Valley herd.

She raised her head and looked across the fields to rest her eyes from the visions. It had been a long, long night. A month had come and gone, and the Shifter's Moon was back. There'd been no attack from the Shifter — at least not yet. And Atalanta had walked the Path from the Moon and across the Gap to warn Arianna in a dream. But there were still three nights left of the Shifter's Moon, when her personal magic would not work — and Arianna was racing toward — what?

Atalanta sighed. Her crystal horn scattered splintered light on the grass.

It was so beautiful, her world! Unicorns stood peacefully throughout the Celestial Valley, as bright as the colors of the rainbow: Blue, scarlet, bronze, emerald, each a jewel of light in the already light-filled land. A sunstruck golden unicorn — brighter than the others — grazed on the hillside at Valley's end. Numinor, the Golden One.

All this beauty. All this could pass away in the next few days.

"What news at Glacier River?" Tobiano marched heavily through the grass, curious as always about matters that didn't concern him.

Atalanta nodded her greetings. The black-and-white-spotted unicorn was as rude as he was nosy. Atalanta's clear violet eyes softened with amusement. Tobiano had a good heart, in spite of himself. "Come and see."

He came and stood by her. Together, they watched Arianna and the Sunchaser take the paddock fence and gallop to freedom in the woods. The collie wasn't with them.

113

"She isn't wearing the jewel?" Tobiano asked.

Atalanta closed her eyes for a long moment. "No," she said sadly. "She is not wearing the jewel. And the dog isn't there. I still don't know what to make of the dog, Toby."

"Huh!" Tobiano's horn was short, but the noise he made through it was loud and brassy enough for a unicorn with a much longer one. "And what are you going to do about that?"

"I did what I could, Toby." She lifted her head and looked at him. Her silvery mane stirred in the soft breeze. "I have already broken the laws of our kind by visiting her on that side of the Gap. That's all I could do. I can't tell her the rest. Not yet. Not unless she crosses the Gap. And if she crosses the Gap, she will be in grave, grave danger. . . . We have no power over the humans at Glacier River, other than the power of dreams. What more could I do?"

Toby looked cross. "You could have told her straight out what's going on," he grumped. "I would have."

"Perhaps," Atalanta said, with a slight edge to her soft voice, "that is why I am Dreamspeaker and you are not. The laws are there for a reason."

"Huh!" Toby said again. "If you ask me —"

"Well, I haven't asked you," Atalanta said, reasonably enough.

"Certain unicorns I know ought to do a little more than just stand around looking into the Watching Pool when there's this much trouble afoot."

114

"If she crosses the Gap, I can do a little more than just visit her, Toby. But she has to cross first. You know that."

"Blah, blah," he said grouchily.

A slight frown appeared between Atalanta's violet eyes. Toby ducked his head, embarrassed. Apparently even he had limits to his rudeness. He muttered a quick, "Sorry!" Then, "We're all doin' our best. I mean, I know you're doin' your best. You lemme know if I can help."

She looked at him steadily. "Would you be willing to walk the Path from the Moon with me to join them? Into Balinor? I have a job for you. Your colors are very . . . usual, Toby. With a little care, you could look just like a unicorn of Balinor. We can disguise your jewel. If you were clever, and I know you can be, no one would guess that you are a celestial unicorn."

Toby looked as if he didn't know whether this was a compliment or not.

"It is very important," Atalanta assured him. "I need to have you tell me what's going on in Balinor. I see only what I ask to see in the Watching Pool. And, Toby, if I don't know what to ask, we could all be in very serious trouble. I want you to walk among the unicorns of Balinor as one of them and tell me of events that I do not know." She leaned close to him and bent her head to his ear. "There is no one else in the herd that could do it."

Toby rubbed his black-and-white horn

115

against the trunk of the sapphire willow tree. He brought his left hind hoof up and scratched his left ear. He yawned carelessly, as if what Atalanta said had been an ordinary, everyday kind of thing. Instead of what it really was. A challenge. An adventure. Leave the Celestial Valley? Walk the Path from the Moon to the earth below? He, Tobiano, the rudest unicorn in the celestial herd? A chance to be . . . a hero?

Atalanta may have smiled a little. It was hard to tell. She said in her gentle voice, "I'd have to check with Numinor, the Golden One, of course. But he would allow you to leave the herd. If you are willing to go."

Toby hummed a careless little tune through his horn to hide his excitement and said, "Sure. Heck. Why not?" And he turned and marched off, rolling through the meadow like a little barrel.

Atalanta turned back to the Watching Pool and watched as Arianna tried to lose herself and her horse in the woods outside Glacier River Farm. She leaned closer to the water, her silvery mane trailing in the starflowers on the bank . . . and watched.

15

ri raced along, her body swaying comfortably. Chase's hand gallop was smooth and swift. She felt as if she wasn't really sitting on his great bronze back, it was as if she were floating. She kept a sharp lookout for woodchuck holes and stones. The stallion was agile and quick, but at this speed even he could trip and fall. She would go to the cave created by the long-ago glaciers in their path to the sea. The cave in the south pasture. Near the meadow where she'd found the first of the strange spiral stones. The south pasture was large enough to hide Chase and her during the day.

It called to her now, stronger than ever.

She shook her head, as if to free it from dreams. Linc knew where the cave was. As soon as he got away from Lori and her father, he would find them. So it was a sensible thing to do.

Wasn't it?

117

She pulled Chase to a half-halt at the edge of the south pasture. It was peaceful under the sun, the uncut hay shifting slightly with the breeze. The cave lay on the far side. The entrance was concealed because the meadow dropped off to a deep ravine, but she could see it with her mind's eye, as clear as anything.

Ari guided Chase through the grass with her knees, the lead line loose over his neck. She listened carefully. Were there shouts in the distance? And was that the sound of another horse?

She felt Chase tense between her knees. His head came up. He whinnied, the call of a stallion to a member of the herd. Someone was after them. Ari leaned over his neck and whispered urgently, "Hush. Hush now, Chase."

She urged him to a swift trot. They reached the meadow's edge, and she slid to the ground. She walked carefully down the slope to the cave, urging the horse along with small murmurs of encouragement. He slid, caught himself, then flattened his ears. This meant he was cross with her, and despite the urgency of her search for the cave, Ari felt laughter bubble up in her throat. "Well, I'm sorry," she muttered. "I know you don't like it when the footing's rough. But this is an emergency, Chase."

He snorted and even seemed to nod his head. Ari wondered again about her ability to catch his thoughts. Was it true that he could speak with her in moments of great stress? Or was it just her imagination?

"There it is, Chase. The cave." She pulled on the lead line. He caught sight of the dark entrance, barely taller that his head. He balked, pulling her backward.

"No, Chase." She kept her voice low, but put all the urgency she could into it. "I know you don't like small, dark places. No horse does. But we have to hide. Just for a while." She stopped herself and listened hard.

Arianna! That whisper on the breeze! She rubbed her hands through her hair. Was the voice coming from the cave?

Ari cocked her head. The voice — if it had been a voice — faded with the wind. And now there was no doubt about it. There was a horse coming through the woods after them. Somewhere north of where they were now, which meant it or they were coming from the farm itself. "Come on, Chase." She tugged at the lead line. Chase backed up, swinging his head back and forth, back and forth. He dug his hind hooves into the ground and pulled away. So it was serious then, his refusal to go into that deep dark place. She loosened the line; Dr. Bohnes always said in a tug-of-war between a fourteen-hundred-pound horse and a one-hundred-and-three-pound human, it should be obvious who would win.

She made her voice firm and low. "Please, Chase. *Please.* For me."

The faraway hoofbeats grew nearer. Then stopped. Good. He or she or whoever was up there wasn't sure which way to go. But she had so little time!

Ari quickly freed the makeshift reins from the knot she'd made and turned the rope into a lead line again. She clipped the line to the ring in Chase's halter and backed herself into the cave, not pulling, just letting him stand. She would let him make his own decision. "See, Chase. Come on, boy. Walk in. It's just a nice hiding place. There's nothing in here."

She stopped herself in midsentence. There *was* something in here. She could feel it. And there was an odor. Faint. Horrible. Just like the stink she had run into the day before, in the meadow and then again in the vet's room. Still holding the lead line, she turned and searched the darkness with her eyes. It had rock walls and a dirt and gravel floor. There was slight trickle of damp from an underground water source.

Was that a low buzzing? A whine? Flies, black flies? Yes! She could just make out a mass of them against the north wall. No wonder Chase didn't want to come in. Horses hated black flies. She backstepped out into daylight. If she soothed him, explained to him, maybe she could ride him in.

Chase's ears pricked forward and he turned his head, listening to something behind him. There was a familiar scrabbling through the brush above. Lincoln poked his head over the lip of the rise and looked down on them. He had escaped the Carmichaels! He barked once. Ari knew that bark: It was a warning. The dog bounded down the slope. He came directly to her, bumped her knee with his head, then whirled and faced the rise. He barked again, and again Ari knew what it meant: Stay away! *Stay away!*

The thrumming of hooves grew nearer. Ari took a deep breath. She would face them, whoever they were. She heard a horse breathing hard and heavy, and a grunt from the animal as the rider pulled him up. His feet scrabbled in the gravel at the lip of the rise, just as Chase's had done. Then Max, the buckskin, fell over the edge. He slid down on his haunches. The rider on his back pulled hard on the reins. The gelding's mouth gaped wide and he twisted his head with the effort to get away from the bit.

Horse and rider tumbled straight toward them. Lincoln threw himself in front of Ari, trying to protect her. Still holding the lead line, Ari leaped backward into the cave. Max made a massive effort to avoid sliding into them. He gave a great heave with his front legs. The rider flew off and crashed into Chase. The stallion leaped forward, startled at the impact. His great chest smashed into Ari. She fell flat on her back, her head hitting the stone wall.

There was an immense, terrifying buzz of a million flies.

She heard Lincoln's snarl of rage.

There was a flash of bright violet, the scent of flowers.

And then . . . she heard nothing at all.

16

Ari woke up. She had wakened like this once before. After the accident. After the terrible crash that had twisted her legs and wiped her memory as clean as a blackboard eraser.

But then, she had awakened to pain worse than fire. Now she woke to sky that was a different blue from any blue she had seen before. To the smells of a forest that wasn't pine — but what?

Cautiously, she sat up. The ache in her legs was familiar: a dull throb in her calves where the scars were, an ache in her right knee. No different, then. No new injuries.

She sighed in relief. A wave of dizziness swept over her and she fell on her back. She fought the blackness. Chase! Where was Chase? A cold nose poked her neck, a warm tongue licked her cheek. She smiled gratefully and wound her hands in Lincoln's ruff. He stepped back and she held on to pull herself upright again. She blinked the dizziness away and looked. Chase stood near. So near that she reached out one hand and steadied herself against his iron-muscled foreleg. He bent his head and whiffed gently into her hair. She got up and dusted off her breeches.

Are you all right, milady?

His voice in her head! Tentatively, she spoke to him. "Chase? Is that you? Or am I dreaming?" She bit her lip and said to herself more than to the others, "Or maybe I'm crazy? The doctors told me they weren't sure why my memory's gone. Maybe I'm just plain nuts."

Chase looked back at her. The nice little wrinkles over each eye were sharply cut with worry. His nostrils flared red and his lower lip was tightly closed. She knew he was upset. She stroked his neck, then quickly checked him over. She remembered falling down, the horse and the dog rolling after her. If either one were hurt, she'd have to run back to the farm for help.

I have no hurt, no wound. But she may be injured. Go to her.

"She? Who?" A groan answered her. Ari looked around.

And she felt as if a giant hand squeezed all the breath out of her. Wherever Ari was, she wasn't at Glacier River Farm anymore.

The sky she'd wakened to not moments before was a purple-blue, unlike any she'd seen before.

She was in a meadow. At least, she was pretty sure it was a meadow. The grass was thick, knee-high, and of a bluish-green that reminded her more of water than anything else. The broad-bladed blue-green grass was as thick and uniform as a carpet.

The meadow itself was an irregularly shaped circle surrounded by dense trees. But the trees weren't any more normal than the grass or the sky. They were tall, with thickly gnarled branches that bent and twisted.

Had she been here before? A second groan, louder than the first, jerked her back to her companions. Lincoln, his tail waving, danced through the strange thick-bladed grass and bent his head to look at whatever was lying there. Ari hesitated. Should she run away?

"I will not," she said aloud. Chase snorted in approval. She cautiously approached Lincoln and whatever he was looking at. She wished she had a heavy branch.

The third groan made Ari stand up straight and march over to the hump in the grass. She knew that voice. And she was well acquainted with the crossness in it. She put her hands on her hips and looked down. "Lori Carmichael! What are you doing here?"

Lori's hair was tangled with bits of twigs and gravel. She wasn't hurt: Ari saw that right away. She was sitting cross-legged, with her head on her knees. And that last groan was exasperated, angry even, but not wounded. The blond girl blinked up at her. Her face was scratched and muddy. "What have you done now?" she grumbled.

"What have I done? You were the one who came chasing after me. And Max. Poor Max. You rode him too hard, as you always do. When you came crashing down that . . ."

"He *slipped*," Lori said furiously. "Can I help it if that dumb horse slipped!?"

Chase walked gracefully through the grass and stood next to Ari, watching Lori with courteous interest. Lori glared at him and got to her feet. Ari suppressed a giggle. Lori's breeches were torn right across the seat. And her underwear was green with little flowers on it.

"What did you do with him?" Lori demanded in a nasty voice.

"With Max, you mean?"

"With Max, you mean?" Lori mimicked furiously. "Who else, stupid? Godzilla? If you think I'm walking back to the farm all bumped up like this, you've got another think coming."

Chase lowered his head and nudged Ari gently. *He did not cross the Gap with us.*

"Gap?" Ari put her hand on Chase's mane. It was silky under her hand. "Chase, what's the . . . Gap?"

I do not . . . I do not . . . recall.

"What are you doing now! Talking to your horse? Great. Just *great*. I told Daddy that accident

126

made you loony, and I was right." Lori took a couple of steps toward them, then looked down to shove Lincoln out of the way. He growled, deep in his throat, but moved aside.

Lori looked around angrily, then gasped. Her face turned white. For the first time she seemed to realize that she — they — were in a place so strange it might have been another planet. "What's going on here?" Her voice quivered. She looked at the trees, with their bizarre branches bent and curled like hair after a bad perm. She glanced up at the purple-blue sky and looked past the trees to the horizon beyond. She flushed bright red and pointed, her eyes so wide Ari could see the whites all around them. "Ari! Ari! *What is that?*"

Ari shaded her eyes with her hands and looked at the sun. It was in the same position in the sky it had been at home, about halfway between the eastern horizon and straight overhead. Which meant Lori was pointing west. Ari wheeled around slowly, almost afraid to look beyond the trees. "Why, it's a village!" she said in amazement.

"What do you mean, a village, Miss Know-It-All? That's not like any village I've ever seen. A village!" Lori was making a huge effort not to cry. She was shaking so hard Ari wondered if she'd shake herself right out of her riding boots.

Ari kept her voice gentle, the way she did when she handled a scared horse. "Those are buildings, don't you think?"

"With grass on the roofs? Don't be an idiot."

"Sure. You've seen pictures. Those are thatched roofs. You know, long grass that's dried and then put on top of a house to keep the rain out."

"I don't like it here. I want to go home. You take me home. Right now! If you don't, I'm going to tell Daddy to buy Chase and you'll never see him again."

Ari ignored her. "Where do you suppose we came out?" she asked thoughtfully.

"Came out? Came out?"

"Well, we're on the other side of the cave, aren't we?" Something Dr. Bohnes had told her about Glacier River came back to her now. "The land here folded and folded again when the glaciers came through millions of years ago."

Chase nodded. *The Gap.*

"So that's the Gap, Chase?"

"Stop that!" Lori shrieked. "Stop that right now!"

"Stop what?"

"Pretending that horse is talking to you!"

"Well, he is talking to me," Ari said reasonably.

"Don't be an idiot!"

Ari walked up to her horse and put her hands on either side of his muzzle. She pulled his head down and laid her cheek against the strange white scar on his forehead. It felt cool, cooler than the rest of him. "Can we go back the way we came?"

He nickered, low in his throat. *No.*

"Do you know where we are?"

On the other side of the Gap.

"Do you know what place this is?"

The wrinkles over his eyes grew deeper. *I . . . I perhaps have dreamed of this place.*

"But you don't know where we are."

Before he could answer, Lori screamed, "Cut it out, cut it out, CUT IT OUT!" She fairly danced up and down in rage. "I want to go home RIGHT NOW!"

"I don't know how to go home, and Chase doesn't, either."

Lincoln whined, lay down on the grass, and put his paws over his eyes. Did he understand what she'd just said? Ari thought she truly would go crazy if he started to talk to her, too. She found herself hoping that the dog hadn't really understood what she'd just said, but that he was tired. Or the sun was hurting his eyes. Or something.

I want to go home, too.

Ari stared at him, her mouth open. *O-kay.* The dog was talking, too. Lincoln's voice was different from Chase's. For one thing, he had an accent. He sounded just like Mrs. Broadbent, the dressage teacher. She came to the farm once a week to teach first level to the riding students.

"Hel-lo," Lori said in an incredibly sarcastic voice, jerking Ari's attention away from Lincoln's newfound ability to chatter. "Earth to Ari. Let's get it

129

straight. You do know what's happened here, don't you?" The tears welled up in her eyes. "We've been abducted by aliens."

"We haven't been abducted by aliens. For one thing, the sun's in the same position it was when we fell through the cave."

"So?"

"So I think we're on the other side."

"The other side of what?"

"Of the farm. A different side. A side . . ." Ari hesitated, "that maybe was here all the time, but the glaciers folded it away. I mean, we can breathe the air and everything, Lori. And I've seen pictures of those thatched roofs in books. I know I have. If we were on another planet, everything would be weird."

"Oh?" Lori's eyebrows rose to her hairline. "You don't think this is weird? *Excuse* me, but this is weird enough for me, thank you very much. Now, let's get out of here."

Ari looked at Chase, standing regally alert, and at Lincoln, sitting majestically, if a little forlornly, on the grass. If they went home, would she be able to speak with them again?

"You do want to get out of here, don't you?" Lori's voice was quavering again.

"Sure. So let's go up to the village and ask how to get back."

"Are you crazy?"

"I don't think so."

130

Lori grabbed her by the shoulders and shook her. "What if they attack us?"

"Why should they?" Ari removed Lori's hands from her shoulders. "Here's what we'll do. Those trees are pretty thick. And the village is on the other side of the forest. So we'll go through the trees and wait until we see some people walking around and see how normal they look. If they look pretty normal, we'll . . ." Ari stopped. "We'll ask for the police station. Then we'll go to the police station and ask our way home."

"Finally, a plan that doesn't sound stupid." Lori folded her arms across her chest and tapped her foot.

"Good." Ari picked up Chase's lead line, whistled to Lincoln, and set off for the forest. "Are you coming?"

"I'm not walking all that way. I'm hot. I'm hungry. And I'm tired. I'm going to ride Chase."

Ari debated. She could drag Lori whining all the way through the woods, or she could put her on Chase and get some peace and quiet. She patted Chase's neck. "Do you mind?"

She sits like a sack of potatoes.

"Just don't dump her off, okay? We've had enough physical stuff this morning." She nodded to Lori. "He doesn't mind. Much. I'll give you a leg up." She crouched and cupped her hands together. Lori put her left foot into Ari's cupped hands. Ari counted "one, two, three" and on the count of three, pushed her hands up. Lori pushed off the ground with her right foot, then swung her right leg over Chase's back. The stallion snorted, tossed his head, and rolled his eyes. Ari raised her hand quietly, and Chase settled down with a grumble. Then Ari crouched down in front of Lincoln.

"You have a pretty good nose, boy?"

We collies have excellent noses.

"That's great. Can you lead us to the village? By scenting the people and . . ." Ari sighed. She'd missed breakfast this morning and she realized she was starved. "And the food?"

Of course. Lincoln's mental tone was lofty. *No problem at all. Of course,* he hesitated, *collies are not bloodhounds, you know.*

"I know."

Nor are we terriers. Terriers have excellent noses. However, a nose isn't everything, you know. There are more important issues for dogs than a great sense of smell. Beauty, for example. We collies are —

"Lincoln?"

— among the most handsome of breeds. . . .

"LINC!"

Yes?

Ari put her hands on her hips and regarded him with exasperated affection. My goodness. Who would have thought her beloved dog was as gabby as this? "Quiet, please. Just find us the village."

132

Right you are. He trotted ahead, plumed tail waving gaily. Ari walked behind him, not so much leading Chase as walking companionably side by side. They crossed the meadow. Linc's gold-and-black back almost disappeared in the tall grass, but the way was soft-going. The blades grew straight and tall. Despite how thick the grass was, it bent easily with their passage.

And the way was almost silent.

It was not as easy once they got to the woods. Inside the forest, the branches intertwined overhead to make a canopy that kept out the sun. The golden leaves held the light, much as a glass holds water.

Ari could see where they walked, but the close-growing trees made their forward progress almost blind. Thank goodness the branches started growing a third of the way up the trunks and the ground underfoot was thickly padded with leaves and not much else. At least they didn't have brush to wade through.

Lincoln's progress was erratic, just as it was when he and Ari went out for walks at home. He stopped and sniffed at piles of leaves, investigated mysterious holes, and occasionally marked the trunk of a tree with his scent, lifting one leg with an intent, faraway expression. The chief difference was that Ari heard all the dog's chatter in her mind, which was addressed as much to himself as to her:

Now that would be a woodchuck hole on the other side of the Gap, but Canis alone knows what animal den this would be. And that trail up the trunk, could have been a squirrel, but are there squirrels here on the other side of the Gap?

She became almost happy with the constant chatter the deeper they went into the woods. The leaves were darker here, the gold deepening to a dull brown. The forest was quiet and alternately dim and dark. Really quiet. And Lincoln's cheerful comments kept her mind from wondering what that dark hump really was at the foot of an especially large tree, or if she'd actually seen a shadow slip between the trunks of two slender saplings.

Lincoln came to an abrupt halt and growled. Ari froze in place. That was Lincoln's "stranger!" growl. The hair along the dog's creamy ruff rippled and stood up.

Chase stopped, ears forward. He curled his upper lip over his teeth.

Lori, a sob of fear in her throat, cried, "What! What is it?"

"Hush!" Ari strained her ears to hear. Flies. Black flies. And that horrible, dead animal odor that she'd smelled three times before.

Lincoln whirled to them, teeth snapping. *BACK! BEHIND THE TREE!*

To her astonishment, Ari heard Chase respond.

What? Chase demanded. *I hide from no thing nor beast, dog!*

Lincoln's tone was grim. *You'll hide from this! Quickly now!*

Ari couldn't stop to think about this new phenomenon. Her dog and her horse could talk to each other.

There was a quiver in the air, just like the beating of a drum. Ari counted under her breath, almost without realizing she was doing it. "One. Two. Three. Four."

"What is it?" Lori was so scared, she almost whispered with terror. Lincoln, cold determination in his eyes, nudged them behind the trunk of the largest tree near them.

The sound in the air grew closer:

"One. Two. Three. Four."

"Something's marching," Ari whispered. She looked up at Lori. The blond girl's face was white. Ari could hear the quick shallow breaths she took. "Easy, now," she said, just as she would to a frightened horse. "Deep breaths. Take very deep breaths."

"ONE! TWO! THREE! FOUR!"

There were voices in the beating of the air. Deep voices, many of them, and all of them marking time together.

Ari flattened herself against the tree, not daring to look around. Lori bent her head into Chase's mane and sobbed silently, her shoulders shaking.

135

Chase kept his head up, his nostrils flared. He was confused and angry. *Horses, milady. And yet, not horses.*

Ari was afraid to answer. Suddenly, Chase started forward, snorting. Lincoln flung himself in the way, pressing the great stallion's body out of sight of the oncoming marchers. Ari huddled between Chase's legs. The ground shook.

She had to see! Ari crawled forward, peering around the huge tree trunk, almost hidden in the leaves piled at its base.

The marchers came through the woods.

Ari stuffed her fist in her mouth to keep from screaming.

There were so many of them — perhaps a hundred. Each was coal black with red eyes, demon eyes. Each had an iron horn springing from the middle of its forehead.

Black unicorns.

An army of them.

They carried fear with them — and terror. It was in the air they breathed, the ground they marched upon. They passed the tree where the companions lay hidden, in pairs. Their flaming eyes stared straight ahead. Their coats were blacker than coal, blacker than the bottom of the night itself.

Ari's mouth was dry. Her breath was short. She may have fainted, just a little, from the utter horror of it.

When she opened her eyes, they were gone. The air was clean and sweet, the ground firm. It was as if they had never been.

"Lori?" Ari was surprised at how calm she sounded. "You okay?"

"I guess." Lori's voice was a mere squeak. "Did you look?"

"I looked."

"What *was* it?"

"Did you look?"

"No." Lori paused. "I mean, yes."

"Well, so you know what it was." Ari knew that Lori had been too scared to raise her head from Chase's mane. If she told Lori that'd she'd seen a herd of black and fire-eyed unicorns, evil in every step they took, the blond girl would dissolve in a sticky puddle of tears. And they'd never get out of this forest.

"I didn't exactly see, I guess. So what was it?"

"Just some . . . ah . . . bears."

"Bears!" Lori sat up with a squall.

Lincoln looked at Ari reproachfully, *Now you've done it. She won't stop shrieking until we get to the village.*

"BEARS!" Lori drummed her heels into Chase's sides. The stallion cocked his head at Ari. *May I dump her, milady?*

"You may not. We will just . . ." Ari sighed, "march on. Maybe she'll shut up when she sees we're close to safety."

137

None of them spoke again. The fear was still with them.

Half an hour later, Lincoln led them to the edge of the woods, and they gazed upon the village for the first time. Ari looked. She couldn't tell if it was safe or not. But there was a sign. And the sign said:

WELCOME TO BALINOR

Ari stopped. Stared. And a cold, cold wind blew over her heart. What was this? *What was this!*

More than a village lay ahead.

She took one step forward. Then another.

SUNCHASER'S QUEST

For John Robert,
from his loving Mary.

1

It was a beautiful day in the Celestial Valley. The sun was at its height over the deep green meadows. A soft breeze rustled the leaves of the sapphire willow trees lining the banks of the Imperial River. The unicorns of the Celestial Valley herd grazed peacefully in the sunshine, each unicorn a flare of brilliant color corresponding to a color of the rainbow. A beautiful violet unicorn with a silver mane and tail gazed down upon the herd from the Eastern Ridge. This was Atalanta, the Dreamspeaker, mate to Numinor, the Golden One, and counselor to the herd. Her deep violet eyes were troubled. Sorrow had come to the Celestial Valley. The herd's ancient enemies were stirring. The threat of war loomed.

Atalanta sighed deeply. In normal times, today would be the first day of training the Dreamspeaker's Disciple. She had already selected a candidate, Devi, a weanling unicorn who already showed the spirit of adventure necessary for the hard life of Dreamspeakers. But she had spoken to Nana, the Herd Caretaker, and told her to cancel Devi's first lesson. These were hard times, and she had to consult with Numinor about what lay ahead.

Atalanta turned and went up the Eastern Ridge to the Cave of Numinor. Below her, the unicorns grazed under the sun. The adults formed a protective circle around the nursery. The babies were a spot of silver-gray right in the middle of the herd. Devi the weanling unicorn looked up and watched as Atalanta disappeared around a curve of the Eastern Ridge. Nana, the Caretaker, had just told him he couldn't meet with the Dreamspeaker for his first lesson, and he was trying to hide his disappointment. "But *why* can't I study with the Dreamspeaker?" he asked in his high, sweet voice. He was careful not to whine. "I've been good."

"You know that the Dreamspeaker has very important matters to attend to," Nana said. Nana was a pleasant, rosy sort of pink. Her horn was a creamy ivory, as were her mane and tail. She was round and soft to nestle up to. "And you know that she always keeps her word. She'll get to your lessons soon, Devi. Just not today."

"Then can I go play?"

Nana sighed. Like all baby unicorns, Devi was a pearly gray color, which would deepen to a rainbow color as the unicorn grew into adulthood. Nana was sure what color Devi would be as a yearling: chocolate-brown with an obsidian horn. Chocolate-brown was the stubbornest color Nana could think of, and obsidian was the hardest jewel. Devi was the stubbornest foal she'd handled in a long, long time. When Devi began his apprenticeship to Atalanta this kind of determination would be good. But for now, it made things difficult. "I don't think you should play today. Why don't you take a nice nap with the others?"

Devi pouted. "I'm not sleepy!"

"You *should* be wantin' a nice rest. If you run around too much, you'll get hot. And if you get hot, you could get sunstroke. And if you get sunstroke, I'll have a conniption. You wouldn't want that."

Since Devi didn't know what a conniption was, he didn't care. Devi didn't think his chances of tiptoeing away for a little adventure without permission were too good, either. Someone would spot him right away.

"If I can't play, can I just walk down to the river?"

Nana pushed out her lower lip. She hated to say no. And she hated to think that it wouldn't be safe. The Celestial Valley had been a haven for her and her kind forever. Until now. For the past three days, the herd had been alive with the terrible news: Entia was on the prowl! Entia, the Shifter, was the enemy of all those in the Celestial Valley and the lands of humans beneath it. He had kidnapped the King and Queen of Balinor, and threatened the life of the

Princess Arianna and the Sunchaser, her Bonded unicorn. Atalanta and Numinor had sent Arianna and the Sunchaser through the Gap to safety at Glacier River Farm, with the help of the loyal villagers of Balinor.

But the haven of the farm had proved to be a trap. Arianna's memory was gone, obliterated by the Shifter's tricks. Ari no longer knew that she was the Princess of Balinor. And worse yet was the condition of the Sunchaser himself. With his horn hacked off in the heat of the battle at the Shifter's Palace, he, too, had lost his memory: He no longer knew he was the Sunchaser, Lord of the Animals in Balinor, and Bonded to the Princess Arianna.

And now the Shifter stalked Balinor — and perhaps the Celestial Valley itself! No, it wasn't safe for little Devi to travel to the river. She shook her head. "I don't think a walk would be a good idea, either."

Devi rubbed his little horn against Nana's foreleg, then nibbled her pink whiskers. "Please?" he said. "I'll be very, very careful."

Nana's lower lip still stuck out. Devi blew softly against her cheek. "I won't go in the water," he promised. "And I'll be very, very, VERY careful."

Nana looked at the meadows filled with unicorns, all within shouting distance if trouble came. She looked at the sky, a clear, deep violet-blue that rivaled the color of the Dreamspeaker's eyes. And Devi was such a rowdy little foal! If he took a walk —

just a short one! — it might tire him out enough so that she could nap a little herself this afternoon. "All right," Nana said. She blew back at him, a soft tickle of breath that made him sneeze. "But you come right back here."

"Hoo-ray!" Devi jumped into the air. Nana chuckled as she watched him trot off. Young unicorns' knees were so knobby when they were small! And their little tails and manes were nothing more than soft fuzz. She bent her head to graze, looking up occasionally to see Devi skipping down to the Imperial River. Then young Lydiana got into a shoving match with Viola-Rose, who'd just barely been weaned, and Nana forgot all about Devi as she settled the squabble.

Devi slowed from a skip to a walk as he approached the banks of the Imperial River. He looked back. Nana was paying more attention to the spat between Lydiana and Viola-Rose than she was to him.

Good. He was safe to explore. He danced a little in the short sweet grass. The trees dropped flowers on the rippling water. Sunlight sparkled off the wavelets. Everything was peaceful.

Peaceful enough for *adventure*.

Devi was upset about the lost Princess. And even more upset about the terrible accident to the great bronze unicorn Sunchaser. A unicorn without his horn! And one who didn't know who he was!

Devi thought, Why not just *tell* them?

Tell the Princess that she's the Princess. Tell Chase that he's the Sunchaser, the mightiest of the Royal unicorns in Balinor and the Lord of the Animals there. And once they were told? Well! The animals in Balinor wouldn't lose their ability to talk and everything would be all right!

Devi stood in the sunshine and formed a plan. He'd been to the Watching Pool, the magical spot that allowed the Dreamspeaker to see events in lands below the Celestial Valley.

He didn't need lessons to be a Dreamspeaker! He could go to the pool, call up the Princess and the Sunchaser, and tell them who they really were! Then they would fight the evil Shifter and everything would be back to normal.

Devi followed the course of the river up the hill, stopping to nibble at a bit of grass, then to nose a pebble along the well-marked path, just in case Nana was looking to see what he was doing. His alert ears caught the sound of falling water, and he trotted a little faster to reach the source. He rounded a large amethyst boulder and heaved a sigh of relief. The Watching Pool!

He stood before the wide pool of clear water surrounded by amethyst rock. Water rushed over the lip of the pool and into the Imperial River. This was the Watching Pool. Devi knew all about it. Every unicorn did. The Watching Pool was where the Celestial herd watched events in the world of humans. But Devi had never been there alone before.

The wind stirred the brush at the side of the pool. The air felt hot. Suddenly, his plan to call Princess Arianna and the Sunchaser through the Watching Pool seemed — dangerous.

He crept nearer.

No one yelled, "Halt!" or "Stop!" or worse yet — "Back to the nursery, little one!" He stuck out his chest and pranced a bit to give himself courage. He was not a little one. He was Devi the Great!

The water fell with the sound of silver bells.

He took one hesitant step, then another, until he reached the broad shelf of amethyst where Atalanta the Dreamspeaker stood each morning to gaze at events in the world of humans. The rock was worn smooth from the hooves of Dreamspeakers standing watch throughout time.

"Ho," Devi said as he bent over his reflection in the water. And, "Ho" again as he saw his own face — tiny horn, wide green eyes, and frizzy forelock.

He could do it! He could call Princess Arianna and the Sunchaser! "I am Devi! The Great!" he piped in his high, sweet voice. He bent his head. Just as he'd seen the Dreamspeaker do, he touched his horn to the water, once, twice, three times. "I call Arianna, Princess of Balinor!"

He stepped back. The water began to spin and darken. With a sudden shudder, the waters convulsed and went black. A sickly yellow-green light glowed eerily in its depths. A terrible odor of decay drifted from the surface. Devi swallowed hard.

"Devi!" came a cross, gruff voice. "Get out o' there, bud!"

Devi jumped into the air. A stout black-and-white unicorn regarded him balefully from the upper slope of the hill. Tobiano, the rudest unicorn in the herd. He didn't like foals at all. Devi tripped and scrambled helplessly against the smooth rock and fell into the pool with a splash.

Devi had never felt fear in his entire short life. But he felt it now. The waters closed over his head. And they were hot — burning hot! He struggled to breathe and gasped, choking on the taste of ash. The evil yellow-green light surrounded him, blinding him.

And then . . . *skeletal hands on his pasterns, pulling him down!*

He screamed, inhaled more fiery water, and, too scared to think, fell into blackness.

He woke to a cool violet light and the scent of roses. He lay still for a moment, blinking, glorying in the sunshine that warmed his withers, in the feel of the soft breeze against his flanks. He was safe on the banks of the Watching Pool. And he'd have to be thankful to the bossiest unicorn in the herd for pulling him out. Well, he didn't care. He was just glad to be alive.

"Well, then, little Devi." Atalanta's voice was gentle, with a crystal chime. Atalanta, the Dreamspeaker! She had saved him! And that cranky Toby was just behind her! Devi gasped, then stumbled upright as fast as he could. "Oh, Atalanta!" he said miserably. He hung his head. "I just . . . I just wanted to help."

"Ah." Atalanta pricked her ears forward and gazed at him with her deep violet eyes.

"Interferin' little one," Toby grumbled. "Send him back to his ma, I say."

"He's very brave, to try to warn Arianna," Atalanta said. "But Devi, do you know what almost happened to you?"

He shook his head.

"The Shifter was after you!"

Devi's eyes grew round.

"Were you scared?" she asked gently.

He thought about this. He was brave. Atalanta herself had said so, and what she said was true. He puffed out his chest a little, took a breath, then caught that deep purple gaze. "Yes." He scraped one forefoot along the ground.

Atalanta nodded. "Wise, as well as brave," she said. "Those were the hands of Entia himself, pulling you down."

"The Shifter." Devi shuddered.

"And now you know why we have a rule about the Watching Pool, Devi. I, and I alone may call at the pool. Because you never know who — or what — will answer."

"I'm sorry." Devi looked up at her. "But Atalanta. Why don't you just tell the Princess who she is? Why don't you help the Sunchaser get his horn back?"

Atalanta bowed her head. Her silky mane flowed over her face, like a light cloud across the sun. "I am doing what I am allowed to do. There is only so much magic to use, and a very few times that I can use it. I am about to use some now. Perhaps you would care to help?"

Devi nodded vigorously. "Oh, yes!"

"Then stand here, next to me."

Devi pranced forward. Then, suddenly shy as the silvery light around Atalanta enveloped him, he dropped his head and stared at his hooves. The left fore was a little chipped, and he rubbed his nose on it furiously. What if she noticed!

But Atalanta was not looking at Devi's hooves. She nodded at Toby. "Are you ready?"

"Guess so," Toby said gruffly. Devi could hear the excitement in his voice.

"Devi?"

He looked up at the Dreamspeaker.

"I am going to open the water. Toby and I are going to Balinor. I will come back alone, for I will not be allowed to stay too long. But Toby will remain there and report to me. I have made arrangements to . . ." She paused, clearly amused at something. "To hook him up with a friend, so to speak."

"How come *you* have to come back? I mean, aren't you the Dreamspeaker?" Devi asked.

"She holds the Deep Magic," Toby said. "It will leave her if she stays too long below. Now me, I have practically no magic at all." He thought a moment.

"Enough," Atalanta said. "Be silent, both of you." She walked to the edge of the pool and struck the water three times with her horn. The water swirled, and Devi held his breath. A vision appeared in the pool of a bronze-haired girl with eyes the color of the sky, and a great bronze horse. A huge collie walked with them. "The Princess, the Sunchaser, and that dog, Lincoln," Atalanta said. "They have just come through the Gap. They are headed to Balinor itself."

"Who's *that?*" Toby grumbled. "That blond kid. How did she get through the Gap?"

"Her name is Lori Carmichael," the Dreamspeaker said thoughtfully. "How odd." She shook herself briskly. "Well, we shall see." She backed away from the pool and raised her head to the sun. Slowly, she rose on her hindquarters until her forelegs reached into the sky. She took a long breath and sang a single note, low, sweet, and throbbing. The waters in the pool parted slowly, as if giant hands were pushing them aside.

The song gathered in strength until Devi closed his eyes with the power of it. When he opened his eyes again, the Dreamspeaker and Toby were gone. Devi leaned over the pool. In the depths, he saw a tiny silver star speeding toward Balinor, and a black-and-white shadow bouncing beside it.

The Dreamspeaker and Toby were on their way to Balinor.

2

Ari, Lori Carmichael, and Chase stopped at the edge of a small field of short grass dotted with flowers. Lincoln, the collie, stood at Ari's side.

"This is your fault," Lori said flatly.

Ari looked at Lori in exasperation. The blond girl was a spoiled brat, no doubt about it. She thought she was the most important riding student at Glacier River Farm. And unfortunately she was — but only because of her father's money.

Lori scowled and stamped her feet. "I said this is your fault! What are you going to do about it?"

"Just let me think a minute." Ari ran her hands through her hair. She didn't have any idea where they were or how they'd gotten here. The last thing she remembered was a frantic ride on Chase from Glacier River Farm to the safety of the cave in the south pasture. But the cave hadn't been safe at all. Some terrible force had pulled her, her dog, and

157

her horse through a tunnel to this place. And that force had also caught Lori and pulled her through.

"None of this would have happened if you'd just let Chase alone," Ari said, trying to keep her voice reasonable. "You didn't have any business trying to lease him. He's mine!"

"What good is a horse to you?" Lori asked rudely. "Your legs got so messed up from that accident that you can't ride him as much as he needs to be ridden anyway."

Ari rubbed her right calf. Both legs had been broken, in what her foster parents, Ann and Frank, had told her was a truck accident. Chase himself had also been hurt; he still carried a white scar in the middle of his forehead from the tragedy. But Ari was healing just fine. She just couldn't remember anything before the accident. Nothing about Glacier Farm was familiar — not even her foster parents. Chase, her horse, was her only memory. "You just had to have my horse, didn't you? I shouldn't have to remind you, Lori, that if you hadn't chased after us, you'd be safe at the farm."

"I wouldn't have had to chase after you if you'd kept up your end of the bargain!"

"I didn't make the bargain. My foster father did. Because we needed the money to pay my medical bills!"

"Oh, shut up," Lori said. "Just shut up! And get us of out here, will you?"

"As soon as I figure out where 'here' is, I'll do just that! Come on, Linc."

The collie darted on ahead, moving quietly through the grass. They were in a flowery meadow, filled with blossoms that were yellow, blue, and deep red. Ari thought she recognized a few of the species. That was comforting. Surely that green and purplish-brown bloom in the shade of the trees was Jack-in-the-pulpit.

On the other hand, the little town on the other side of the field was not familiar at all. And that was not so comforting.

The village looked strange. For a moment, Ari wondered if Lori was right. Maybe they *had* been abducted by aliens. A wide dirt path ran straight down the middle of it. It was hard to tell at this distance, but the path appeared to end at a long, low, rambling structure made of wood that was too big for a house. Ari could make out a sign on a post in front of a big front porch. Maybe it was a hotel.

The left side of the path was lined with three-sided sheds. Some were big, some were small, but all contained many kinds of items. One shed had a spinning wheel out front. The shelves inside held brightly colored piles of yarnlike stuff. Several of the sheds had fenced paddocks attached. One of them held a few milk cows; another goats. And there was a bread shed, a fruit shed, a vegetable shed.

Houses — at least Ari guessed they were

159

houses — clustered on the opposite side of the dirt path like bees in a hive. The huts were round, with straw roofs. Most of them had bricklike chimneys. It was a warm morning, but smoke rose from a few of the huts and Ari guessed that the people here used wood fires to cook.

There were people in the village. That was a plus. And there was the smell of vegetable stew and melting cheese and freshly baked bread. That was a double plus.

But the women were dressed in long flowing gowns. . . .

Ari's mouth dropped open. Just like the dinner plates in Ann's kitchen!

And the men wore boots, tights, and loose shirts that looked as if they were made out of rough cotton. Some had short cloaks that were attached at the shoulder and fell to the waist. Ari had never seen clothes just like this before, or houses and shops and hotels.

"What is this place?" Lori said crossly. She shifted irritably on Chase's back. "What a dump! Where's the police station? This doesn't look right."

"I think it's because there are no power lines," Ari said. She realized she'd been clutching Linc's ruff. "No telephone poles, nothing like that."

"No cars, either. How do these people get around?" Lori gave a scornful sniff.

Shank's mare, Chase said. At Ari's puzzled look, *It's an expression we horses use for the way men walk. With two legs and those silly shoes you wear. I have no idea how your shoes stay on without nails, milady.*

Ari didn't know quite what to say to this. She didn't know what she should do, either. Just walk down the dirt path and say, "Hi"? She and Lori were both dressed in denim shirts, breeches, and boots, so they didn't look as out of place as they might have. Jeans, T-shirts, and sneakers would have been very noticeable.

"So what do we do now?" Lori complained. She glared at Ari, pouting.

Chase looked at her with his wise brown eyes and breathed out softly.

Lincoln settled down on his haunches, scratched furiously at one ear, then looked at her expectantly.

Ari looked back at the three of them. *She* was supposed to decide?

"Well." Ari twirled a strand of hair with one finger. Then she twirled a strand of hair with the other. She squinted her eyes and tried to look thoughtful. Like a leader. She folded her arms across her chest and gazed sternly at the village.

What should they do? Just walk in?

The noise from the village was what you'd expect. People talking and laughing. Somebody was hammering metal somewhere, and the clangs split the air. One of the milk cows mooed in a thoughtful way while a woman in a long brown skirt with a shawl over her shoulders milked it. There was a jingling noise underneath all of this. It sounded just like the harness Ari used at Glacier River Farm when she hooked the pony to the cart. The jingling came from the woods to their left. Ari turned around as the sound grew louder.

"Morning! Morning, ladies!" A man driving a horse and a four-wheeled wagon waved to them as they trotted past. Except the horse wasn't really a horse.

It was a unicorn! A stout, black-and-white spotted unicorn, with a short black-and-white spiral horn coming straight out of the middle of his forehead! His harness was made of scarlet leather and his eyes were hazel. They widened at the sight of two girls, a collie, and a bronze stallion standing at the edge of the wood. He stopped and nodded to them.

The man driving the wagon jiggled the reins. "Move on, Toby. We're late — I say we're late with these vegetables." The man was very fat, with a smiling red face and a huge, curled mustache. He wore black loose-fitting trousers tucked into the top of heavy brown boots. His dark brown shirt was loose, too, but not loose enough to hide his enormous tummy.

"Hold on a minute, Samlett," the unicorn said in a very bossy way. Then, in the rudest voice Ari had ever heard, "And who, may I ask, are you?"

162

Lori shrieked. It was a faint shriek, mostly because she was too scared to get much breath into her lungs, but it was a shriek.

Toby scowled. "You are addressing a unicorn," he said loftily. "And that's how you pay your respects? By yelling?"

"It's talking," Lori gasped. She closed her eyes for a second. Her face was whiter than ever. "Oh, my. Oh, my. It's talking. It's a unicorn and it's talking. I want to go home."

"Well, Toby *does* talk a bit rude," Mr. Samlett admitted. "Hasn't been with me long, so there's not too much I can do about the way he talks, milady." He chewed one end of his mustache. "Rude to the others, too. And uppity. But there you are. It's like they say. Unicorns will be unicorns."

"I don't mean the way he's talking! I mean the fact that he's talking at all!" She threw Ari a poisonous glance. "I suppose *you* think it's perfectly normal."

"Now, your maid doesn't think a thing you don't want her to think," Mr. Samlett said nervously. "Don't get in an uproar, milady. Too fine a morning for that."

"Maid?" Ari said. "You think I'm her maid?"

"Well," Mr. Samlett said, "stands to reason, don't it? I mean, don't it? She's ridin' as fine a unicorn as I've ever seen in these parts, and you're doin' the walkin'." He leaned forward, squinting at

Chase. "Except, by gum. I say by gum. He don't have no horn, Toby."

"No, he doesn't," Toby said. He had a very odd expression in his eyes as he looked at Chase. Respect? Fear? Pity? Toby shook himself hard, as if to clear his brain. Then, resuming his former manner, he said, "Any fool could see that, except maybe you, Samlett."

"He's a horse," Ari said. "Not a unicorn."

"Looks like a unicorn to me," Mr. Samlett said. "Only he's got no horn. What happened to your horn, friend? If you don't mind my askin'."

Chase nudged Ari with his nose. *Say nothing for the moment, little one. We don't know how horses are treated in this place. And I — I cannot remember.*

"He doesn't talk," Lori said. "And you're both idiots. You heard her, he's a horse."

"Whatever you say, milady." Mr. Samlett rolled his eyes. "S'pose if he don't have a horn, he don't talk, neither. Didn't used to hear of such things. Not in Balinor. All the animals talk in Balinor. But the troubles are here, sure as you know it. More and more you hear of animals losin' their speech. Next thing you know, humans won't be able to talk, either. I say we won't be able to talk, either."

Ari bit her lip to keep from laughing. It might be a mercy if Mr. Samlett couldn't talk. But it was very sad about the animals.

He gave his mustache a final tug and asked Lori, "You and your maid headed into Balinor?"

164

"I'm not . . ." Ari began. Chase nudged her warningly. Toby, to everyone's amazement, began to laugh. When unicorns laugh (or, as Ari discovered later, sneeze, cough, hum, sing, or cry), they laugh through their horns.

"Now what stickerburr's under your saddle?" Mr. Samlett asked the unicorn genially.

"If there were a stickerburr under my saddle, do you think I would have agreed to pull this rickety old cart?" Toby demanded. "I would not. Why I'm laughing, I'll keep to myself for the moment. Ask this — lady — and her 'maid' and her dog and her hornless unicorn to come along to the Inn for breakfast."

"Ain't he something," Mr. Samlett said admiringly. "Never met a fellow with such a way with words. Well, how about it, milady?"

"Who, me?" Lori said. "I mean, yes. I want breakfast." She lifted her chin in the air and said in a highly snobbish way, "Breakfast for me and my maid. And a bath."

Lincoln growled under his breath, then tapped Ari's boot with his paw. She glanced down at him.

No baths!

Ari laughed and rumpled his ears. So Balinor, as Mr. Samlett called it, may be a different place, and they were in a different world, but some things were always the same.

3

They all rode down the dirt path through the village. Toby led the way, trotting briskly along while Mr. Samlett jounced in the cart. Once in a while, he would say, "Whoa, there, Toby." This had no effect whatsoever on the unicorn's speed, of course.

Lori rode behind the wagon on Chase. Chase held his head high, his neck arched. His silky mane flowed down his withers almost to his knees. His chestnut coat glimmered in the bright sunshine. Lincoln pranced along at his side.

Ari walked behind them all. She could see the torn spot in the back of Lori's breeches, but the flowered underwear was only visible when Lori tried to show off by posting bareback on Chase. Because she wasn't a very good rider — and because with all their adventures, everyone was tired — she posted once or twice, then gave it up. But she sat in a very lordly way, which made Ari chuckle to herself.

Mr. Samlett knew everyone in Balinor. Crutch, the Weaver, and his wife, Begonia. The vegetable man, the fruit girl with oranges, lemons, and peaches for sale. Even the milk cow, Falfa, said "Happy good morning" as they all went by.

Mr. Samlett said, "You should have heard the cow talk last week. The troubles have fallen on Balinor, sure enough. Something," Mr. Samlett continued, "has to be done."

Toby headed straight for the long, low wooden building at the end of the street, as Ari thought he would. The unicorn veered to the right as they approached the building. They passed the post with a sign hanging from it. Under the carving of a noble white unicorn with gold mane and horn, Ari read:

THE UNICORN INN

FINE FOOD, GOOD BEDS, STABLES

SAMLETT

The Inn was surrounded by flower gardens on three sides. Toby drew the wagon to the rear of the building. Here the yard was paved with worn red brick. There were stables on two sides with stalls that were much the same design as those at Glacier River Farm, with an upper and lower door. The upper doors were all open to the sunshine. There was an area for parking carts, wagons, and buggies on the third side of the yard. A large watering trough ran down the middle of the brick. Toby stopped in front of the trough, lowered his head, and drank some water.

Mr. Samlett heaved himself out of the wagon and gave a sharp whistle. Three or four heads poked out of the open stall doors.

Ari drew her breath. They were all unicorns. One was fine-boned, elegant, and satiny black. The nameplate on her stall door read BRYANNA. Her horn was solid ivory. A sapphire jewel glittered at the base of her horn, just where it met her forehead. The unicorn in the stall next to her looked very similar to the Belgian draft horses Ari knew at home. He was big, muscular, and solid, with a curly brown beard under his chin to match his curly brown mane.

Ari couldn't see much of the third unicorn, who shifted slightly in the dimness of her stall. But she had an impression of cool, violet grace and a silver mane. And she knew — she couldn't say why — that the unicorn inside was a mare.

"Bother. I say bother." Mr. Samlett looked as mournful as a man with a cheery red face could look. He whistled again. "Where is that dratted stable boy?"

"Gone to his mother's house for his name day," Toby said. "He told you that this morning, you boneheaded bozo. But did you listen? No. And do we have more guests with no human to care for them? Yes." He gave a derisive "blaat!" from his horn. "Now what are you going to do?"

"Why, I'll muck out and water them myself. I say myself." Mr. Samlett rubbed his chin. Then he tugged at his mustache. Ari noticed that he tugged at his mustache often. Maybe it helped him think. "Trouble is, I got lunch to make, and floors to sweep, and beds to see to. Here! I got an idea." He walked over to Chase and looked up at Lori. "How were you goin' to pay, milady?"

"Pay?" Lori gazed down at him, her eyebrows lifted in nervous astonishment. "Why, by credit card, of course." She drew her eyebrows together in an alarmed way. "That is . . ." She patted her breeches pocket. "If I brought it . . . oh!" She felt the tear in her breeches. "Oh, no! My pants are torn!"

"The maid will fix 'em for you," Mr. Samlett said. "Don't worry about that. Thing you want to worry about is how are you going to pay me? For the breakfast. Yes, the breakfast."

Lori pulled her father's credit card from her breeches pocket. She waved it at Mr. Samlett. "With this. I assume you take Visa?"

Mr. Samlett didn't look as happy as he had before. "I don't know a thing about this, milady. Not a thing. Now, you tell me what your house is, who your papa is, and maybe I can send him the bill. But the thing is, if that's all you got for money — why, it isn't. Money that is. Not in Balinor."

"This is money everywhere," Lori said loftily. "Check with the bank."

"With the bank? Why'n the name of Numinor himself would I want to go the riverbank? I say the riverbank?"

Toby cleared his horn with a loud "blaaat!"

This made everyone jump. But it got their attention. "Do you have any way to pay for your room at the Inn?"

"My fa —" Lori stopped herself, then bit her lip.

"Her father!" Mr. Samlett said. "And who might your father be, milady? Are you one of Lord Benterman's kin, perhaps? From the House of the Wheelwrights?" He jerked his thumb at Chase. "That unicorn . . ."

"Horse," Ari corrected him.

". . . is such a fine specimen even without his horn that you must be related to the Lords of the Roadways. I say the Roadways."

"We can't pay you," Ari said. "But we would be grateful if you would give us shelter for the night."

"Well now, well now." Mr. Samlett rubbed his hands together. "If you sold me that fine uni —"

"*Horse*," Ari said firmly. "And he's not for sale, Mr. Samlett. But if you don't have a stable boy, we can work for our food and shelter."

"Work?" Lori said. "Don't be ridiculous."

"Of course *you* won't have to lift a finger, milady. I say a finger. But your maid here looks like a fine strong girl, and I do need a stable hand." Mr. Samlett beamed. "How lucky we found one another! I need a stable hand, and your mistress needs a soft bed and a warm fire, for it will be cold tonight. And it all works out for the best. I say the best. You, girl . . ."

"Ari," Ari said, as firmly as she had said "horse."

"Ari!" he said with what he obviously thought was an amazing amount of generosity. "You can sleep in the grain room. There's a nice lot of old sacks in there, should keep you and the dog pretty warm. I say pretty warm."

"And Chase?" Ari asked. "May I work to put him in one of the empty stalls?"

"A hornless unicorn? And one that doesn't talk? My goodness no, my girl. He can stay with the milk cow in the village, or in the field out back. I say out back. He'll get plenty to eat, never you fear."

So Ari — with kind but firm instructions from Mr. Samlett — set about earning their meals and a place to sleep.

Mr. Samlett insisted that Lori go to her room, take a hot bath, and eat a meal. Ari, he said, could begin her stable duties right away and join them all in the Inn for supper.

With Lincoln at her side, Ari put Chase in one of the small paddocks near the stable yard and made sure that he had water. Mr. Samlett showed her where the hay was stacked. It was beautiful hay, thick, properly green, that looked so delicious Ari could have eaten some herself. She hauled two large flakes out to the stallion and dropped them in front of him.

"I don't know about this hay, Chase," she said.

171

"I probably shouldn't give you too much. What if you get colic on this strange food?"

Chase turned it over with his nose. *It smells like summer, milady. I will be careful how much I eat. But it is beautiful.*

"You'll be all right while I go to work?"

He dropped his muzzle in her hair and breathed out twice. This meant he was contented, so Ari and her dog went back to the stable yard. There she found out what a help it was being able to talk to Lincoln. He fetched her the broom, so she could sweep the brick yard, and carried the water buckets when she emptied the watering trough and cleaned it.

When the sun was straight overhead, a bell clanged. Mr. Samlett came out of the Inn, carrying a wooden bowl of delicious vegetable stew, a hunk of mild cheese, and bread. Ari sat on an overturned bucket and shared her meal with Linc. The unicorns in the stalls had pushed open their stall doors (there were no latches or locks) and gone for a stroll in the market. All except the one who lurked in violet and silver shadows, who had no name on her door. Ari could see the tip of her crystal horn glinting in the sunlight, but nothing else. She swallowed her last spoonful of stew, rinsed her bowl in the trough, then walked to the stall.

"Hello?" she said tentatively.

There was no answer. Just a slight shifting in

172

the lavender shadow and a stir in the fragrant air. Ari peeked in.

The most beautiful unicorn was asleep in the straw! She was the color of the sky just as the sun goes down, a murmur of lavender, violet, and blue. Her cheek lay on a silk pillow. Her delicate legs were folded under her belly. Her silvery mane rippled over her back and touched the fresh sweet straw on the floor. But it was the horn that drew Ari's fascinated gaze. It was long and translucent, twisted like a seashell. A diamond gleamed at the base.

Ari held her breath. The stall was magnificent. A silver-bordered mirror was hung on one wall while an ornate silver bridle and silver velvet saddle hung on racks on another. There was even a silver manure bucket tucked neatly in the corner. "Wow!" Ari said softly.

Linc reared up and put his front paws on the edge of the stall door. At the sight of the unicorn, his ears went up. There was an eager, adoring look in his eye. He dropped to the ground outside the door in a crouch. Ari bent down and ran her hands over his silken head.

"Are you okay, Linc?" she whispered.

It is the Lady! The Dreamspeaker of the Celestial Valley! He closed his eyes. *And I have seen her! I am the luckiest of dogs!*

"Well," Ari said in a low voice, so as not to wake the unicorn from her nap, "why doesn't the

173

luckiest of dogs help me with the manure buckets? There's a lot to do to tidy up before those other unicorns come back. And Mr. Samlett said they like their stalls cleaned before the evening meal. So let's get cracking!"

All the buckets were emptied, the straw raked and turned over, the mirrors in each unicorn's stall polished until they shone. Ari left the violet unicorn's stall for last, to give her the maximum time to sleep. But when she tapped timidly at the stall door, she discovered the lovely being had gone out, perhaps to join the others, perhaps to wander by herself in the woods.

Finally, with the sun just touching the edge of the western horizon, Ari's work was finished.

Mr. Samlett came bustling out of the Inn door. "This is just a fine job, a fine job," he beamed. "Now, come in a bit before the dinner hour, will you? You will want to wash and change, I expect. And my good wife found you a proper kirtle."

"Sir?" Ari asked, bewildered.

"Ah, I forgot. Your mistress said you were from the north." He shook his head. "Strange customs they have up north, up north. And you lost your luggage in that stream, besides. We will give you something to wear, instead of those boys' clothes you had to borrow. But you must come and see your mistress now. She desires your presence."

"She does, huh?" Ari said a little grimly. It was just as well that good old Lori had "desired her presence." They'd better get their stories straight about who they were and where they came from. Although she had to admire the fib about losing their clothes in the stream, whatever stream that may have been. None of the women or girls she'd seen in Balinor wore breeches.

Ari had thought quite a lot about their predicament while she had been sweeping, stacking, washing, and mucking out. Someone in Balinor had to know about the Gap, and how to get back to Glacier River. But she needed time to figure out who to ask. She had seen that Balinor had its bad side, just like the dangerous parts of cities near Glacier River Farm. Those red-eyed unicorns had been terrifying. And then there were these mysterious troubles, with animals losing their ability to talk. She wanted to find out a lot more about this place before she went around telling people they were from another world. And if Mr. Samlett gave them clothes to help them look more like the people who lived here — it'd be a great help. They'd be in disguise.

"Well, girl?" Mr. Samlett demanded.

"I'm sorry, I was thinking of something else," she explained. "Thanks very much for the loan of the clothes, and yes, I would like a bath. And sure, I'll go see that bra . . . I mean, Mistress Lori now."

Ari liked the inside of the Inn right away. The whole place was made of solid wood — wood floors, wood tables and benches, wood walls. A wide flight of stairs in the middle of the room led to the second

175

floor. A huge stone fireplace took up the entire south wall. There were several people sitting around the big room, all of them adults. Ari kept Linc close by her side.

"You go right up them stairs and turn right. Your mistress's room is number twelve. My good wife gave her your new clothes. And the bath is just down the hall."

Ari ran lightly up the stairs, Lincoln clicking along behind. She tapped at door number 12 and pushed it open.

"Oh," Lori said, "it's you." She sat on a bench in front of a small fireplace.

The room was small, with a low ceiling, a small window, a huge bed, and a chest against one wall. Lori had changed her torn breeches and shirt for a long blue dress that buttoned all the way to a high neck. Her riding boots — scratched and muddy — lay in a tangle of clothes on the floor. "You can pick those up and polish them." She pointed to her boots.

"You wish." Ari sat down on the bed. She was tired.

"Well? You're my maid, aren't you?"

"Forget it, Lori. I'm in no mood. And it wouldn't hurt for you to help with the chores."

"What? A lady like me? No way. It'd shock them out of their little leather sandals." She stood up and roamed around the room. She bit her lower lip. "Have you figured a way out of this mess?"

"Not yet. But I will. What kind of story did you tell Mr. Samlett?"

"That we were traveling from up north and some bears scared us and we lost our luggage in a stream."

"Bears? What if there aren't any bears here!"

"You told me there were bears here. And Samlett didn't know what I meant until I told him about the sound of the marching." She shuddered.

"What did he say then?"

Lori's voice was so low, Ari could hardly hear her. "There are things that walk these woods. Terrible things. And we are not to go out at night." She shivered. "I believe him, too. I'm not setting foot out of this place until you figure out a way to get us out of here."

"Did Mr. Samlett's wife leave some clothes for me?"

Lori pointed to the chest. "In there."

"And the bathroom?"

"Bathroom! Ha!" Lori's laugh was scornful. "You call a big bucket and a little bucket a bathroom?"

"A big bucket and a little bucket?"

"One to wash in and one to ... you know. Anyhow, take a left in the hall when you leave. And you can leave anytime soon."

Ari, who had opened the chest and was examining the contents, said in an absentminded way, "I'll take this skirt and this jacket. I'm going to leave

177

my boots on. Then I'll go downstairs and hang out. See if I can find anyone to talk to."

"Fine," Lori snapped. "Just fine. Leave me here all by myself. I've been by myself all day."

"Oh, for goodness' sake. Look, Linc will keep you company while I wash up. And then we'll go downstairs together, okay?"

Lori gave a pitiful sniff. She had her usual mean expression, but there were big tears in her eyes. Ari sighed. "It's going to be fine."

"It is NOT going to be fine! What if we never get home?"

Ari folded the skirt and jacket in her arms. "Don't you worry. We'll get back. I know we will."

"I'm not moving out of this room until I find out we're going home."

Ari rolled her eyes, left the room, and stood in the hall. The very air here smelled different from the air at the farm. Wood torches burned in holders on the walls, so even the light was different.

Would they ever get back to the farm? Ari rubbed her face with her hands. She was tired. So tired.

She bit her lip. The thought was strong in her, strangely persistent.

She didn't want to go back. Not yet. Not yet.

There was something about this place that called to her heart.

4

Lincoln waited patiently outside the wash-room while Ari bathed and changed. The dark red skirt had pretty embroidery around the hem but was a little big around the middle, so she rolled up the waistband. The blouse was made of a soft, off-white cotton and had full sleeves and a scoop neck that tied with two strings. The leather vest fit snugly and it would be nice and warm as the evening cooled. She wound her hair up on top of her head and clipped it with her barrettes. The only real problem were her riding boots. Her socks were filthy after the long day of adventure, but there was no way she would wear her boots without socks. So she pulled her socks on and her boots and opened the door.

She was ready.

Lincoln was lying on the floor, cleaning his

179

little white forepaws. When she came out, he jumped to his feet and met her, head low, tail wagging. *You look like one of them!*

"Is that good or bad, Linc?" She sighed. "Are *they* good or bad?"

If they are bad, his thought was fierce, *I will bite them and bite them!*

"Thanks. I think."

She paused at the top of the stairs. The room was lit by torches. A big log burned in the fireplace. The great wooden door to the outside opened and closed as people came in. A draft of cold air drifted up the stairs and Ari shivered. She was glad she had on the leather vest. It was cool here in Balinor, once the sun set.

The room was filled with townspeople. Some drank from wooden cups, others ate bread, cheese, and peaches. Could she slip among them, unnoticed? Would they talk in front of her, a stranger? They all seemed to know one another.

She surveyed the room. Bread, cheese, peaches. Of course! She could walk around with a wooden tray and pretend to be a waitress. Nobody really paid too much attention to waitresses.

She ran lightly down the stairs and took a platter of peaches from the sideboard near the kitchen door. Then she watched the group of jabbering people carefully. A tall man with gray hair stood talking in the very center of the room. His clothes were expensive: Soft leather boots came to his knees and the short cloak over his shoulders was trimmed with pearls. His hair was gray and he had a neatly trimmed beard. The men around him seemed to be listening carefully to what he was saying. A woman stood there, too. She was tall and slim with dark hair and black eyes. Her face was smooth. Ari had never seen such a perfectly white complexion. Dark jewels winked in her hair. She and the man looked like important people from the way they dressed and acted. It would be smart to start with them, Ari thought.

Ari edged her way through the crowd, offering the tray of peaches with a smile. She stopped right in back of the man with the pearl cloak, then picked over the peaches with a frown. "Oh, my," she said, to no one in particular, "several of these have brown spots." She picked up peaches, examined them, then set them down again.

All the while she was listening.

"The Shifter's forces grow bolder every day," the tall man said. His voice was low, but urgent. "I had word the Demon herd moved through the King's forest today. In broad daylight."

"Aye, I heard that as well," the woman said. Her voice was quiet and distinguished. "But you should not call it the King's forest, milord Lexan. Not even here at the Unicorn Inn, where we think we are safe. It's the Shifter's forest now."

"But we are the King's men here," said another man.

"And the Queen's," the woman responded. "Wherever they may be."

"May the One Who Rules us all bless them both." That was Mr. Samlett. Ari tucked her chin down and turned the peaches over and over. The Innkeeper sounded anxious as he asked, "There's been no word? No word at all of where the cursed Shifter has hidden them?"

"They remain hostage. No one knows where." That was Lord Lexan again. "Our only hope is the Princess herself. I tell you again, we must beg her to come from the safe place, to lead us against the Shifter and his devil army."

"She's only a girl, my brother," Lady Kylie said. "About the age of my own daughter. I would not put a mere girl in danger. That is why the Resistance appealed to Numinor to send her away."

"And because of who she is, we must bring her back again! I tell you, that lying usurper has broken every oath he gave after he stole the throne! All would remain as it had when the King and Queen ruled," Lord Lexan said. "There would be no reason to fight. The only difference would be that *he* would ride the Lord of the Unicorns at Midsummer. That only *he* would place the Crown of Balinor upon his head. And look how long he kept his word — a mere three months! And now what is happening? The Shifter's men stormed my manor not three days past! They ravaged my crops, stole my hay and corn, burned my barns. And the unicorns. The unicorns'

182

language is disappearing. Without their language, we will not be able to speak with the animals who live in the forests and on our farms. Already the animals of our kingdom are losing the ability to speak. The Lord of the Unicorns has disappeared. His mistress, the Princess, is in hiding. I tell you, we must bring her back. We must ride against the Shifter!"

The crowd murmured in agreement. Lincoln pressed his head against Ari's knee. *Just our luck. We arrive right in the middle of a war.*

"It seems a lot more important than our being lost," Ari said to him. "And it's sad about the animals. The unicorns especially."

I don't know what we can do about it. Lincoln yawned. *I'm tired.*

"It might be better to see what we can find out in the morning," Ari agreed.

"Peach, girl?"

Ari looked up. The man in the pearl-encrusted cloak was smiling at her. Lord Lexan, they had called that woman's brother. "May I have a peach?" he asked Ari.

"Why, yes, sir. Of course, sir." Ari offered him the tray. Lord Lexan narrowed his gray eyes at her. "You aren't from Balinor. I don't believe I've seen you before."

"Um, no, sir. I'm from up north. We just arrived today."

"North? That's Arlen's territory. The Lord of the Six Seas. Are you from his House?"

From the way he said "House," Ari was pretty sure he didn't mean a little hut with a straw roof. He meant a castle — or at least a mansion. He looked kind, and he looked as if he might know a bit more about this world than Mr. Samlett. She took a deep breath and said recklessly, "Well, sir, my friends and I. We're from north of the Gap."

The room went still as a graveyard. Everyone stared at her. Lincoln growled.

Ari was scared, but determined not to show it. She stuck her chin up a little. "Do you know the Gap, sir? Actually, my friends and I would like to go home, except we don't seem to be able to . . . to . . . find . . ." She stopped talking. Lord Lexan's face was as grim as death.

"Samlett!" he snapped.

The crowd around Lord Lexan parted to reveal the Innkeeper. His chubby face was drawn tight with fear. "I didn't know, sir. I swear, I didn't know, sir."

Ari cleared her throat. She hoped her voice wouldn't shake. "Is there something wrong with the Gap?"

"Wrong with the — ha!" Lord Lexan flung his head back and laughed. But it was not a happy laugh. It was definitely an angry laugh. "She is young to be a spy, is she not, Samlett?"

Mr. Samlett's normally red face was pale. "You know, girl, surely you must know. The Shifter is from beyond the Gap."

"Oh," Ari said. "Um, no, I didn't know. Who is the Shifter?"

"She claims not to know? Ha!" The woman whose voice had seemed so kind pushed her way past Mr. Samlett and grabbed Ari's chin with one ringed hand. She tilted it up so that the flickering torch light fell on it. "She looks innocent. More than innocent. She has a look of the Royal family itself. This is the Shifter's work, I swear. It is well known that he can take any shape. Any form. That he moves among us unannounced, to spy and do his filthy work of destruction. I say we lock her up. We lock her up and let justice deal with her!"

5

"That's a bit fierce, my dear. All over a mere girl?" Lord Lexan put his hand on the angry woman's back. "I don't think the young girl quite understands what she's saying, Kylie."

"She doesn't look like a simpleton to me," the Lady Kylie snapped. "Far from it."

"Thanks, I think," Ari muttered. Which was worse? To have people think she was an idiot or to be locked up? It seemed safer to be an idiot. She dropped her mouth open, to look as stupid as possible. "Peaches, milady? I — oops!" She tilted the tray and the peaches spilled all over the floor. A particularly ripe one rolled against Lady Kylie's velvet shoe and splattered. The people nearest Ari backed up. A few of them bent down and began to pick up the peaches. Ari kicked the ripe peach away from the outraged Kylie, then she stepped on it. Ripe peach squished all over the floor.

"Clumsy fool!" Lady Kylie hissed.

"Now then, now then!" Mr. Samlett wiped his perspiring face with a large red cloth. "And such a good stable hand, too! Nobody cleans stalls like this one, milady."

"Then confine her to the stables! And keep her out of the way of the gentry!" Lady Kylie's smooth face was drawn tight with irritation.

"Sorry, milady," Ari said. She pretended to sniff. Then she wiped her nose with her sleeve. Lady Kylie made a disgusted noise.

Mr. Samlett made shooing motions. "Isn't there work for you with your mistress, girl?"

"Why don't I check on the unicorns, sir?" Ari suggested. She wanted out of this room. There were things she had to discuss with Chase.

"Fine. Fine! Just don't smear them with ripe peaches. I say ripe peaches. Especially the unicorn with the crystal horn. You must take great care around her, girl!"

"Crystal horn?" Lady Kylie said sharply. She narrowed her eyes. "And who might that be, Samlett?"

"Oh, a very beautiful unicorn, milady. Very beautiful. My cart unicorn Toby made the arrangements for her lodging. He is working to pay for her room and board. I haven't actually met her, of course," he added in a bewildered way. "She never seems to be in her stall when I go to see if the arrangements are satisfactory. But I've seen the crystal horn and the jewel on it."

187

"A unicorn with a servant?" Lady Kylie sneered. "I've never heard of such a thing. And Balinor unicorns don't have precious jewels on their horns. Just those of the Royal court. And they all disappeared when the King and Queen did."

"The unicorns who live in the Celestial Valley have jewels on their horns," someone at the back of the crowd said.

"Legends!" Lady Kylie scoffed. "Mere legends."

"Oh, no, milady," Samlett said earnestly. "Why, you don't believe in Numinor and the Rainbow herd?"

"I believe in what I see," Lady Kylie snapped. "And if our unicorns need to believe in gods and goddesses that don't exist, that's fine with me. But I have seen the Royal unicorns, Samlett, when milord Lexan and I attended the King and Queen at court. Before the troubles began. And if there's a Royal unicorn in your stable, man, she should not be here at this Inn!"

"That's true," Lord Lexan said with a slightly puzzled air. "If she is one of the Royals. Could it be, Samlett? Do you have a Royal unicorn at your Inn?"

"I didn't dare ask!" Mr. Samlett said.

"We will ask her now!" Lady Kylie said. "I've never heard of such a thing! A Royal housed in *your* Inn, Samlett. It's ridiculous."

"It's a very fine Inn, milady," Mr. Samlett protested.

188

"Take me to her at once!" Lady Kylie stamped her foot. A bit of peach flew up in the air. "If what you say is true, I shall invite her to our manor house. Where she will be in company fit for her, Samlett!"

Ari was amused to see that Mr. Samlett could walk backward and bow at the same time. He backed and bowed across the stable yard, apologizing to Lady Kylie and Lord Lexan all the way. Ari followed them, keeping well back so that Lady Kylie wouldn't notice her. Lincoln pattered unobtrusively behind them all.

But when they reached the stall, the beautiful unicorn was gone.

"She was right here, milady!" Mr. Samlett protested. "The light from the torches isn't very good. Maybe she's in the back. I say in the back of the stall."

But the violet unicorn wasn't there. The silver bridle was gone from the wall. All that remained was the scent of flowers.

"You've been drinking too much of your own punch, Samlett!" Lord Lexan said.

"I didn't believe him for a minute!" Lady Kylie sniffed. "A Royal unicorn here!"

"These are strange times," Lord Lexan observed. "Come, my dear. It's late. We should be heading back to our home. Samlett, ask our unicorns if they are ready to be hitched to our carriage."

"If they will hear me, milord," Samlett said apologetically. "I'm afraid that when I turned them

189

out to pasture this morning, I say turned them out, they spoke very little to me."

"Outrageous!" Lady Kylie said. "Our unicorns losing their ability to speak? They wouldn't dare!"

If she were a unicorn of Lady Kylie's, she wouldn't speak to that horrible woman, either, Ari thought. Then she volunteered, "Shall I go ask them, Mr. Samlett? It's the pair of matched chestnuts in stalls three and four, isn't it?"

"You go ask them, girl. I say ask them. And then hitch them up, if you would."

"It's Ari," she reminded him firmly.

Lady Kylie gave her a suspicious glance. Ari slipped out of the stall before Lady Kylie could question her further. She and Linc walked down the brick path to stalls three and four. Lord Lexan's unicorns were both there, dozing peacefully. Ari looked at the first over the half door, which was open to the fresh night air. His name was written on a piece of slate attached to the lower door — NATHAN. She suddenly felt shy. It seemed so odd to be talking to unicorns!

"Excuse me," she said tentatively. "Hello? Nathan?"

Nathan jerked his head up, startled out of sleep. He nodded at her. He was short and powerfully built, with well-muscled hindquarters and sturdy legs.

"I'm Ari, the um . . . stable hand. Lord Lexan asked if you were ready to draw the carriage home."

190

"Home," Nathan said in a confused way. His voice sounded rusty, as if it hadn't been used for a while.

"Shall I hitch you and . . ." She ducked her head to take a look at the nameplate on stall three. "And Orrin up to the carriage?"

"Orrin," Nathan said more clearly.

"Nathan?" Orrin stuck his head out of his stall. He looked exactly like Nathan. Ari wondered if they were brothers.

The carriage harness was hung on Orrin's wall. Ari took both unicorns into the courtyard and backed them into the carriage shafts. Then she hitched up the harness. Both unicorns stood placidly and did whatever she asked.

"What are you doing? I say what are you doing?"

Ari jumped. She didn't hear Mr. Samlett come up behind her. "Hitching the unicorns up," she said. She wanted to add, "Isn't it obvious?" but didn't.

"But *you* are guiding them!" Mr. Samlett said. "It's as if they don't know what you want them to do! Oh, dear! I say oh, dear! I wonder if Lord Lexan will be able to get home!"

"They're very well-trained unicorns," Ari offered. "I'm sure all he has to do is use the reins."

"Use the reins? I say use the reins!"

"That's how you communicate with a ho . . . I mean, a unicorn. Isn't it?"

191

"Not in Balinor," Mr. Samlett said. "No, not in Balinor. And where did you say you were from again?" Ari waved her hand vaguely in the air. "Up North?"

Ari stayed well out of the way when Lord Lexan and Lady Kylie got into the carriage. It was a bit of a comedy. Lord Lexan took up the reins and said, "Home, Nathan and Orrin."

Both unicorns just stood there. It looked as if Nathan had fallen back asleep.

"We said *home!*" Lady Kylie said sharply.

Nothing happened.

"Cluck," Ari suggested.

"What!" Lady Kylie glared at her.

"Go like this." Ari made a clucking noise. Both Nathan and Orrin jerked their heads up at the sound. "And then flex the reins like this." Ari shook her hands into the air. Lord Lexan tried it. The unicorns moved off, slowly, in an erratic manner.

"Well, at least they are headed home," Mr. Samlett said woefully. "Hard times, my dear. I say hard times. How did you learn not to talk to unicorns and still get them to help you?"

"Um," Ari said. "Well, I ride quite a bit. At home."

"Of course. Your own unicorn cannot speak. So you must have learned these things."

"He's a horse," Ari corrected him firmly.

"Whatever you say. You must teach me how to do this," Mr. Samlett said. "If the troubles con-

192

tinue, we are all going to need to learn this unspoken language. I say all of us. Well, I'm for my bed, my dear. You gave me good help today. I say good help. If you want to leave that demanding mistress of yours, you'll always have a job here, I say always. I need someone like you. In times like these." He shook his head, sighed, and went back to the Inn.

Do we go to sleep now, too? Linc asked.

"Not yet, boy. I need to see to Chase."

You always think about Chase first! He looked up at her, eyes soft and pleading. *It's dangerous in this place. I can smell it. I can hear it. We should go back to the room where Lori is. It's safe there.*

Ari knelt down and ran her fingers around his ears. "I don't know that it's safe anywhere, Linc. And I have to see to Chase. He needs me."

I need you, too, Linc growled.

Ari laughed. "We need each other. All of us. And that includes Lori. Come on now, I need to find a currycomb, if they have currycombs in Balinor. I'll brush Chase and then I'll brush you."

Linc located a very nice currycomb with a wood back and soft wooden teeth. Ari collected a bucket of oats and a bucket of fresh water. They found Chase alert in his paddock, ears up, eyes facing the north.

"There's no moon tonight," Ari commented as she gently combed out his mane.

That isn't good, her stallion replied. He bent his head and breathed gently into her hair.

193

"Why not?"

Chase shifted restlessly on his feet. *I don't know. I think I knew once, but I've forgotten. As I've forgotten so many things. But there is danger when there is no moon.*

Ari commanded Chase to "stand," then went to work on his coat. After a moment he said, *There is magic here in Balinor.*

"I know. I wonder if that's why you can talk to me all the time now. But I wish you could talk out loud, Chase. And Linc, too. And there's another thing I wish. I'd like to meet that unicorn, the one with the crystal horn. But she's gone from her stall."

There is mystery here, Chase agreed. *And something bad is out there, milady. I can feel it.*

Ari straightened up and listened hard. The night was quiet. "I'd say the whole thing was a mystery." She shrugged her shoulders and yawned suddenly. She was tired, and she hurried to finish up.

She ran her hands down Chase's right foreleg, then tapped his ankle. Obediently, he lifted his hoof. She brushed the dirt and stones out as well as she could. She brushed out his other hooves in turn. She'd have to find a hoof pick. "If they have currycombs in Balinor, they must have hoof picks," Ari said cheerfully. "There. You're all set. I brought you some oats, and fresh water and . . ."

"ARI!" It was a woman's voice, high and commanding.

Lincoln jumped to his feet and growled. Ari

194

felt Chase come to full alert beside her. "Yes?" she called. "I'm over here!"

"Come back to the Inn! Now, if you please!"

"It's Lady Kylie," Ari said. "I suppose she's forgotten something. Or maybe the unicorns just turned around and wandered back here. Sleep well, Chase."

Ari! Don't go!

She looked up at him. There was a line of worry between his eyes. "Why not?"

He stamped the ground. *I don't know! By the moon, I don't know. If I could only remember!* He raised his head and whinnied, a long, angry call full of frustration.

"Hush!" Ari said. "You'll wake everyone up." She smoothed his forelock, her fingers tender over the white scar.

"Girl!" Lady Kylie shrieked. Ari looked over her shoulder. The Inn door was open, and Lady Kylie stood there, a dim figure against the light from inside. Her hands were on her hips.

"I'll be right there!" She gave Chase a final pat. "I'll see you in the morning. Come on, Linc." She climbed through the fence boards, Linc wriggling after her. She jogged toward the Inn, hoping that Lady Kylie and Lord Lexan hadn't decided to stay the night. She'd have to unharness the poor unicorns again, and she was really tired. Behind her, Chase let out another long, loud whinny.

"Yes?" Ari said as she came up to the angry woman.

"Come in here, please." Lady Kylie stepped aside. Ari walked into the room. A chill prickled the back of her neck, and she stopped. Linc pressed close to her side.

Something was wrong. There were people in the room, as there had been earlier in the evening. But those had been the townspeople of Balinor. These men and women looked the same — at first glance.

Maybe it was the air in the room that was confusing. Perhaps Mr. Samlett had placed a wet log on the fire by mistake, because the whole room was full of a sort of thin, oily smoke. Not smoke, exactly, but a brackish haze. It made it hard to see who these people were.

Ari squeezed her eyes shut and opened them again. Everyone except Lady Kylie was dressed in long cloaks. The hoods were drawn over their heads so that she couldn't tell the men from the women.

The fire blazed up suddenly, revealing the face of what Ari thought was a little boy beside the fireplace. Ari backed up. The short ones weren't children. They were very short adults with twisted faces.

"Where's Lord Lexan?" Ari asked. "Is . . . um . . . anything wrong?"

"Oh, yes, there's something wrong," Lady Kylie hissed. She moved closer. The fire blazed up again. The flames were reflected in her eyes.

Ari was suddenly very afraid. "Tell you what, milady," she said. "Maybe I'll just go up to my room. . . ." She edged backward toward the stairs.

"We know who you are." Lady Kylie opened her mouth to smile. Ari swallowed hard. The woman's teeth were sharp and pointed like a fox.

"Get her!" Lady Kylie commanded.

The cloaked figures gathered together slowly, like droplets of oil forming a pool. Lincoln barked, and barked again. Suddenly, the collie was a whirlwind, teeth bared, eyes hot and angry. He growled and bit, moving as fast as the wind.

The crowd fell back. Someone screamed.

Run, Ari! Run! Lincoln shouted.

"I won't leave you here!"

You must! A hand reached out to grab her. Its nails were long and pointed. Lincoln darted forward and sank his teeth into it. Blood flew around his jaws. *Go now! Go now! I cannot save us both!*

"I can't leave you!"

THEY DON'T WANT ME! THEY WANT YOU! RUN!

Ari picked up her skirts, ran for the back door, and pushed it open. Lincoln, a whirlwind of teeth and claws, kept the crowd at bay. She fell outside gasping. Thank goodness there were no latches here. She turned for a last look at her gallant collie. What she saw then would haunt her for the rest of her life. Lady Kylie came at the dog with a flaming

197

torch. She whirled it once around her head, then brought it down with all her might onto Lincoln's silken head.

The collie yelped and fell like a stone to the floor.

The door swung closed in Ari's face.

Ari fought the urge to open the door and plunge into the crowd. "Keep calm, keep calm," she muttered to herself. If she went back in, she would be captured. And there would be no way at all to help Linc. But if she went for help . . . where was Mr. Samlett?

Ari pulled a heavy bench in front of the door. The crowd pounded against it. It wouldn't be long before they broke it open. She spun around. A hiding place! She had to find a hiding place!

Starlight shone on the brick yard, bleaching the ruddy bricks. The white light fell on the stable doors, closed now against the cool night air. The top of one door swung open. A low, sweet voice called out, "Arianna. Come here."

The door behind her bulged with the force of angry blows. The bench shifted out.

"Ari. You must come here. Now."

Ari ran. She flung herself over the bottom half of the stall door and fell into the straw. She landed on her leg, and bit her lip so she wouldn't scream. She heard the Inn door burst open with a terrible *cra-a-a-a-ck!* She picked herself up and peeked over the door. People poured into the yard.

A few carried torches snatched from the rough-hewn walls of the Inn. They swung the torches in a wide circle.

"She can't have gone far!" Lady Kylie shouted. "Check the stables!"

"Arianna. Lie down. I will cover you with the straw." The twilight-colored unicorn drifted toward her, as if she were dancing on air. "Come. Do as I say."

6

"But . . . how do you know my name?" she asked shyly. The Dreamspeaker, poor Linc had called her. She seemed like a goddess, encased in silvery light.

"Hurry."

Ari flung herself into the straw. The unicorn bent her lovely head. The crystal horn flashed as she used it to toss straw over Ari.

Someone thumped urgently on the unicorn's stall door.

"And who disturbs me?" the twilight-colored unicorn asked.

"Lady. We beg your pardon. But we seek a young girl. With hair the color of bronze, and eyes like the sky." Lady Kylie again. Ari wondered why she'd thought the woman sounded distinguished. There was something horrible about her voice. Something snakelike.

200

"And you seek her here? Go away. Do not disturb my rest."

There was a long pause. Then, "Lady. We must obey of course. Will you bless our search? She is a traitor, this one, and a spy."

"I bless all searches for traitors and spies. Now go. Leave me."

There was a respectful murmur from the crowd outside. Ari held her breath. There was a sound of many footsteps, marching away into the night. Ari let her breath out softly. Long moments went by, then the bell-like voice said, "You may come out now, Arianna."

"I'm not a traitor or a spy. I don't even know what's going on!"

"I understand. Come out."

Ari emerged from the straw. A pale light surrounded the unicorn, and although there were no lamps or torches, Ari could see her clearly. She stood near her mirror. To the girl's dazzled eyes, there seemed to be two violet unicorns before her.

"You left the ruby. On the other side."

Ari's hand went to her throat. "The necklace Lincoln brought me when I was in the hospital? Why . . . how did you know about that?"

"You shall see." The unicorn turned to the mirror. She arched her neck and blew out softly, twice. The mirror clouded over, then rippled, like water in a shallow stream. "I am Atalanta. As your friend the collie said, I am sometimes called the

201

Dreamspeaker. This is all I have of my Watching Pool," she added. "But it will do for now."

"But the Gap. If you know about my necklace and where I left it, you know about the Gap. Please, milady. Can you . . . Will you send me and my friends back?"

"Come and see."

Hesitantly, Ari looked into the mirror. She didn't see anything at first, just the still surface of the water. It was weird, looking into vertical water. The water rippled, as if a stone had been dropped into it. Ari gasped. She was looking at herself in her bedroom at Glacier River Farm! She watched as she took the ruby necklace from her neck and put it carefully into her dresser. Then, the vision in the mirror shifted to Dr. Bohnes's clinic, and the note she'd written on the window: SELL THE DOG LEASH!

"That was a mistake," the unicorn said. "Made with good heart, but a mistake nonetheless."

"Why?"

"Watch again." Atalanta breathed out once, sharply, as a mare does when calling a foal out of danger. The water rippled, darkened.

Ari drew back with a gasp. Unicorns with fiery eyes paraded through the forest. She shuddered. "Ugh. I saw them today. The Demon unicorns."

"The Shifter's work," Atalanta said sadly. "My herd mates, once upon a time. But that is not a story

202

to tell you here and now." The coal-black horde of unicorns marched across the watery screen, a grim and terrible sight. The leader of the column whirled suddenly, then brought his head up, as if he knew he was being watched. He turned slowly, slowly. Ari shrank back. The unicorn's head, rimmed in fire, blacker than the depths of the deepest cave, filled the Watching Pool mirror and stared directly into Ari's face.

"I know that eye!" she gasped. "Oh, please, please! Take it away! Turn it off!"

Atalanta blew once on the water, a sharp explosion of breath. The evil vision vanished. "Yes, you know that Eye. That is Entia, or one of the forms that Entia takes. He is what was searching for you, in the meadow at Glacier River. That Eye, the Eye of the Shifter, is looking for you everywhere. He will stalk you, search for you until he finds you."

"But why?" Ari burst out. "Why me? I haven't done anything."

"It's not what you've done. It's who you are." The unicorn stepped closer, so close that her long mane, as light as dandelion seeds and as soft as rose petals, draped Ari in a magical veil.

"Do you not remember, Arianna?" She blew gently onto Ari's face, just as Chase did when he told Ari that he loved her.

The last six months tumbled through Ari's mind like gravel falling down a slope: the days before she learned Chase could talk to her, when she was just Ann and Frank's foster daughter, Dr. Bohnes's friend, Frank's best worker in the stable.

And then — some memories came back. They were erratic. Like fireflies winking off and on, on and out. But there were memories. Just enough. The days before Glacier River Farm.

The days when she had lived here, in Balinor.

"I'm that Princess they talked about," Ari said dully. "I remember some of it now. Oh, I remember now. There was no accident. There was no car wreck. The Shifter caught me. Caught my mother, the Queen. Hid her, kidnapped her, sent her away. Stole my father, the King. And he has gone from the Kingdom to the Caves beneath the Six Seas, where no one has gone before."

"Yes, my dearest dear." Atalanta's amethyst eyes were sad.

"And I . . . I am Arianna." She raised her head, a sudden hope flooding her. "My brothers? Tace and Bren?"

"The Princes were taken, too."

"Oh, no. Oh, no." Ari sank to her knees in the straw. She remembered now. She wished she hadn't. The Palace, with its reflecting pools and large gardens. The white stone terrace overlooking the sea. Her mother . . . no. Too painful, the memories now. That last day. The day of the Great Betrayal . . . the shouts and screams of terror. The Shifter himself, a

204

terrible shadow, grabbing her, flinging her through space.

She cried hot tears. "Why, you were there, milady. You took me through the Gap."

"We sent you, yes. With the help of the people of this village."

Ari was bewildered. "But why didn't they recognize me? I mean, if the people here are, as they said, the King's men. And they helped me and my family as best as they could. . . ."

"They've helped you more than you know."

"But why didn't they know who I was tonight!?"

"You have been gone from Balinor awhile, Arianna."

"Yes. Lord Lexan said that traitors could be among us, among my people, and we would never know it because the Shifter can change the way people look." Ari frowned. "That woman, the one that grabbed me first . . ."

"Kylie. The one who looks for you even now, with part of the evil army? One of His. Yes. She knows who you are. That's why she returned for you just now. And you have grown up since you've been gone, Arianna. You have changed. Many may not recognize you."

"My goodness." Ari put her hands to her head. Her mind was whirling. "The Shifter!" Rage welled up in Ari like a lava flow. Poor Lincoln! And she hadn't even had time to grieve! "My dog's been hurt." Tears flooded her eyes. "And Lady Kylie." The name sent a shiver of horror through her. "The Shifter's High Priestess."

"And your mother's friend. Before the Great Betrayal. Yes."

"My mother's friend! It can't be!"

"You will find the truth, Arianna. But it will take you a long time. Your memory will return slowly. It was lost in the terrible struggle. I do not know if you will ever regain it completely. And it may be at great cost to you and those you love."

The tears came back. Ari swallowed hard. Princesses didn't cry. Or did they? "There already has been a terrible cost. My dog is hurt, maybe dead! My family the same! I hate the Shifter! I hate him!"

"You must put aside your hate, Arianna. Hate will not save you or your people."

"Hate makes me strong," Ari said through clenched teeth.

"Hate blinds you. Hate is a tool of the Shifter." She laid her horn on Ari's shoulder. The crystal horn was a warm, living thing. With the touch of it, rage and terror ebbed out of Ari. Wondering, she raised her eyes to Atalanta. "You must listen to me, child. I haven't much time. Stand aside, please."

Ari slipped out of the way. As quiet as a whisper, Atalanta collected herself. She stood at attention, her neck arched, her hindquarters tucked, her back supple and slightly arched. And she sang, one long, lyrical note: "I call the Sunchaser."

"Chase." Ari stared at Atalanta. "Chase. *Chase is the Lord of the Unicorns!*"

Atalanta didn't reply. She stood as if carved in amethyst rock, her violet eyes on the open door to the stall.

Ari heard the distant sound of a horse jumping a fence: a short gallop, a moment of suspension, the moment of landing. Then she heard a familiar set of hoofbeats on the brick yard.

Chase appeared at the open door. He wasn't even breathing hard. His dark eyes searched and found Ari. Then he looked at the unicorn. Without a sound, he sank to his knees, great head bowed, forelegs knuckled against the straw.

"Sunchaser," Atalanta said. "It is hard to see you like this." She took a few steps toward him. The tip of her horn touched the scar on his forehead. Chase trembled. Sweat patched his withers. But he didn't lift his head.

"His horn is gone," Atalanta said sadly. "And his jewel is lost. Without them, he cannot hear me. Without them, he cannot speak."

Ari cleared her throat. Her voice was small and lost. "He can talk to me," she said.

Atalanta widened her violet eyes. "Indeed?"

"Yes. I hear him in my mind."

207

"Ah." The unicorn's tone was skeptical.

"It's true," Ari said. "Chase. Chase. Lift your head. Do you know who this is?"

A goddess, milady.

"He says you are a goddess," Ari informed her.

Atalanta looked thoughtful. "When did this happen?"

"On the other side of the Gap. At Glacier River Farm. At first I thought I was imagining it. And it only happened in moments when he was angry or upset."

"That is true of all horses, of all unicorns, whether they have personal magic or not," Atalanta said. "It is true in Balinor, and in all the worlds of humans and animals."

"But here," Ari insisted. "Here I can talk to him anytime." She added, politely, because Atalanta didn't seem to believe her, "It's true."

"If it is, then this is more of the magic I do not understand."

"There's magic *you* don't understand?"

"There is."

Ari swallowed. She had seen a little of the Shifter's magic, and it scared her. "Is it *bad* magic?"

"I don't know."

This was surprising and very unsettling. Atalanta smiled at Ari's expression. "There is a lot of magic about, Princess. Magic greater than my own. Even I must obey the laws of the One Who Rules humans and animals alike. Well, I must think about this. But it doesn't change the task you must accomplish."

"I think I know what it is. We have to find Chase's horn."

"Yes, Arianna. Without it, the people and animals of Balinor will lose all their ability to speak to one another. It is the unicorns who supply the link, you know. Between humankind and animals. Without you and the Sunchaser that link is broken."

"Okay," Ari said. "Where is it?"

"It was broken into several pieces. There is one here." Atalanta bent her head and nudged a nest of straw aside with her horn. A small stone glimmered in the white light shed by the unicorn's body.

Ari picked up the spiral stone with gentle fingers. "Why, I have two of these," she said. "I found them. . . . No, I believe now that someone — was it you? — wanted me to find them at Glacier River Farm." She fumbled in her skirt pocket. "Here." She withdrew the stones. "They were in two places: one in the south pasture, the other in Chase's grain." To her astonishment, two of the three pieces fit together.

"Samlett went through the Gap, at great risk to his own life, to leave these pieces for you. He hoped that once you touched them, felt them, that you would remember. There is magic in these pieces. He thought perhaps this magic would overcome the Shifter's work. Because it is the Shifter who made you forget. Do you know where the rest of the horn is?"

Ari's voice was hushed. "The Shifter has them."

"More or less." Atalanta's tone was dry. "The Sunchaser's horn was broken off in the battle on the day of the Great Betrayal. The day the King and Queen of Balinor were kidnapped, exiled. The day you yourself were sent to safety at Glacier River Farm, and the stallion with you."

Tears rolled down Ari's cheeks. Memories of her family and her life at the castle were tumbling back thick and fast now. But they were patchy, like morning fog on a river.

"Chase is the Lord of the Unicorns. And he is paired to you for life. But he cannot rule again — will not be himself again — until the horn has been restored to him."

"The Sunchaser is mine. My friend. My companion. The hereditary Lord of the Animals in Balinor." Ari pressed her hands to her temples, in an agony of thought. Would Chase become like Atalanta? Magical? Encased in celestial light? And if he did, would she lose the Chase she knew and loved right now?"

Ari blinked back tears. Atalanta's eyes were gentle. "The One Who Rules us all set the laws for us a long time ago, my dear. You are the Firstborn Princess. The Link to the Unicorn . . ."

"The Speaker for the animals here. And without me. Without Chase . . ."

"The power of speech is gone. The animals here will become like those at Glacier River. The world there is a world of humans only. When the great ice mountains moved through the world, so many millions of years ago, all humans and animals were linked in spirit. But a small part of that world was saved, split off, when the ice mountains plowed the land. The world on the other side of the Gap changed. Humans and animals lost the ability to speak to one another. But *not* in Balinor. Here, things are as they were at the beginning of time. And here, humans and animals are linked. By you. By the Sunchaser."

"Until the Shifter came."

"And if you do not do all you can to restore the Sunchaser's horn to him, this world will become like all the others. Where animals cannot speak. Where men are divided from nature. Where there is no magic at all."

Ari examined the three pieces of horn in her hand. She would set aside thoughts of losing Chase to magic. Her task now was to help him.

"You see this diamond at the base of my horn? This jewel contains a unicorn's personal magic. Without it, we are nothing. Without it, we are . . ." She paused. "Horses. Well enough for the world of humans. Not enough for Balinor."

"The ruby necklace?" Ari faltered. "Is Chase's magic in the ruby necklace?"

"Yes. The one you left behind."

"Oh, no! I had no idea! I have to go back and get it?"

"If you wish him to regain his power."

Ari couldn't look at the Dreamspeaker. And she couldn't ask the question that was tugging at her heart: Will he be the same? Will he be as remote from me as you are now, Dreamspeaker? She had no right to ask that question. Chase must regain his horn and his jewel. He had lost it. Without it, he would not be himself. And she couldn't deny him that. "I *must* go back and get it."

"If you can. Already the Shifter's army moves against us. The way to the Gap may be blocked."

"And the other pieces of the horn? Where are they?"

"The Sunchaser fought gallantly on the day of the Great Betrayal. His horn was splintered into four pieces. Mr. Samlett, who is a leader of the Resistance, picked up these three pieces and saved them to send to you. The other piece fell out of his hands."

"Fell where?"

"Near the Palace moat. The same Palace where the Shifter now rules through the Eye of Entia."

"I see now." Ari stood up as tall as she could. "What do I have to do, Atalanta? Tell me."

"Well!" said a sharp, all-too-familiar voice. "The first thing you can do is get that miserable Lori Carmichael down here. She's screaming her fool head off up in that room."

Ari whirled. Chase scrambled to his feet. A little woman with white hair and rosy cheeks stood foursquare in the doorway. A little of Atalanta's pure light reflected off her wire-rimmed glasses.

Ari sprang forward with a shout and gave her a huge hug. "Dr. Bohnes!" she cried. "Oh, Dr. Bohnes! Thank goodness you're here."

"Goodness has nothing to do with it," the vet said tartly. She turned a shy glance to Atalanta and bobbed an awkward curtsy. "Milady."

"Eliane," Atalanta said. "It's good to see you."

"It's wonderful to see you!" Ari burst out.

"Do you really think I'd leave you to your own devices? Who's going to rub your legs for you, so that they will get stronger and heal? And besides, I had to give you this." She dug into the pocket of her shabby shorts and held out her hand.

"Well, Eliane," Atalanta said. "I am pleased."

"Oh, Dr. Bohnes!" Ari's fingers shook as she picked it up. "The ruby necklace. You brought the ruby necklace!" It glowed brightly as she held it up. Chase brought his ears forward and looked at it attentively.

"You do not remember this?" Atalanta asked him.

Chase snorted. *Ari! She is speaking to me!*

213

"About the ruby, Chase. It is yours, after all. Do you recall how and where you lost it?"

He shook his head.

"I was afraid of this," Atalanta said. "It is going to make your quest that much more difficult, Sun-chaser."

"What do we have to do?" Ari asked. "Just tell us, please, milady."

"It will be dangerous. But there's no help for it." Gradually, the glow around the Dreamspeaker had been getting more intense. It was becoming difficult to see her in the white light. Ari shaded her eyes with her hands. "I don't have much time, Arianna. Please listen. There is an old man on the far side of the woods — some two days' journey from here." The light grew brighter. All Ari could see now was the intense violet flare of the unicorn's eyes. Her silvery voice faded. "He is Minge, the Jewel-wright. Take the necklace and the horn to him. He must fashion them together, make them as whole as he can . . . and then . . . the other piece at the Palace moat will join them. . . ."

She disappeared in a flare of radiance. The stall was dark. No one said anything for a moment. Then Dr. Bohnes clapped her hands together. "Come on, then. There's a great deal to do before morning."

7

"You're a what?" Lori demanded.

"Firstborn Princess, Link to the Unicorn, the Speaker for all the animals here." Dr. Bohnes's fingers were gentle as she probed Linc's still body. He was breathing, but just barely. Ari watched, her hands clenched so hard the nails dug into her palms. Ari and the vet had sneaked quietly into the Inn after putting Chase back in his paddock. They'd taken Linc upstairs to Lori's bedroom. There, as Dr. Bohnes had said, Lori was having a major temper tantrum.

When the noise of the attack on Ari broke out, Lori had dragged the big chest across the room to barricade her door, then crawled under the bed to hide. At first, she'd been so glad to see Ari and Dr. Bohnes that for a minute, she'd behaved like a nice, normal person. Then Dr. Bohnes had told her briefly what the riot had been all about.

"I don't believe it! A Princess? Get real!" But her eyes wouldn't meet Ari's. And she backed away from her. "And this . . . this unicorn with the magic that told you all this stuff. Where is she now?"

"Gone back to the Celestial Valley," Dr. Bohnes said. "Her kind aren't allowed to stay here long. Well." She got up and dusted her knees. "That was a crack on the head, to be sure. He's alive, but just barely. It's going to take awhile for that head to heal."

"Can you do something?" Ari asked softly. Lovingly, she stroked the cream and bronze fur. Linc's eyes were closed, his breathing deep and slow.

"Time is all he needs. You know what that's like. It took awhile for those legs of yours to get as good as they are now. And I wouldn't call them one hundred percent."

Ari dropped her head in her hands. She was so tired. And there was so much to do! "This is impossible, Dr. Bohnes."

"Not impossible. And it's a lot to ask of anyone. But we have to do it. We have to. For if the Shifter wins . . ." For a moment, the sparkle drained out of the old vet's face. Ari had never thought of Dr. Bohnes as old. She was always filled with life and energy, striding around, snapping out orders, her tough old hands amazingly gentle when they massaged Ari's hurt legs. But now — the wrinkles in her face were deep. The skin beneath her bright blue

216

eyes sagged. "Do you know me, child? I know you don't remember everything yet. You won't. Not until the Sunchaser gets his horn back and the two of you return to the way you were meant to be. Bonded for life. But do you remember me?"

"Why, yes," Ari said slowly. "I think I do. You were my nurse."

"And Chase's caretaker."

"That's right. And . . ." Ari smiled a little. "My father called you 'a little bit of a wizard.'"

"More than a little. Yes, Arianna, I am a wizard. Not enough, I'm afraid, to protect you entirely when we start our journey to the forest's edge tomorrow. And my power's getting less as that devil Shifter's power grows here." She sat heavily on the bed and rubbed her back. "Old bones," she sighed.

Ari sat down next to her and rubbed Dr. Bohnes's back and shoulders, just as the vet had rubbed Ari's own legs. "Is that better?"

"No, it's not better," she said sharply. "Nothing's going to be better until your mother and father are back on the throne, and you and Chase are bonded again. Nothing's going to be better until the Shifter is driven back to the Caves beneath the Six Seas." A reluctant grin brought some of the sparkle back. "But your hands are young and strong. And that does feel good on my old bones. And we aren't down yet! Not by a long shot."

At Dr. Bohnes's insistence, they settled down to sleep, even though morning was close. The vet and Lori shared the bed. Ari rolled up the borrowed cloak and lay near the collie. She drifted off to sleep, troubled by dreams of a searching Eye. She woke with a start, staring straight into a pair of brown eyes.

"Linc!" She got on her knees and softly stroked the collie's ears. "How are you feeling, boy?"

My head hurts.

"I'm sure it does. Don't try to get up. I'm going to get you a little more water and a bit of breakfast. You have to eat, you know." She got to her feet and rubbed the sleep out of her eyes. Pale light came through the window. She looked out. Rain today, if she was any judge. Dr. Bohnes snapped awake and rolled out of bed, grumbling. She grabbed her backpack and stamped out the door to the washroom.

Ari pulled on her boots and brushed her hair. None of them had had the strength to get out of their clothes the night before, and she felt grubby. "Lori?" she asked quietly. "You awake?"

"Uh! Leave me alone."

"I'm going to ask Mr. Samlett for some food for Linc. Will you watch him? Hold his head if he gets sick. Dr. Bohnes said that happens with a concussion."

"You want me to hold the dog's head if he barfs? Aagh!" She sat up. She was a mess. Tears from the night before had smeared on her cheeks. The scowl on her face didn't improve her looks at all.

"I won't be long. Then you can wash up."

"Okay, okay." She brought her knees up to her chin and wrapped her arms around her legs. She was frowning, but at least she was frowning at Linc.

Ari slipped downstairs and went into the pantry. It was early. Mr. Samlett was already in the kitchen unloading a basket of eggs in a wooden bowl on the big table in the middle of the kitchen. He dropped one on the floor as Ari came into the room.

"Oops!" Ari said. "Hang on, Mr. Samlett. I'll clean that up."

"Milady! Oh! Milady!" He waved his hands in the air. Two more eggs rolled off the table and smashed on the flagstones. It was getting to be quite a mess. What was this milady stuff from Mr. Samlett? Ari glanced over her shoulder. Had Lori come down? She was going to get a good talking to if she'd left Linc alone. Nope. Lori wasn't there. She turned back to see Mr. Samlett on his knees in front of her. "Forgive me," he sobbed. "Oh, forgive me! And I said you were such a good stable hand! The best, I said, and you the Princess." Big tears ran down his red cheeks.

Ari bit back a laugh. "Now, Mr. Samlett. Who told you?"

"Eliane Bohnes!" he sobbed. "Just now. She's out in the yard getting a cart ready for you. I say a cart ready for you. A cart! That's all you ask of me. A cart! And I called you the —"

"The best stable hand you'd ever had. Please

get off your knees, Mr. Samlett. It feels really weird to have you down there." She extended a hand to help him up. He got to his feet with a groan. "Now, I understand I have you to thank for many things, Mr. Samlett. You helped me through the Gap. You saved as much of the Sunchaser's horn as you could. And this Inn is the heart of those loyal to my father and mother and me. I have one more thing to thank you for. Do you know what it is?"

He shook his head woefully.

"For giving me a job when I needed one!"

His eyes went wide. Then he began to chuckle. The chuckle turned into a laugh. He was still laughing when Dr. Bohnes stumped into the room.

"Put a cork in it, Samlett," Dr. Bohnes said. "We're going to need provisions for a three-day journey in addition to that cart."

"Three days? You and Her Highness are leaving?! You can't!"

"Hush!" the old vet commanded. "You keep Arianna's return to yourself, if you please. It's far too dangerous here as it is. You must not tell a living soul, Samlett. Do you understand? All our lives are at stake."

Samlett bowed to Ari. He was completely serious now. "I do, Eliane."

"All right, then. I'm going to take you upstairs, Samlett. You'll have to take care of Linc the dog while we're gone. I want to show you what to do."

Mr. Samlett's lower lip stuck out like a baby's. "But the dog doesn't talk!"

"So? It's one of nature's creatures. And deserving of your compassion. Eh, Samlett?"

"He talks to me, Mr. Samlett," Ari said quietly. "He's from beyond the Gap. The place where you and the others took me to save me from the Shifter. And even if he couldn't talk, I would not want to be Princess of a Kingdom where one being was considered more worthy than another."

"Well put," Dr. Bohnes said. "Now, if you're finished being Royal, Ari, get your rear in gear. The sooner we find that Jewelwright, the better!"

The next half hour passed in a flurry of activity. Mr. Samlett swore to call the Guild of Balinor Dog Physicians if Linc became the slightest bit worse. Ari prepared food for the journey and packed a small kit of brushes and hoof picks for Chase. Dr. Bohnes had not only commandeered Samlett's best cart, but cajoled the spotted unicorn Toby into pulling it.

Lori dawdled around the fringes and sulked. "How long are you going to be gone?" she asked for the umpteenth time.

Ari was just about finished in the kitchen. She added a second bag of dried fruit to the pack she was loading. Weight shouldn't be too much of a problem if they were driving, rather than hiking. And it wouldn't do to run out of food. Dr. Bohnes had suggested they travel the out-of-the-way roads, because no one knew where the Shifter's forces were. And it was easier to hide evil in large towns than small ones.

"Ari?" Lori demanded. "Or don't you answer to anything but 'Your Highness' these days?" She swept a mock curtsy.

"Sorry, Lori. I was counting dried apples. Dr. Bohnes isn't exactly sure where we have to go. But she thinks it's near here. I'll show you." She pulled out of the backpack the small map of Balinor that Mr. Samlett had given them.

"We travel through the forest —"

"The same one we came through when we landed in this forsaken place? Where those so-called bears were?"

"There isn't any other way to get south," Ari said. "From there, we go through what Mr. Samlett called 'a bit of a swamp' and what Dr. Bohnes called a 'mucky bog.' I don't know anything about it, to tell you the truth. If I ever did, I don't remember. Anyhow, we come out into the small village of Luckon. It's quite near the Palace, I understand. So if we can get Chase's jewel and horn repaired . . ." She trailed off. After the jewel and the part of the horn in her possession were merged, she and Chase would have to go to the Palace to find the last part of the horn.

She shook the thought away.

"Anyway," she finished briskly. "That's it."

"So I suppose I'll come along," Lori said sulkily.

Ari's mouth dropped open. "You? Are you sure you want to?"

"Why not? Do you expect me to stay here? Without money? That Samlett character said he'd give me a room, all right. As long as I mucked out stalls and scrubbed the kitchen floor. Forget that."

"But, Lori. It might be dangerous."

"Old Bohnes is a wizard, isn't she? And who's going to mess with a Princess? That is, if you are a Princess, which I don't believe for one second flat. Besides . . ." She muttered something Ari couldn't catch.

"Sorry. I didn't hear you."

"I said I'm scared to stay here by myself. I saw those creeps go after you last night. If those jerks come looking for a thirteen-year-old girl and find one, they aren't going to believe me when I tell them it isn't me."

"Mr. Samlett knows."

"Phooey. And frankly, Ari, who looks more like a Princess? You or me? I don't want to risk staying here alone, thank you very much."

Ari shrugged. "Suit yourself. I guess I'd better add a little more food."

The sun was over the eastern hills by the time they were ready to go. Toby backed himself into the shafts of the little cart Mr. Samlett had given them. It was bright blue, with two wheels and a sign on the side that read: THE UNICORN INN FINE EATS! Dr. Bohnes hopped onto the double seat and took the reins.

Lori climbed in and sat beside her. Mr. Samlett loaded the last of the packs into the back of the cart. Ari, who had saddled and bridled Chase with the tack that had come from Glacier River Farm, swung into the saddle with difficulty. Her legs were more than usually cramped this morning. She saw Dr. Bohnes eyeing her, but the old vet didn't say a word.

"Milady!" Mr. Samlett tugged shyly on her stirrup. Ari looked down at him. "Take this," he whispered. "Just in case." He drew a thin leather scabbard out of his sleeve and slipped it into the top of her boot. "It was your father's."

She caught the glitter of a gold-encrusted hilt. A powerful memory swept her: a tall man, broad-shouldered, his blond head thrown back in laughter. His well-shaped hands pared an apple. He cut off a slice and offered it to her on the blade of his knife.

This knife. Her father's.

She stared down at the scabbard, which was almost completely hidden by the top of her boot. She touched the ruby jewel, concealed beneath her skirt. She set her jaw. She tapped her heels into Chase's side and rode to the head of the cart. "Move on out, Toby. We're ready."

8

The blue cart and its passengers didn't get a lot of attention as they rode through the village on their way to the forest. Ari and her hornless unicorn did, however.

Dr. Bohnes drew to a halt in front of a thatched three-sided shed. Bunches of dried herbs hung from the shelves. Bottles with mysterious contents stood in disarray on the counter facing the dirt street. A thin woman with curly brown hair and serious gray eyes was sitting on a stool as the procession stopped. She got up and dropped a polite, perfunctory curtsy. The sort of curtsy, Ari realized, that was part of the general manners of these villagers. She was on horseback — or rather, unicorn-back — so she nodded in return.

"I have nothing to help you, miss," she said. "And never have I seen such a thing. A hornless unicorn! What terrible times we live in."

225

"We didn't stop for that," Dr. Bohnes said gruffly. "How are you, Leia?"

The woman bent forward. Her eyes widened. Dr. Bohnes raised a cautionary finger to her lips. "Eliane! Is it you?" she whispered.

Dr. Bohnes nodded, and said loudly, "Mistress Leia, I've heard you have fine teas for sale. I would like some peppermint, if you please."

"Why — ah — certainly, Eli . . . Mo . . . I mean, madam. Will you come to the back with me? You can make your own selection there."

"Ari?" Dr. Bohnes motioned her off Chase with a commanding forefinger. Ari dismounted and followed the two women into the depths of the shed.

Once out of the sight of passersby, Dr. Bohnes gave Mistress Leia a quick hug. "It's good to see you well."

"And you, Eliane! I'm glad to see that you are safe. I've heard such terrible rumors!"

"That's why I've stopped to see you. You know more about what's going on in Balinor than any ten Samletts. I need to know what lies in the way of our getting to see old Minge."

"The Jewelwright?" Leia's eyebrows drew together in a frown. "Why would you want to see him?" She went on, with a rush, "Is it true, Eliane? That the Princess is lost, perhaps dead? That the Sunchaser has lost his jewel?" She gasped. Her hands went to her mouth. Her gray eyes met Ari's blue ones. "Your

226

Highness!" she exclaimed. She sank to the floor in a profound bow.

"Oh, my," Ari said uncomfortably. It was hard getting used to this. She hoped every single person they met wasn't going to drop to the dirt like a lopped-off cabbage every time her identity was revealed. On second thought, she'd be glad if the Shifter and his gruesome pals did that instead of trying to cut off her own head like a cabbage.

"Please get up, ma'am," Ari said.

Leia raised her head. There were tears in her eyes. "We thought we would never see you again!" she said softly. "Your mother, the Queen? Your father?"

"We don't know anything at the moment, Leia," Dr. Bohnes said briskly. "Now, get up and give us the news, there's a good woman. Where is the Demon herd? And what about Sistern?"

Sistern. Another memory rocked Ari. Tentacles. A huge beak. One single yellow-green eye. A scaly, slimy thing that could travel in water as fast as it could on land. She drew a shaky breath.

"No one's heard a thing about the Demon unicorns, not since they passed through the King's forest yesterday."

"And they were headed north," Dr. Bohnes murmured. "We are headed south."

"Sistern now dwells in the moat outside the Palace." Leia shuddered. "They say he was maimed in the battle on the day of the Great Betrayal. That he

227

can no longer walk on land. That is why . . ." She bit her lip. Her face was pale.

"Why what?" Dr. Bohnes demanded.

"That is why the Shadow King flies at night."

"What's this? The Shifter has bred a new monster? With wings?"

"They say it's the Eye of Entia. In a new and more horrible form. The Eye can see far now, above the land. Perhaps to the gates of the Celestial Valley itself."

"Have you seen this winged Shadow?"

"Once. I didn't see it as much as I felt it passing. Like a cold, cold wind, Mother Eliane. And I could not move for fear."

"Humph." Dr. Bohnes tugged at her lower lip. "That's all the news?"

"All except this." She turned to Ari and curtsied a third time. "We are so glad for your return, Your Highness. The hearts of the people are with you."

"We'll need more than their hearts before this is over," Dr. Bohnes said bitingly. "Keep the news about Arianna to yourself for the moment, Leia. But when the time comes . . ."

"When the time comes . . ." Leia echoed. She raised her fist in the air. "We will fight!"

9

"We will fight," Ari murmured to herself. They were deep in the forest. The air was still. Dark was coming on, and Dr. Bohnes was on the lookout for shelter from the moonless night. They had taken the wrong turn a few hours back.

"You said we wouldn't have to spend the night here," Lori complained. She drew her cloak around her and shivered. "I'm freezing."

"The worst possible night to be out with the Shifter's forces looking for you," Dr. Bohnes said to Ari. She jiggled the reins over Toby's back. "Step out, Toby. That shepherd's hut can't be too far from here."

"Your directions were awful," the unicorn threw over his back. "Past the cove of pine trees, you said. Then north by northeast, you said."

"I was right," Dr. Bohnes said flatly. "It's you who can't tell north from south, Toby."

229

The unicorn stopped in his tracks. "Hey!" His voice had the patient reasonableness parents use with idiot children. "You face north, right? If you face north, south is in back of you. East is to the left of you."

"East is to the right of you," Dr. Bohnes said. "I told you before."

"Left! Left! Left!" Toby stamped his right fore-foot each time he hollered. Ari burst into laughter. "And what's so funny?" Toby asked icily.

"You are," Lori said. "I've never seen such a boneheaded unicorn in my life. For one thing, you can't even tell your left foot from your right foot, which means nobody can understand how we got so lost in the first place, because when you were wrong you were right."

"Right here," a scratchy voice said.

Everyone jumped.

"Where did that come from?" Lori demanded.

"From the bush. Over there. To your *left*," Toby said sourly.

Ari looked to her right. The bushes twitched.

It's a human, Chase said. *And beyond him, I think I sense the shepherd's hut.*

"How can you sense a shepherd's hut?" Ari asked.

The wind blows around its shape. And there are movements in the forest. Vibrations on the floor.

The vibrations change when there is a structure there. I feel those movements through my hooves.

"Right here," the voice said again. The brush parted. A man with wild hair and a very dirty face peered at them dubiously. "You who I bin expectin'?"

"Whom have you been expecting?" Dr. Bohnes sounded grim.

"Travelers. In need of a place to sleep. They say you'll pay."

"Who says?" Lori asked sharply. "And if you don't take Visa, forget it. I don't have any money, and they don't, either."

"Them." The man jerked his chin up. Ari craned her head back and looked into the trees. A flock of crows hopped silently overhead. One of them blinked his beady eye at her and said, "Toll! Pay the toll! Pay the toll!"

"We have a few pennies," Dr. Bohnes said. "Is the place clean?"

"Yes'm."

"And do you have water?"

"Yes'm."

"Then we accept your offer of hospitality."

"Huh?"

"We'll pay," Lori clarified. Then, not so quietly that he couldn't hear it, "Moron!"

The grimy man said his name was Tomlett. This appeared to reassure Dr. Bohnes, who questioned him at length about his family as he led the way through the forest to the shepherd's hut.

"He's a member of one of the Forest Clans," she said as they settled inside the hut. The old vet had made a brief inspection of the hut, informed Tomlett in no uncertain terms that it wasn't clean enough, and sent him off to draw water. "A distant relative of Samlett's, in fact."

"That's all right, then," Ari said.

"Maybe," Dr. Bohnes said, "and maybe not. Most of the Forest Clans are independent. They couldn't give a hoot about who hangs around the Palace." She rubbed her hands together. "Lori. Get the dried apples and the corn pancakes from the packs and serve the food."

"Me!" Lori said indignantly.

"You. Ari will see to the unicorns. I'm going to take a nap." She sat down and leaned against the wall with a groan. "These old bones," she said. "These old bones." She dropped asleep instantly.

Ari went outside to make sure that Toby and Chase had enough forage for the night. Lori came out of the hut grumbling, and unloaded the packs from the cart. Toby was still hitched. Chase grazed restlessly next to him. Ari went over and began to unbuckle the lines from the shafts of the cart. Toby stamped his foot and said, "Stop."

"Do you have a stone in your hoof?" Ari asked. "Let me get the hoof pick."

"No stone. There's something going on I don't like."

Without thinking, Ari's hand went to the knife in her boot. "What is it?" she whispered softly.

"Look up."

Ari gazed upward.

"Don't be so obvious about it, Princess!" Toby said.

Ari rubbed her nose casually. She stretched her neck this way and that. She rolled her shoulders, put her arms over her head, and yawned.

All the while she battled fear. "The crows," she whispered to Toby. "There are thousands of them in the trees. And Toby, their eyes . . ." She shuddered.

"Demon eyes," Toby agreed quietly. "They've found us. Or Tomlett's betrayed us. Get those two out of the hut and into the cart."

Ari? Chase stood at full alert, gazing into the trees. *There is danger here.*

"Would you tell him not to hang out a *sign!*" Toby grumbled. "Tell him to keep on grazing, like nothing's happening. If those birds attack . . ."

"What do they want?" Ari whispered back. She caught the eye of a large crow. It glittered like a banked coal. His pinfeathers stuck up all over his back. He chattered at her, "Pay the toll! Pay the toll! PAY THE JEWEL!"

Ari stopped herself just in time. She almost grabbed the jewel around her neck. And if they

233

saw where it was hidden, the birds would attack for certain.

"Food's ready," Lori announced. She stood at the door to the hut.

"Get Dr. Bohnes," Ari said as normally as she could.

"She's asleep."

"There's something wrong with Toby's hoof."

The black-and-white unicorn nodded vigorously. The harness jingled wildly as he shook his head. "I want a doctor NOW!" he said.

"Oh, all right!" Lori flounced into the hut and a few moments later, Dr. Bohnes stumbled out. She yawned, scratched her head, and stamped over to Toby. "Which foot is it? Right or left. What the heck am I asking you for, you don't know the dif —"

Ari grabbed her hand and squeezed it. The vet's bright blue eyes narrowed. Ari jerked her chin upward, ever so slightly. Dr. Bohnes nodded. "Lori," she said curtly, "get the hoof pick and bring it to me. Right now."

"I'm eating!"

"And this unicorn's lame. Move it."

"Aaagh!" Lori slammed back into the hut.

"Bring the whole pack, Lori," Ari suggested in what she hoped was a casual tone. Her palms were sweating. She wiped them down the sides of her breeches. Chase, who had been grazing nearer and nearer in ever-smaller circles, nudged her in the back with his muzzle.

We must ride, milady. We don't have much time.

"Oh, Lor-ri!" Ari looked up in pretended exasperation. She probed the trees as she chattered. Hundreds of crows gathered in the trees above. Perhaps thousands. What unnerved her most was the silence in which the birds gathered. All except one. The bird with the demon eyes, who chattered, "Pay the toll! Pay the toll! PAY THE JEWEL!"

"Here!" Lori thumped the backpack on the ground.

"Move!" Ari shouted. In one fluid motion, she drew her father's knife from her boot and leaped onto Chase's back. Dr. Bohnes clambered into the wagon and jerked Lori after her by her long blond hair. As soon as he felt their weight in the cart, Toby took off at a dead run.

And the crows attacked. Screaming, cawing, their wings were like a tidal wave. They flew down from the trees straight at Ari and Chase. The great stallion reared, and Ari realized with a pang that he was trying to spear the birds with his horn. But he had no horn! She stabbed upward with her father's knife, slashing the air.

A memory flooded her. She was in a high, white room. Her brother was there. He held a stick in his hands. "Thrust home!" he cried.

"Thrust home!" Ari yelled. She sliced at a huge bird flying straight toward Chase's eyes. Feathers fluttered into her hair. "We must run, Chase!"

I. Do. Not. Run. From. Battle!

"You have no horn!" Ari shrieked. She slammed her heels into his sides. Shocked, Chase took a great leap forward. The crows rose in a whirlwind after them, cawing. Ari slammed her heels into him again. "Run!"

They raced off after the cart. Chase thundered through the woods, dodging trees, leaping over fallen logs, splashing through pools of water. The forest grew denser. Thicker. The crows fell behind. Ari could hear their frustrated shrieks. But the trees were too thick for the birds to penetrate without getting caught in the branches. Chase slowed to a walk. His great sides heaved in and out. His withers were covered with sweat. Ari bent forward and patted his neck. He stopped and quivered.

Do you hear that?

"What?" She held her breath. She heard shouts, ahead of them through the trees. "It's Toby and the others! They're in trouble!"

They raced through the trees to try to save the others.

10

Toby had run straight into the swamp. He was just a few feet from shore when he realized they were sinking. The mud was thick and sucked at his hooves with a slow, inexorable force. He thrashed slowly, and with purpose. Lori clung to the sides of the cart and screamed.

Ari pulled Chase up just in time. His left forefoot slipped into the muck. He pulled it free with a surge of his powerful muscles. Ari slipped off her stallion and stood in despair.

"Do something!" Lori screamed. "We're sinking!"

"I can see that," Ari said. Dr. Bohnes, her hands steady on the reins, looked at her and smiled. "Do you think you can throw the lines to me? I can tie them to Chase's saddle and he can pull you backward."

"Too heavy, even for him," Dr. Bohnes said. The cart slipped further into the ooze. "Pull Lori out first."

"But . . ."

"No buts. The way she's wriggling around, she's making us sink faster."

"Lori," Ari called. "LORI!"

"What!"

"I'm going to throw Chase's reins to you!"

"I'm going to die!"

Ari gave up trying to talk to her. She was glad now, that she never had to use a bit with Chase. He was wearing a nose band, a head stall, and nothing more. She just hoped the leather would hold. She searched the ground beneath her feet for a heavy rock. She found it. She tied the end of the reins around it, and tossed it into the cart. It hit Dr. Bohnes on the back. The old vet slumped forward. Ari stood frozen in fear. Dr. Bohnes shook her head and then reached around and handed the reins to Lori.

The cart sank another twelve inches into the muck. Toby was still struggling gallantly. His muzzle was just above the slime.

Lori held onto the reins, too scared now to scream.

"Okay, Chase," Ari said.

The great stallion pulled back. Lori flew out of the cart and landed half in and half out of the mud. Ari pulled her to her feet, took the reins, and threw them out again to Dr. Bohnes.

The vet crawled forward and tied the reins around the shafts of the cart.

"Dr. Bohnes! Bohnesy!" Ari clenched her fists to keep from screaming.

"We can't leave him here," Dr. Bohnes said. "And there's no one to tie the reins to him once I'm out."

"You. Go. Ahead," Toby said. His voice was thick with mud.

"Okay, boy," Ari said. "Pull!"

Chase backed up. He tugged. The cart moved up, then settled back into the swamp.

"For me, Chase. For me!"

Chase pulled again. The muscles swelled on his haunches and sweat broke out on his neck. His eyes bulged with effort. The cart rose and sank, then rose and sank again. Slowly, miraculously, it started to come out of the swamp. Chase pulled steadily. Ari was afraid to look at Toby, but she couldn't look away. The black-and-white unicorn was almost completely under the mud. All she could see was his horn, sticking bravely up, like a flag.

"Hurry, Chase! He can't survive under there very long!"

Blood ran out of Chase's nose. The edge of the cart reached firm ground. Dr. Bohnes quickly climbed out to safety.

Ari grabbed the edge of the cart with both hands and cried, "Pull, both of you. Pull!"

They all put their backs into it. Finally, the cart rolled free. Ari leaped forward, but she was too late. The reins slipped off the shafts.

Toby was gone, except for the tip of his horn.

Ari wound the reins around her waist, and plunged into the swamp. She sank to her chest almost immediately. Dr. Bohnes's hands were firmly around her shoulders. Lori grabbed her right arm. With her left, she searched under the mud. After a few terrible moments, she found a leather strap, and a warm hide underneath. "I've got him!" she gasped. She tied the reins around the belly band of the harness.

"Pull!" Dr. Bohnes shouted. "Pull for your lives!"

With a tremendous groan of pain, Chase dragged Toby out of the swamp.

The spotted unicorn lay dreadfully still. Dr. Bohnes took the edge of her shirt and quickly wiped the mud from his nose and mouth. His eyes were closed. "But he's still breathing," Lori said timidly. "Look!"

It was true. His flanks heaved in and out with the harshest of breaths. Dr. Bohnes crouched over him for a long anxious moment. Then his eyes flickered open. He gave a great cough. Swamp mud poured out of his mouth and all over Lori's feet. The blond girl crouched down and smoothed the forelock away from Toby's eyes.

"You — told — me — to — take — a — left!" He coughed.

Then he gave a sigh and fell peacefully asleep.

They were delayed two days while Toby recovered. Ari wanted to ride Chase to the nearest village for help, but Dr. Bohnes refused with a curt shake of her head. "We must all stick together now," she said.

"We don't have enough food for three days," Ari said.

"Skimpy rations aren't going to bother *me*. They'll have to do."

Lori opened her mouth to whine, looked at poor Toby lying asleep on the grass, and shut it.

And from there on in, she stopped complaining. Ari was amazed. She helped clean the cart, helped wash out their clothes, and even helped Ari wash her hair.

Finally, Toby coughed up the last of the swamp mud, and they proceeded around the swamp to the village of Luckon, where the Jewelwright Minge lived.

"Except he don't live here no more," the Innkeeper of Luckon said. The Inn was situated on the outskirts of the village. Lori greeted the prospect of a hot bath with a squeal of relief. As Dr. Bohnes

241

disbursed the necessary funds to the Innkeeper, Lori ran upstairs to take a bath. Toby and Chase relaxed in the outside paddock, eating good green hay for the first time in almost a week.

"Sure he does," the serving girl grunted. "He lives somewhere around here. He comes in here all the time."

"Every day?" Ari asked.

"Sure. Most weeks. Sometimes every other day." The serving girl had bright red hair and a lot of freckles. She also talked a lot. She talked incessantly for the next three days, while Dr. Bohnes, Chase, Ari, and Lori waited for the Jewelwright. Toby, much quieter since his near-death experience, slept a great deal.

On the morning of the fourth day, Dr. Bohnes told Ari their funds were running out. "And I don't like being in one place for too long," she added. "Word travels fast, even in country villages like these. And you know that the Palace isn't all that far away."

"Is it?" Ari asked vaguely. Not much of her memory had returned. "Have I ever been in Luckon?"

"Once. Long time ago. Just before the Ceremony of the Bonding." Her wise eyes wrinkled in thought. "You don't remember that?"

"With Chase, you mean. No, I don't remember that. And Dr. Bohnes, I'm worried. His . . . his speech seems to be going. I mean, I can't really talk with him anymore."

Dr. Bohnes nodded. "Doesn't surprise me."

"Isn't there anything we can do?" Ari got up and moved restlessly around the Inn. This place was not nearly as comfortable as the Unicorn Inn in Balinor. The wood floors were never clear of straw and mud. And the food was awful.

"Nothing," Dr. Bohnes said. "We can do nothing without the jewel and mended horn."

11

Numinor, the Golden One, went down the hill at an impatient walk, his hooves striking sparks from the granite gravel on his way. The unicorns of the Celestial herd raised their heads at his approach, then melted silently into the trees when they saw how he looked.

"Atalanta!" he called out. "Atalanta!" He jumped the huge bore of a fallen tree with an angry flick of his tail.

"I am here, milord." The Dreamspeaker moved as she always did, quietly, gracefully, like a flower on a stream, but she seemed tired, and her eyes were cloudy.

Numinor snorted, then reared. He came to earth with a thump. "And I am here, and so are all the others! *But where is the Jewelwright?*"

"I have looked. I have watched. I cannot see him."

Numinor's great golden head sank against his chest. For a moment, he said nothing. "Then what more can we do? Is it time for us to march? Has the Shifter taken the Jewelwright? Must we follow the Path from the Moon to Balinor, an army which that world has never seen before?"

"Others have gone that way, milord. They have left the Valley on the Path from the Moon, and have gone below." She said no more, but waited.

"The Demon herd, you mean."

"Yes. Pride, milord. A fatal thing, especially in Kings."

Numinor raised his head to the setting sun. The Shifter's Moon was done for another month, and now the Unicorn Moon, the Silver Traveler herself, shone brightly even as the sun went down. "They left, the dark ones of the rainbow. And were not allowed to return." He dropped his head and looked intently at the Dreamspeaker. "How shall we know? How shall we know, Atalanta, when it is time to march? What if I make the mistake that *he* —"

"Hush," Atalanta said. "We will not speak of it now."

Numinor raised his left foreleg to strike the ground, then visibly restrained himself. "Where is that Jewelwright?" he trumpeted. "I command that you appear!"

Atalanta looked at him, a grave expression in

her eyes. He could command all he liked, the Golden One. But the Jewelwright listened to his own music and played his own tune.

Like Arianna and Chase, the unicorns must wait.

12

The fourth day at the Inn in Luckon dragged on. Finally, just as the sun was setting, a little old man plodded up to the Inn on an incredibly ancient unicorn.

It was a mare. But an old, old mare. Older than her master, it seemed. Both of them had hair sticking out of their ears, grizzly beards, and sway-backs. The old man gave her neck a pat, then walked into the Inn.

"Hey!" the red-haired serving girl said. "There he is. Minge. Where you been?"

"Out," the old man said. He settled himself on a bench under the window.

"You want coffee?"

"What d'ya think I want. River water?"

This sent both of them into giggles.

"Say," the serving girl said. "There's some folks been looking for you."

"That right?"

"Um. Over there." She jerked her thumb toward Lori and Ari, who were staring openmouthed at him. This was Minge, the Jewelwright?

Minge ambled over. He wore baggy pants, a floppy hat, and a patched gray shirt. "Hey," he said.

"Hey, yourself," Lori replied. She looked at Ari. Ari looked at her. They both burst into giggles.

"You folks have a job for me?"

Ari's giggles died away. "Yes," she said soberly. "I do." She pulled the ruby necklace from around her neck, drew it over her head, and held it in her palm.

Minge bent over her hand. His breath tickled her palm. He smelled like tobacco, sweat, and tired food. "Uh-huh," he said. "That's a unicorn's jewel, that is." He backed up and looked at her. His eyes were gray and very, very wise. They were amazingly youthful in his ancient face. "You have something else for me, then."

"Yes." Ari pulled the three pieces of Chase's horn out of her pocket. "Do you . . . can you . . . it's so important, Mr. Minge."

"Yuh. Hang on, just a second." He took both the jewel and the pieces of horn from Ari. He tottered back to his bench, where the red-haired serving girl stood with a tankard of coffee. Ari started forward, in protest. Minge drained the tankard, wiped his mouth firmly with the back of his hand, then tottered back to where the girls were sitting.

248

He sat down close to Ari. He held his hands out, the jewel in the left hand, the horn in the right. Slowly, he brought his hands together. A puff of crimson smoke escaped from his clasped palms. He opened his hands.

The jewel held the half horn like a candlestick holds a candle.

"He out back?"

Ari knew who Minge meant. "Yes. In the paddock."

She and Lori followed the old man out the door and around to the small fenced area that had been Chase's home for the past few days. The great stallion's coat was dull, his eyes remote. When Ari tried to talk to him now, he listened with a puzzled air, as if hearing the murmur of wind or water. If she had any doubts about restoring his horn to him, they were long past. She couldn't stand to see him this way.

Chase raised his head as they approached.

"Well, now," Minge said. "Well, now." He eased himself through the paddock gate and walked up to Chase. He passed his left hand over the stallion's face, then put his right hand on the white scar.

He stepped back.

Chase shook his head, bewildered. He opened his eyes. He looked full at Ari, his eyes dark and full of feeling. And he spoke to her, his voice strong and resonant with feeling. "Milady," he said, "I have returned to you."

249

13

Clouds obscured the moon outside the Sun-chaser's paddock. Ari walked as silently as she could. Dr. Bohnes had made her take off her riding boots — too noisy and the noise might attract the enemy! — and replace them with soft sandals. Nobody had been able to find any clean socks, so Ari's toes were bare. Her feet were cold. She wore her breeches, a clean white blouse, and the leather vest.

She tried not to jump at the normal nighttime sounds: the scrabble of small creatures in the brush, the sweep of an owl's wings, the shifting of branches in the evening breeze.

"Chase?" Ari whispered.

"I'm here, milady." His great shape moved toward her, a darker shadow in the night. The moonlight glimmered softly off the horn on his forehead. She could see the jagged edge where the final piece would go.

If they found it.

If they returned alive.

Chase bent and breathed into her hair. Ari slipped her arms around his neck. "We go for the rest of your horn tonight," she said into his ear. "And it's a terribly dangerous thing to do."

"I am with you, milady. As always."

"I brought sacking with me, Chase. I must tie the bags around your feet, to muffle the sound of your hooves." She stood with her back to his head. She ran her hand down his foreleg and pinched lightly behind the coronet band, just as she did when she cleaned his foot with the hoof pick. He lifted his forefoot immediately and rested it on her bended knee. She worked rapidly, not wanting him to know how painful this was to her scarred muscles. She slipped the burlap bag over his hoof, wound baling twine several times around his ankle, then tied it off in a knot. She slipped a finger between the twine and his skin, to make sure it wasn't too tight. Unicorns, like horses, were very vulnerable to swollen legs if their hooves were wrapped too tight. She muffled all four hooves in turn, then straightened up with a sigh. Dr. Bohnes had wanted to massage her legs; she had missed her regular sessions. There just wasn't time.

He knelt before her, the iron-hard legs folding gracefully under his belly. She slipped onto his back and tapped her heels lightly into his sides. He rose like a ship pitching on the waves, bringing his haunches well underneath him, and rising to stand tall. Ari settled herself onto his back. Yes, there was the slight depression behind his withers that just fit her long legs. She straightened her back and brought her seat well under her. She flexed her knees and Chase walked out.

"Shall we jump the fence?"

"Too noisy," Ari said quietly. "Are you ready?"

"I am."

They moved out quietly. The sound of his muffled hooves was very faint on the dirt path. Dr. Bohnes had explained the directions to the Palace over and over again. "You must be silent," she had said. "The Shifter's beings are all around your old home."

Home! Ari thought. Am I really headed home? She wouldn't call it home again. Not until her parents were restored to their thrones. Not until she and the Sunchaser walked the Palace gardens together. Until then it was the Shifter's Palace they journeyed to — not home.

They traveled out of the village to the main road to Balinor. Ari looked for the crossroads sign, at the junction of the Queen's highway and a narrow path that led to . . . what was it Dr. Bohnes had said? Pellian, that was it. The Manor of the House of the Fifth Lord.

The road traveled up and up. Then it dipped down to the valley where the Palace lay beside the River Fallow.

Twice during the journey, they slipped off the road and hid. The first was to avoid a party of villagers, out on some late-night errand. Chase heard them long before she did.

"Will we hide or fight?"

"Easy, Chase. I hope we won't have to fight tonight. If we do . . ." She didn't want to think about it. She and Dr. Bohnes had discussed the best way to retrieve the remainder of Chase's horn for hours. Finally, Ari had won the argument. The two of them must go alone. That way, they had the best chance of remaining hidden. And finding the final piece and slipping away in the night.

The second time, it was Ari who pulled them over into the trees.

"I hear nothing," Chase said.

"I don't hear anything, either," Ari whispered. "I just feel it. We have to get out of the way!" She rode him deep into the brush. He picked his way with care, avoiding branches, stepping into soft piles of leaves. Ari finally drew rein and sat as still as she could, listening.

"What is it, milady?"

The back of her neck prickled. A cold wind stirred. She stared up at the moon. Clouds were forming overhead, thick and sullen. The wind picked up and stirred her hair with cold, cold fingers. She scanned the sky and then jerked in alarm. There! There it was! A huge shadow crossed the moon, dimming its bright face. The shape was . . . what?

She was afraid to look, but she didn't dare look away. A winged horse — no, a unicorn. Blacker than the night sky. With burning sockets where its eyes should be.

The Shifter's Eye. Looking for them!

Ari whimpered, but bit it back. This thing had destroyed her family and home. And she would face it, someday! The terrible shadow moved back and forth, a slow sweep across the moon.

Ari buried her face in her hands, almost too scared to move. Time passed. She didn't know how much. But the cold wind died away. Night sounds returned to normal: the squeak of small mice in the grass, the whoop of a night bird hunting. She tapped her heels lightly into Chase's sides.

"Is it far now, milady?"

"A mile, maybe less."

They rode on in silence. They began to descend into the valley. Clouds covered the moon and the way was dark. A cluster of houses and shops lay just outside the Palace grounds. Some of the Royal household lived here; the farrier who shod the unicorns, the tailor in charge of the seamstresses who made the Royal family's clothes. And there was a park by a bend in the River Fallow, where Ari and her brothers used to play when they were younger.

Houses and shops were silent and dark. "No one dares to go abroad at night now," Lord Lexan had said, that long-ago day at the Unicorn Inn. "Except in armed groups." And it was so. If anyone behind the barricaded doors heard them pass, they wouldn't come out. Too many evil things stalked the night.

Chase stopped a short way from the Palace. Ari realized with a start that it was small, as Palaces go. She'd been away too long, and had seen too much of the outside world. The twin towers that guarded the front gate loomed much larger in her mind than the reality. And the moat was smaller across than she'd thought. With care, Chase could jump it.

"And so we arrive," Chase said.

Ari didn't say anything, afraid to speak aloud. A yellow-green light glowed from a window in the peak of the castle. That had been her parents' quarters. The light was sickly, disgusting. She knew who lived there now.

A slow shuffle came from the top of the wall surrounding her former home. A sentry or a guard? Coming closer.

She drew the reins out to either side of Chase's head and tapped her heels against his hindquarters. He backed up until she loosened her legs and drove her seat lightly into his back. Then she flexed her right calf, raised the right rein, and he broke into a canter, almost noiseless because of the burlap sacking on his hooves.

She checked him at the edge of the moat, rose onto his withers, and drove her heels hard into his sides. He jumped. For a moment, they hung suspended over the moat. She bit back a yell. Out of the corner of her eye, she caught a glimpse of a scaly back, a gruesome tentacle.

They landed with a thump on the other side of the moat. The shuffling overhead stopped.

Ari slipped off Chase's back and drew him into the shadows of the castle wall.

"Who goes there!" The voice was grating. Whoever it was breathed like a hissing snake. "I said, who goes there?"

"Garn!" Another voice, higher, but just as sibilant. "You find somethin'?"

Two of them. Ari's hands were cold. She had no weapon, except her father's knife. Wouldn't have another weapon until they found the rest of Chase's horn.

If they found the horn.

"Dunno," said the voice above her.

She felt, rather than saw, a pair of red-coal eyes peer over the edge of the wall.

"Maybe it's Sistern. Yo! Sistern! Want a night-time snack?" Something flew off the castle wall and landed in the moat with a splash. The water erupted with a roar. A scaly head rose from the moat. Ari couldn't see it as much as smell it. Hot breath, like a stinking furnace. Scaly arms, with claws at the ends, flailed in the air. There was a gulp! And whatever the guard threw over the wall was gone.

"Told ya, Garn. It's just before dawn. And Sistern gets hungry just before dawn."

"You think that's what I heard?"

"Sure of it."

"You got any more of what you threw to her?"

"It's been dead awhile," the guard said doubtfully. "But yeah."

"I'm a bit hungry, too. Think I'll go get me some."

"Don't you eat all of it, hear?"

"I'll eat what I can before *you* get there."

Ari heard scuffling, a few blows and snarls, and then the sound of the guards moving away. She waited until everything was quiet.

Where do we look? For one terrible moment, despair overwhelmed her. The danger was so great! It was so dark! Ari swallowed hard, collecting her thoughts.

Ari was glad she and Chase could still communicate without words. She responded with her knees, pressing him forward, guiding him around the base of the castle wall. She kept her eye on the jewel at the base of Chase's horn. It will warm, Dr. Bohnes had said, when you are close to the missing piece of the horn.

Chase jigged impatiently under her. He hated moving slowly. It wasn't in his nature. *You must let me walk on!*

Ari couldn't speak aloud. She kept light, firm hands on the reins. He balked.

She flexed the reins, right, left, right, left. He half reared, then plunged forward. She loved Chase's

257

proud spirit, but now was not the time! She did what she'd never done before and jerked hard on the reins. There was no bit in his mouth, but she knew to him it was a punishment, that she would fight him.

The ruby flared hot on Chase's forehead. He leaped forward with an eager whinny. It was loud. Too loud. Ari gasped in fear.

Above them, the guards shouted an alarm.

She jumped off the stallion's back, stumbling slightly as she landed in the dark. She turned, almost blind in the darkness, and stumbled against the wall.

She reached up and felt the ruby. Stone cold.

She started forward, her hand on the jewel. The jewel heated up. It was like some mad game of blindman's bluff. She couldn't see!

The stallion blundered along behind her, seeking the lost piece of horn as frantically as she did.

Torches flared on the castle wall. Shouts, curses, oaths streamed from the running guards.

The jewel flared hot and wild. Ari stumbled and threw her hand out to break her fall. Gravel slid underneath her hand. She fumbled desperately, her heart thudding. And there it was!

There it was, warm under her hand. The final spiral stone.

She heard the iron gate groan open, the thud of many running feet.

"Keep calm, keep calm, keep calm," she muttered. "Bend down, Chase! Come down!" It didn't matter now that the guards heard her speak. They'd been discovered — and if she just had a little more time!

The great horse bent his neck. Trembling, she fit the spiral stones together. . . .

And there was a burst of rainbow light. It arched high and wide, tumbling the astonished guards back on their heels. It arched to the stars and back again, lighting the countryside like the most brilliant display of fireworks ever seen. It lit the guards, short, misshapen gnomes with blackened faces and wild white eyes. It lit up the great bronze horse himself.

And then, he was a horse no more. His horn sprang from his forehead like a beautiful spear. The ruby glowed at its base.

"ARIANNA!" Chase shouted. "ARIANNA! COME TO ME!"

14

Ari never knew where her scarred legs got the strength. But she sprang onto her unicorn's back. Chase reared and screamed a challenge to the sky.

He turned on the gnome guards and scattered them with quick thrusts of his warrior horn. Ari clung to his back, wild laughter in her throat.

The guards scattered like leaves before the storm of the Lord of the Unicorn's wrath.

The Sunchaser leaped the moat. Ari clung to his mane. They raced into the darkness, past the darkened village, to the freedom of the forest beyond.

The night sky over Balinor was a rich river. The full moon floated there, calm and quiet. Her shining rays lit up the countryside below, flooding the road with silver light, making the forest impenetrably dark.

Ari bent low over the neck of her racing stallion, afraid to look behind. Were the grotesque guards of the Palace following? Moonlight glinted off Chase's horn. If they did follow, if they did try to pull her from the stallion's back, if she had to fight again, it was worth it! The great unicorn was whole again, his horn restored. Chase had fought the guards as if he'd been born to battle. His iron hooves had lashed out again and again. He had used his horn like a sword, thrusting and shoving the scar-faced gnomes aside. And then they had leaped the moat, springing to freedom.

Chase bent to the left, thundering around the curve in the road that took them away from the Palace. Ari felt the stallion shudder. His head dropped as his breath came in deeper gasps. She slid one hand along the side of his muscular neck and felt the sweat run through her fingers like heavy rain. She sat up and drove herself lightly into the saddle to slow him. "Easy, boy. Easy, Chase."

"We — must — get — to — the — village." His voice was deep, like a bell. But he was very close to exhaustion. She'd forgotten what his voice had sounded like, all those long months she hadn't known who she was. All those long months he couldn't speak.

"It won't help if *I* have to carry *you*," she said softly. "Come on, Chase. Walk, please. Walk."

He slowed down. She could feel him trembling. He stopped.

"Walk on, Chase."

"Be quiet, Arianna, and listen. I want to know if we are being followed."

"Just for a moment, Chase. You're too wet to stand in this breeze. You have to keep moving to cool off."

"A cold won't matter if we are captured."

Ari flexed the right rein and tightened her right leg against his side. Obediently, he swung in a circle, then halted, head up, ears forward, staring toward the west where the Palace lay. Ari held her breath, listening as intently as she could. A dawn breeze was coming up, rustling the leaves of the trees in the forest. There was a thrashing from the brush at one side of the road. Ari jumped and Chase moved forward in response.

"Keep still, milady."

"Sorry," she muttered. "I don't hear anything strange." She kept her voice to a whisper. "No gnomes or anything."

"And I?" He turned his head. The moonlight shimmered on his horn, glanced bright light from his eyes. His mane flowed over her knees. "I hear shouts, in the distance. From the Palace. Shouts of rage."

"Your ears are better than mine."

He didn't answer this, but she could feel him stiffen with outraged pride. Well, of *course*, he seemed to say.

Suddenly, a shriek split the air. A cry of terror. In the west, a dark shadow rose above the tops of the trees. It was huge. It blotted out the moon. Ari gasped and bent over Chase's neck, to hide in his long mane.

"Look up," he said. His voice was kind but firm. "And see what happens to those who fail the Shadow King."

Ari forced her eyes open. If Dr. Bohnes was right, if she really was the Princess, then she had to face the unfaceable. The giant shadow circled the trees. Beneath the terrifying spread of those wings, she saw a tiny figure dangling. The shriek came again, more faintly now, and then the little figure dropped, spun away, falling out of sight. The cry was cut off abruptly.

"The guard?" Ari asked, her voice shaking. "The one that didn't hear us until it was too late?"

"One of them, at least, will never guard the Palace gates again." He jerked his muzzle up. "Did you hear that? They shut the gates. I think we are safe for now."

Ari sighed. "We have to get back to the Inn, Chase. But slowly. You really do need to cool off."

The sun had poked slim pink fingers over the horizon by the time Chase and Ari returned to the Inn in Luckon. Ari had never been so tired. She slipped off Chase's back and drew him to the darkness of the barn. Except the sun seemed to have followed them inside. Or maybe that lazy Innkeeper had stuck some lanterns around. If only she could *sleep*! But she couldn't sleep until she curried Chase, put a blanket on him, and then found Dr. Bohnes and Lori. She patted Chase's neck and yawned.

"Oh, my gosh." Lori's voice was high with excitement. "Oh, my *gosh*!"

Ari's eyes flew open. "You guys waited up?"

Dr. Bohnes snorted. "Of course we waited up. We were worried sick."

Ari yawned again. "I'm *sorry*! I just can't keep my eyes open. Here, Chase, step outside for a second so they can see your horn."

"You're kidding, right?" Lori was awed. "I mean, look at him, Ari. Haven't you even looked at him?"

"Well, if you'd been chased by trolls and flying monsters and huge squi —"Ari stopped herself. She looked at her unicorn. Really *looked* at him.

Even in the darkness of the dirty barn, he glowed like a bronze moon. The elegance in his neck, shoulders, and hindquarters was like the exquisite cut of the ruby jewel.

"Hooves," grunted Dr. Bohnes. She unwound the muffling sacks from Chase's feet. The burlap seemed to fall away. His hooves were solid bronze.

"Good," Dr. Bohnes said. She rapped his right forefoot with her knuckle. "Hard as it should be. Excellent." She hoisted herself to her feet with a loud groan. "Well, milady. What do you think of the Sunchaser now? Do you see any changes?" She shot Ari a glance full of understanding. "So, then."

Ari put her hands behind her back and walked around her unicorn. He was taller, surely, and his mane longer. His tail was a silky banner, falling to the ground behind him. His eyes were a deeper brown, almost mahogany.

But they were the same eyes. Chase's eyes. Filled with warmth. Understanding. And that unbreakable spirit.

He snorted and bent his great head. She felt his breath in her hair, and flung her arms around his neck. "No," Ari said. "No changes." She kept her head hidden, so they couldn't see the tears. "He's just the same, inside." She fought for control of her voice. "So, it's over."

"Over?" Dr. Bohnes settled her glasses firmly onto her nose. "Over? Not by a long shot. Grab some grub and sleep fast, ladies. You've got another quest coming up. Right on the heels of this one."

"Uh-uh," Lori said. "No more quests. This one was enough for me, thank you very much."

"Um. What is it, exactly?" Ari asked.

"Your scepter, Your Highness. The Shifter's hidden it somewhere. And there's no finding the King and Queen until you get the scepter back."

"Scepter?" Lori said interestedly. "Royal?"

"Yep." Dr. Bohnes smiled.

"Ah — and would it be the kind of scepter that had jewels on it?"

"Quite a few, as I recall."

Lori put her arm around Ari's shoulder. "Princess, buddy, old pal," she said happily. "On with the quest!"

VALLEY OF FEAR

1

Atalanta walked up the Eastern Ridge toward the cave of Numinor, the Golden One. She had grave news for him, and her steps were slow. The sun flooded mellow light across the top of the mountains surrounding the Celestial Valley. Atalanta's mane, tail, and horn glowed pale silver in the warm light. She was the Dreamspeaker, the Lady of the Moon, counselor to the unicorn herd of the Celestial Valley. The silver-white radiance was hers alone. The light of neither sun nor moon ever changed it.

Atalanta paused in her journey up the hill and looked down into the valley. The Celestial herd was settling in for the night. Each herd member was a different color of the rainbow. Their colors glowed like the dying embers of a campfire in the setting sun. Several gathered under the Crystal Arch, the long bridge that extended up to the cloud home of the One Who Rules and down to the humans' land of Balinor.

Atalanta's heart swelled with love at the sight of her home. The Celestial Valley, the Crystal Arch, and the unicorns themselves had been there for thousands of years. If she could only be sure that they would be there for thousands more!

Atalanta's forelock fell on either side of her crystal horn, shadowing her violet eyes. She paused, deep in thought. She was worried about Princess Arianna and her bonded unicorn, the Sunchaser. All had been well until the evil Shifter rose from his lair in the Valley of Fear to take over the throne of Balinor.

That had been a year ago. And for the unicorns and the people of Balinor, there had been nothing but grief and terror since the Shifter had kidnapped Arianna's parents, who were the rightful King and Queen. Arianna's brothers, the two young Princes, had also disappeared.

Atalanta had sent the High Princess and the Sunchaser beyond the Gap to safety at Glacier River Farm before the Shifter could get at them. The High Princess and her unicorn were the last hope of Balinor. Without them, there would be no way to bring the people and animals of Balinor together to overthrow the Shifter and his army.

Even as Atalanta approached the cave of Numinor, the Shifter hunted the Princess in Balinor.

Atalanta didn't know if Princess Arianna and her companions would make it back to Balinor Village from their recent journey. True, Tobiano, a Celestial Valley unicorn, was with Arianna and the Sunchaser as guardian and guide. And the human wizard Eliane Bohnes also accompanied them. But the Shifter could take any form — any form at all. How could Arianna and the Sunchaser fight an enemy they couldn't recognize? And the travelers were more than two days away from the village and safety.

Relative safety. Even the village of the Inn of the Unicorn, the home of the Resistance fighters against the Shifter and his army, had traitors among the thatched-roofed houses, spies on the cobblestone streets. No one was safe in these times.

Atalanta stood a moment longer. The sun set behind the Eastern Ridge and the last glow of sunlight faded. Atalanta raised her head and looked at the crescent moon riding low in the purple twilight. The Silver Traveler was faint and on the wane. Another week and she would be gone from the sky in her monthly journey around the earth. Then would come the time of the Shifter's Moon — which meant, of course, there would be no moon. A time when evil magic ruled, and the magic of Atalanta was at its lowest ebb.

The Shifter's Moon was no time for war. If there was ever a time for war. And Numinor would want to fight, once he heard what Arianna and the Sunchaser had to do now.

Atalanta shook herself and snorted gently into the twilight. She had to talk Numinor out of the impending war. If the Celestial unicorns were to attack the Shifter's forces, it had to be at a time and place when victory was possible. Arianna and the Sunchaser didn't have their full magical power, and that time wouldn't come soon.

Unless they accomplished the coming quest.

Atalanta resumed her journey up the hill.

The entrance to Numinor's cave was guarded by unicorns selected for their swiftness and courage. There were two sentries for each eight-hour shift. The two there this evening were from Atalanta's own color band of silver and white. They stood at attention in the courtyard, one at each of the two pillars that supported the entrance arch. The courtyard was paved with smooth, flat rock flecked with gold, which glittered in the low evening light.

Atalanta nodded to Ash, who guarded the left pillar, and spoke a word of greeting to Dusty, who guarded the right. Both sentries bowed deeply to her, forelegs to the ground, jeweled horns touching the pathway.

Atalanta walked across the courtyard, her silver hooves striking a barely audible chime. She heard the rhythmic pacing of Numinor in his cave, caught the now-bright, now-shadowy golden glow of his coat as he walked restlessly back and forth. She looked at Ash, then Dusty. "Would you leave us for a moment?"

The two faded obediently into the twilight.

Atalanta struck her horn gently against the pillar supporting the entrance arch. "Numinor!" she called. Her voice was low and sweet. In the depths of the cave, the sound of restless pacing stopped, and Numinor moved to the entrance. His coat was the gold of the sun at high noon. His horn was a shining spear. A deep yellow diamond — rarest of all jewels — glowed at the base of his horn.

Atalanta trotted forward. She gave Numinor the traditional formal greeting: They stood muzzle to muzzle for a brief minute, then she blew twice on his cheek. Her long silver mane swirled across his withers and mingled with the gold of his coat.

"Atalanta." Numinor's voice was deep and deceptively calm. Atalanta could smell the anger rising off him like a mist, could see anger in the sheen of sweat on the muscles of his great chest. He took a deep breath and rumbled, "You have news?"

"Yes." She backed away to see him better. Numinor's eyes were a rich mahogany-gold. She could see the angry pulse throbbing in the great vein at the side of his neck.

"The Sunchaser has his horn back," Numinor said abruptly. "The ruby jewel with his personal magic has been restored to the base. Now! *Now* we can attack! We will grind the Shifter to dust beneath our hooves! We will spear his army with our horns!"

"Now is *not* the time," Atalanta said, her own voice deliberately calm. "Let us stand and discuss this calmly."

"What is there to discuss, Atalanta? Now that the Sunchaser has his horn back, he and Princess Arianna are bonded again. The people and animals of Balinor won't lose the ability to speak to one another. And now they can work together to overthrow the Shifter. And we of the Celestial Valley will be there to help them — as we always have been."

"I wish it were that easy. Yes, the Sunchaser has his horn again. But this was just the first step, Numinor. You know the law of the One Who Rules Us All. Arianna and the Sunchaser are a Bonded Pair. They are the source of all bonds between humans and animals. Arianna is one half of that bonding. And she does not yet recall all of her past — she herself has not reclaimed her role as Princess."

"You must tell her, then. Help her remember."

Atalanta shook her head with a wry, regretful gesture. "I would have done that long before this if it would work. Explaining her past doesn't mean that her memories will be there. You know that, Numinor. You haven't forgotten what else was lost when the Shifter attacked the Royal Family and destroyed the Sunchaser's horn."

"The Scepter!" Numinor's words rumbled and echoed around the cave. "The Royal Scepter!"

"Yes. Without *that,* the Princess will never remember all of who she is. Without the Scepter, the Sunchaser himself will not come into all of his magic. Arianna must find it. The power of the Princess and her Bonded unicorn are inextricably linked together."

Numinor ground his teeth, then bowed his head in acceptance. "What must be, must be." His whole body quivered with the need for action. "Where is the Scepter to be found?"

"It was torn from the Palace during the fight following the Great Betrayal."

"I know that," he said impatiently. "But do you know where it *is,* Atalanta?"

The Dreamspeaker nodded reluctantly. "We unicorns cannot rescue the Royal Scepter. We unicorns can't touch it or even help her get to it. It is Arianna's quest. She must go and find it."

"Where is it, then?!" Numinor struck out with one great foreleg. A gold flame leaped from the spot where his hoof hit the floor. "She must get it back. You can tell her where it is, at least."

"I am afraid to tell her."

"But why?"

"The Royal Scepter of Balinor," Atalanta said slowly, "lies across the Sixth Sea in the Valley of Fear, hidden in the Castle Entia." Her violet eyes clouded with tears. "It lies at the very heart of the Shifter's evil. No one who has ever gone to the Valley of Fear has ever come back —" She stopped, and the next word was so soft that Numinor barely heard it: "— alive."

2

"I'm homesick," Lori Carmichael said. "Home-sick, homesick, *homesick*!" She and Arianna lay on their backs around the campfire, looking up at the crescent moon. Dr. Bohnes had disappeared into the night some time ago on a search for food to augment the meager rations they were carrying. They had left the Inn of Luckon to travel back to Balinor Village with as many provisions as they could carry in the unicorns' saddlebags but their supply was low.

Lori scowled angrily. Her blond hair was matted and her face was dirty. "We're stuck here in the cold and damp while we wait for food. Somebody didn't plan this very well, if you ask me."

No one answered her. The Sunchaser and Toby grazed nearby. Ari, her head propped up on a saddlebag, watched Chase through half-closed eyes. His ebony horn was almost invisible at night, but his bronze coat caught the gleam of firelight. It was amazing, the transformation that had come upon him with the restoration of his horn and the jewel at its base. The muscles of his chest were more sharply defined. He seemed taller. His mane rippled down his withers like a river of bronze water. His hooves were solid bronze that never chipped or cracked. A subtle light came from him — no matter what the time of day or night — so that he seemed to move in a pool of bronze starlight.

Chase raised his head and looked across the fire at her. She smiled at him.

Chase! she said with her thoughts.

Milady! he replied.

I miss Lincoln, she thought. *I'm anxious to see my dog again.*

Dr. Bohnes said he will be waiting to greet us when we get back to the village, Chase thought in answer. The unicorn dropped his head to the grass again and went on grazing.

"Didn't you hear me?" Lori demanded. The blond girl sat up abruptly, a scowl on her face. She pulled angrily at the twigs in her hair. "I said I want to go home. Back to Glacier River Farm. And I want to go now!"

"Yes," Arianna said, "I heard you." She sat up and rubbed her calf. They had been on the road three days since the battle to regain Chase's horn at the Palace, and her legs were hurting again. She rolled the left leg of her breeches up and pulled her sock off. The campfire didn't provide a lot of light, but she could see the scar spiraling down from her knee to her ankle. Why did her injury hurt so much, six months after the leg had been set? Wasn't she ever going to be free of the pain?

"I suppose you're going to tell me you can't talk because you're in *soooo* much pain," Lori snapped.

"That's more than enough," Tobiano said sternly. The black-and-white unicorn gave a short, angry snort through his horn. "You ought to be ashamed of yourself."

Lori had the grace to look embarrassed. "Sorry," she muttered. "I didn't mean that like it sounded."

"Her Royal Highness was lucky to survive the trip through the Gap to Glacier River Farm with just two broken legs," Toby continued, "and I don't recall that Her Royal Highness extended a written invitation to you to come here to Balinor, did you, Your Highness? No, Lori, you just showed up here all by yourself. Driving Her Highness to distraction with your whining."

"It wasn't my fault," Lori said. She tried to look virtuous and only succeeded in looking bratty. "I fell through the Gap by accident. Who knew that your stupid magic was going to drag me through that tunnel into a place where horses with horns stuck on their heads do nothing but *yak, yak, yak* in my face all day long!"

Toby, who was short, stubby, and extremely

sensitive about the fact that he didn't have the elegance of his herdmates in the Celestial Valley, swelled up like a rooster. "I," he said, "am a *unicorn*. I am *not* a horse with a horn stuck on my head, you rude little girl."

"Toby," Ari began, "we only have a few more days on the road before we get back to the village. Please, let's —"

Toby snorted furiously. "Whine! Complain! Whine! Complain! That's all you ever do!"

"Be quiet!" Ari shouted.

Toby shut up like a clam about to be dropped in a stew pot.

"I'll vote for that," Lori grumbled.

Ari threw her blanket from her shoulders and rose stiffly to her feet. She didn't feel like a princess at all. She was tired, hungry, and she hadn't had a bath for three days. She rubbed her hands over her face, scrubbing at the grit of three days' travel. She wanted her dog. She wanted to be clean. She didn't want to face any more danger — especially if there would be danger to Chase or even to the horrid Lori. Ari still didn't remember much about her past as a Princess — but wasn't it supposed to be easier than this?

She put her hands on her hips and surveyed Lori with a sigh. "Homesick? I can understand you being homesick."

Lori stuck out her chin and turned her back. "Well? Don't *you* want to go home?" Her voice was thick with tears. "Don't you miss your foster parents?"

"You miss your mom and dad, don't you?" Ari thought about Lori's father, who was red-faced and loud. Her hand went to the knife in the scabbard at her belt. Mr. Samlett, the Innkeeper at Balinor Village, had said the knife belonged to her own father. The King. The King of Balinor.

Why couldn't she remember him more clearly? She had flashes of memory: a huge man, with a blond beard and a laugh to shake the ceiling. And her mother, the Queen: quiet and fragrant with the scent of roses around her like a cloak. But she couldn't remember any more, no matter how hard she tried. Why did all her memories drift like fragments of cloud across the sun?

A soft chime, like a silver bell, sounded in the depths of the woods behind her. Sunchaser lifted his head, eyes wide and dark, and stared off into the trees.

Lori flung herself onto a log near the campfire. She clearly hadn't heard the quiet ringing. "I guess you want to stay here in Balinor, since everyone here believes you are their long-lost Princess."

"I don't feel like their long-lost Princess. I don't *want* to be their long-lost Princess." Ari was scared. She was afraid of the Shifter, afraid of the trouble being the Princess would cause her friends.

What if she just couldn't do it? What if she

just stood up, announced that she wanted the normal life of a normal thirteen-year-old, and took Chase and went off to be herself?

She avoided looking over at Chase. Dr. Bohnes and the Dreamspeaker, Atalanta, had told her that Chase was now Lord of the Animals in Balinor. Or would be, as soon as she assumed her rightful place on the throne. Would he want an ordinary life? What was his rightful place?

Ari scrubbed at the ground with her worn sandal. They'd been wearing nice, ordinary riding breeches and boots when magic flung them through the Gap. Now Ari wore a long red skirt, a soft muslin blouse, and a leather vest that Dr. Bohnes called a jerkin. One of the leather straps on her rough sandals had come loose. It dragged in the dust as she scraped her sandal back and forth.

Lori watched her for a long moment, then asked, "If you don't feel like a Princess, what *do* you feel like, then?"

"Lost," Ari said slowly. "I feel lost. It's a terrible thing when your memory comes and goes like summer rainstorms. They tell me I'm the Princess. I remember just a few things about being Princess. Something of the Palace before the Shifter's forces took over. My father's face. My mother's presence. But all I really know, Lori, is that Chase is mine. Chase will always be mine. Everything else . . ." She shrugged. "It's as if it happened to someone else.

And I don't feel homesick because I don't know where my home is."

The bell-like chime called again. Lori was oblivious to the sound. Ari listened, holding her breath so that she could hear even the slightest whisper. She looked at Chase. His head was up, his eyes eager. So! He had heard it, too. She looked at Toby. Stout little Toby, rude and belligerent and a little comic.

But at the moment, Toby didn't look comic at all. He looked stern, and a little frightening. He stared at her, his brown eyes commanding her to go.

The bell sounded a third time.

Third and last.

"I have to go," Ari said.

"Go? Go where?" Lori asked crossly. She darted a glance at the trees surrounding them, then she whirled and glared at Ari. "Into the woods? Are you crazy? This . . . this Shifter person is all around here, or so that crazy old veterinarian said."

"Dr. Bohnes is not a crazy old anything," Ari said evenly. She took one step toward the woods, then another. What was calling her? She looked at Chase.

You must go alone, he thought at her. *I will come if you need me.*

"But . . . what is it?" Ari whispered.

Chase said nothing, but gazed at her with his deep, dark eyes. Lori, unconscious of anything but her own grievances, chattered on, "All right, all right. So, Dr. Bohnes says she was your old nurse here in Balinor or whatever. But Ari, back at Glacier River — back *home* — she was the vet at your farm." Her eyes followed Ari as the bronze-haired girl moved slowly toward the woods. Lori's voice rose and she spoke faster and faster. "And who knows what she really is, this Dr. Bohnes? Who knows what *anyone* really is in this crazy place. . . . Ari! Come back here! Don't you dare leave me alone with this talking horse!"

"Unicorn," Toby said, his tone unexpectedly deep. "Let Her Royal Highness go, Lori Carmichael. This is no business of yours."

Ari stepped out from the comforting glow of the fire and into the woods. The pale light of the crescent moon didn't penetrate here. She stood a moment until her eyes adjusted to the dark. There was the rustle of a small creature in the brush, the faint scent of damp leaves, the strong odor of pine needles.

Ari cleared her throat and said, "Um . . . hello?"

A shadow shifted to her left. Ari grasped the knife at her side, willing herself to stand still. "It's Ari — I mean, Arianna," she said aloud. "Did . . . did someone call me?"

Silence. She began to wonder if she'd imagined the crystalline chime of the bell. And then,

288

deep in the woods, a lavender-blue light began to glow. The light was soft at first, and dim. Ari walked toward it, careful not to scuff the leaves in her path, careful to move as quietly as she could.

A breeze lifted the leaves in the trees, and a scent of flowers came to her, a scent she had smelled before. Her heart began to beat faster. She recognized that blue-white radiance — didn't she? And that smell of flowers that never grew upon this earth . . . that was familiar, too.

She crept toward the light, which was growing steadily stronger now, until it illuminated the very tops of the trees. The source was — where?

There. At the foot of the tallest oak in the forest, or so it seemed to Ari. A faint sound of trickling water came to her. She stopped and shaded her eyes with her hand.

The most beautiful unicorn stood beneath the oak. Her coat was a milky silver shadowed with violet light. Her mane swept in a long fall to her knees. Her head was bent, so that Ari couldn't see her eyes, and her crystal horn just touched the surface of the water in a small stream trickling past her hooves.

"Atalanta," Ari breathed.

The Dreamspeaker raised her head. Her deep violet eyes smiled. She nodded once and then spoke, her voice as gentle as the fall of petals.

"Come here, child."

"The Lady of the Moon," Ari said. "They call you the Dreamspeaker. You rescued me from the mob at the Inn. The mob led by Lady Kylie."

"Come closer, Arianna, and sit here at my feet. You must learn your fate."

3

"Sit down, my child," Atalanta said.

Shyly, Ari curled herself at the unicorn's feet. Surrounded by the Dreamspeaker's magical radiance, her doubts and fears ebbed away. "I missed you," she said. "I wish you could be near me always."

"I am here now." Atalanta settled gracefully onto the forest floor, hindquarters tucked under herself. Her forelegs curved around Ari's back. Ari settled into the silky warmth of the unicorn's side and twined her hand in Atalanta's silver mane. "Now tell me, Arianna. What is troubling you?"

Ari looked deep into Atalanta's violet eyes. There could be no holding back in her response. Those purple eyes could see lies and evasions and half-truths. "I don't want to be the Princess!" she said. "Part of me knows that being the Princess means giving up things. I will always have to think of

291

others first. I'll have to *do* things for others before I do things for myself. I won't have a life of my own!"

"That is true," the Dreamspeaker said calmly. "But there are great rewards in fulfilling your destiny, Arianna. There is both peace and love within you, my child. Those feelings, those qualities will come to full flower when you work for the benefit of your people."

"What if I can't?" Ari asked. "What if . . . what if I become cruel and selfish?"

"What will be, will be, Arianna. We all feel cruel and selfish at times. Greedy. Angry. Spiteful. But you have a choice, don't you? You aren't at the mercy of your feelings. You also have a brain and a heart. You can decide for yourself. You have been afraid before."

"Petrified," Ari agreed.

"You conquered the fear. You made a choice to be brave. And you succeeded. You have another choice now. Can you bear what I am about to tell you? And can you make the right choice this time, too?"

"I don't know if I can," Ari said humbly. "I'm awfully scared."

"You'd be a fool not to be frightened, Arianna. And you are not a fool. True bravery, genuine courage, comes from enlightened fear. Do you understand me?"

"I think so," Ari said. "It's easier not to know if something's going to be truly bad. But I'm not as scared when you're here. This — whatever it is that I'm going to have to do now — can you come with me?"

"No."

"No? Just no?"

Atalanta's eyes seemed to smile, but her gentle voice was firm. "I am the Dreamspeaker. You are the Princess of Balinor. It is not within my power to do other than I am doing now. I am a guide, Arianna, a counselor. I cannot be other than I am. Tell me, do you wish to return to Glacier River Farm?"

"Do you mean — I could?"

Atalanta nodded slightly. "Yes. You could."

"But . . . my parents. Who will find them if I don't?"

"There are those in the Resistance who will try."

"Will they rescue them? Find my father and make him King again? Find my mother and my brothers?"

"Perhaps. Perhaps not."

"Chase and I would have a better chance to find them?"

"Yes. It is what you were born to do. But first, there is one task you must complete. *If* you can do it. If you can go on this quest and return in triumph, then the people of Balinor will rally around you and the Sunchaser. And there is good reason for that, Arianna. You and the Sunchaser have a hereditary magic that is given to no others in the kingdom. This

293

is why the Shifter is afraid of you. Why he and his army of phantom unicorns are looking for you even now. But yes, if you wish to return to Glacier River, to cross the Gap to safety, I can contrive to send you both back. But Chase must give up his horn and his personal magic. And you must renounce your claim to the throne. Forever."

"I would be an ordinary girl," Ari said. "I think I might be better as an ordinary girl than as a Princess, Dreamspeaker. Trying to remember what it was like to be a Princess is like trying to grab water. The memories spill right out of my mind. And I feel silly when people curtsy to me. I'm embarrassed when everyone calls me 'Royal Highness.' I don't feel very royal."

"I see."

"Could I be an ordinary girl?"

"It is your choice, Arianna. Anale and Franc would continue to be your foster parents. You could live at Glacier River Farm and go to school there. You could train horses. Teach the young on that side of the Gap to ride. Perhaps" — Atalanta's tone was thoughtful — "perhaps tell them tales of legendary unicorns."

For a moment, Ari lost herself in a safe and reassuring dream. Her memories of Glacier River Farm were clear, distinct, and recent. She remembered the green meadows, the gray barns and white fences. And the horses — nice, ordinary horses named Cinnamon and Scooter and Duchess. She could go to school, make friends with other ordinary girls.

And the Sunchaser, too, would be an ordinary horse. And perhaps, at night, dream of the life he was meant to lead. Lord of the Animals here in Balinor.

She couldn't do that to Chase. She couldn't change his destiny. Or her own.

Ari sighed. "Well," she said. "I guess not. I suppose I'd better do what I have to do."

"You are certain?"

"No. I'm not certain. I'm scared. But I'll do it. Whatever it is, I'll do it. You're sure you can't come with me?"

Atalanta shook her head. Her mane swept over Ari's cheek.

"So Chase and I will be all alone?"

"Not quite alone. There are four who will travel with you and the Sunchaser. You will be the Company of Six." She was silent, and then said with an odd hesitation in her voice, "I believe there is one other who will help you. But I am not certain of this. She is part of the deep magic. You must seek advice from the Old Mare of the Mountain."

The words sent a strange thrill through Arianna. Her breath caught in her throat. "Who — who is that?"

Atalanta closed her eyes for a long moment. "I cannot tell you more. Not now." Her long lashes swept up, and her deep violet eyes held Ari's. "This is a great task you are asked to do, Arianna. Some of it involves the deep magic. I have not been permitted to see all. That will be revealed to you in time — I have seen this in the Watching Pool, and what is in the pool is true. I can only hope that the four who travel with you and Chase will have magic of their own. I can only hope that you will see the Old Mare. But, just in case of trouble that I have not foreseen, I am permitted to give you this. To use only in time of your greatest need." Atalanta dipped her horn into the stream, then tossed her head. The sparking water whirled in a tiny vortex around the tip of her horn, then coalesced into a starry point. "Hold out your hand, my child."

Obediently, Ari held her hand out. The starry tip of Atalanta's horn fell into her open palm. Ari looked at it, fascinated. The tip had formed into a small flask filled with diamond-clear water. She closed her hand around it. It was cool, as cool and chilly as rain.

"This is the Star Bottle. Use it only when all is dark and there seems no hope. This — and your own courage, Arianna — should be enough. With these, you will not be alone." She nuzzled Ari's hair gently, the breath from her muzzle soft and fragrant. "You must ask me, child, what this great task will be. I will wait until you are ready."

Ari swallowed tears of fright. She snuggled into Atalanta's side. If only she didn't have to be the

Princess! If only she could lie here with the Dreamspeaker, safe and content forever!

The unicorn lay quietly with her, the soft sounds of her breathing as comforting as the sounds of waves at the seashore. Finally Ari said, too loudly, "Please, tell me."

"You must find the Royal Scepter. Do you remember it?"

Ari stared straight ahead, concentrating. "I think so. It's not very big, is it? About the size of a riding crop."

"It is made of rosewood and set with lapis lazuli."

"And there's a carved unicorn's head on the top."

"Yes."

Ari focused as hard as she could on the elusive memory. The Scepter had special powers — she remembered that, at least. "Chase!" she exclaimed. "The Scepter is a visible token of my bond with Chase! It was passed to me when we bonded."

"When you find it, you will come into all your powers as High Princess. Your memories will return to you. All of them. You and the Sunchaser will have full use of the Bonded Magic." The silver light around Atalanta began to dim. Ari tightened her hold on the unicorn's mane. "What's happening?" she cried.

"I must return to the Celestial Valley," Atalanta

said. The light was fading faster now. "The Scepter is in the power of the Shifter, Arianna. You and the Sunchaser must return to Balinor Village and prepare for a two-week journey to his home in the Valley of Fear. You must travel in disguise all the way, for the Shifter's spies are everywhere."

"Disguise?" Ari asked.

"When you journey through Balinor and the lands beyond, you will go as ordinary citizens of Balinor. As soon as you reach the Valley of Fear, you must appear to be soldiers of the Shifter's army."

"So there will be no battle," Ari said. She relaxed a little. This sounded possible. "Do we walk to the Valley of Fear then?"

"Samlett will take you in the cart to Sixton, a village on the shore of the Sixth Sea. There you will ask for Captain Tredwell, of the ship named the *Dawnwalker*. He will equip you with the soldier's disguise — he's been to many strange places, Captain Tredwell! And he will take you to the Valley of Fear."

"The . . . the . . . home of the Shifter," Ari faltered.

"Yes, Arianna." Atalanta got to her feet. Ari rose with her, and released her tight hold on the unicorn's mane. "His true home. Where his true form lies. The being who occupies your own Palace is only a shadow of his evil. Not the evil itself."

Ari's mind was whirling. "Can Chase and I do this?"

"The Sunchaser has known for some time about the Valley of Fear. And of the need to find the Royal Scepter."

"He never said anything to me."

"He knows — as I do — that the decision rests with you."

Ari didn't know anything about the Valley of Fear. And she was pretty sure she didn't want to know. The ghouls who guarded her own Palace now that the Shifter had taken the throne of Balinor were horrible — not even human. She supposed that the Valley of Fear was filled with ghouls worse than those she and Chase had just fought.

"Yes," Atalanta said, as if reading her thoughts. "The Shifter's army came from the Valley of Fear before they occupied Balinor. There is still a garrison there. But you will have as much help as Numinor and I can give you.

"First, I have spoken to Numinor. We will create a diversion as soon as you reach Sixton. A band of Celestial unicorns will walk the Path from the Moon to Balinor for the first time in our history. We will appear on the grounds of the Palace in Luckon, and we will lead the Shifter on a merry chase."

"You won't fight?" Ari asked. "You're sure?"

"We are not ready," Atalanta said simply. "Although Numinor is quite angry about it. We cannot fight until you and Chase are a fully Bonded Pair again. While we are leading the Shifter and his soldiers away from the Palace, you and your five com-

299

panions will enter Castle Entia and reclaim the Scepter." Atalanta's light was almost gone. Ari could barely see her in the dark, just the crystal horn, which glowed with blue-white light. "You must enter the Valley of Fear. Follow the lava path to the Castle Entia itself. Take no food or water into that place. The Scepter lies concealed beneath one of the Shifter's greatest victories."

"One of his greatest victories?" Ari asked, bewildered. "What is that?"

But only the glow was left. Atalanta herself was gone.

There was no answer. Just the gentle spill of water over rocks in the stream. And then the trickling water stopped, and there was no sound at all.

Great grief and fear welled up in Ari's heart. The feelings were so strong, tears came to her eyes. She bit her lip, hard, and then she coughed to keep from crying. She tucked the Star Bottle into her scabbard, next to her father's knife.

She went back to the campfire, and to Chase. There was so much yet to be done.

4

"Where have you *been*?!" Lori shrieked as Ari walked out of the woods and into the warmth surrounding the campfire. "I've been all by myself here!" Lori wrapped her arms around her chest and shivered. "The fire's going out."

"I told her to get more wood," Toby said.

"*You* get more wood," Lori said angrily. "What am I, your slave?"

Toby's affronted expression was such a perfect example of "What? The great *me*?" that Ari had to laugh.

"What's so funny?" Lori scowled.

"Why don't we all gather some wood," Ari said diplomatically. "I'll take Chase and you take Toby, and we'll pick up enough to last the rest of the night."

"I don't want to," Lori sulked. "There are *things* out there in the woods."

"True enough. But if we go together we'll be safe, I think. I have my knife, and Chase and Toby have their horns."

"Listen! Just listen! Can't you hear that horrible howling?"

One long, mournful cry split the night. Then came another howl. Chase lifted his head. His ears swiveled forward. He whinnied a challenge. A chorus of howls came in response. Despite herself, Ari shivered.

"Wolves," Lori said, with the sort of satisfaction people get when the worst has been confirmed. "A pack of them."

"Dr. Bohnes isn't back yet," Ari said with concern. "And she should have returned by now." The chorus of howls cut off, and then there was a yelp. Ari set her mouth in a firm line. "Forget the firewood. We'd better set out and look for Dr. Bohnes."

"No need," Chase said. "She's almost here."

Chase's ears were keener than those of humans. It was some minutes before Ari heard the steady tromp of Dr. Bohnes. The tough little vet stamped out of the bushes and came toward them. She had a load of firewood on her back, and she clutched a large bag against her chest. Her white hair was damp with sweat.

"Oh, Dr. Bohnes!" Ari cried. She ran forward and grasped the bundle of firewood. "Stand still a second, so I can take this off your shoulders." She lifted the bundle off the doctor's shoulders, and Dr.

Bohnes sat down suddenly. "You should have taken Toby with you," Ari scolded gently.

"It's not heavy," Dr. Bohnes gasped. "Just got a little winded coming up the rise. I had help most of —"

Suddenly, Lori pointed a trembling finger behind Dr. Bohnes and shrieked.

"— the way," Dr. Bohnes finished. She glowered at Lori. "Hush, now. They don't like screaming. Hurts their ears."

"Hurts *whose* ears . . . oh!" Ari said. Three long shadows slunk into the light of the dying fire.

"Wolves," Toby said. "Phuut!" He lowered his horn menacingly.

"Stop!" Dr. Bohnes commanded him. She held out her hand. "Rufus. Tige. Sandy. Come and meet Arianna and the Sunchaser."

The wolf in the lead was larger than his two fellows. All three had thick gray coats, freckled with rust and white. The tip of the leader's tail was reddish brown. They moved cautiously, heads low to the ground, sharp teeth visible in wolfish grins. The wolf with the red-brown tail looked up at Dr. Bohnes. His eyes were yellow, with round black pupils constricted to pinpoints by the firelight. Dr. Bohnes nudged his thick fur with her toe. She beamed affectionately at him. "Good old Rufus," she said.

"May we see them?" His voice was mellow and slow.

"Arianna! Stand up straight, girl. This is Rufus, leader of the Forest Pack. Rufus and Tige, this is Her Royal Highness, Arianna, Princess of Balinor." Dr. Bohnes dropped the sack she was carrying with a thud. The third wolf howled mournfully. "And Sandy, too. Sorry, Sandy. Anyway, I promised them they could have a look at you and Chase. They've been loyal supporters of the Crown, of course."

"Um," Ari said. "Uh . . . welcome." This didn't seem very princesslike. And now, because she was committed to her fate, she might as well try being a little more — impressive.

But she didn't feel very impressive. Her skirt was grubby and spotted with sticker-burrs. Her blouse had a big grass stain on it. And her hair was a mess. She stood up a little straighter and deepened her voice. "Welcome, loyal subjects of the Crown." She ignored Lori's giggle with what she hoped was Royal dignity.

"And there!" the wolf behind Rufus whispered in excitement. He gazed, quivering, at the Sunchaser. "Your Majesty!" All three wolves dropped to the ground, then rolled over, exposing their tawny bellies. They lay with their forepaws in the air, gazing adoringly — upside down — at Chase. Ari bit back a giggle. This was exactly the way dogs behaved.

Chase, Ari admitted to herself as she watched, really knew how to handle the Royal dignity part of being Lord of the Animals. He stood proudly, confident but without arrogance. Every muscle in his great body was defined under his glistening bronze coat. The ruby jewel at the base of his horn gleamed like a banked coal in an inviting fire. His ebony horn shone.

"Your Majesty!" Rufus said. "A word!"

"Please come forward." Chase had just the right combination of wisdom, majesty, and kindliness in his voice. Ari smiled at him. He half-lowered one eyelid in a mischievous wink. Rufus rolled over onto his feet. Head low, tail wagging gently, he walked toward the Sunchaser. Rufus had his own kind of dignity, Ari noted. He was respectful without being servile. He had the right kind of pride, too: pride in himself and his kind, without being aggressive. Sandy and Tige followed two strides behind their pack leader. The two of them waited until Rufus stood directly in front of the Sunchaser.

"You may sit," Chase said.

Rufus sat first, forepaws together, ears up, eyes leveled at Chase's chest. Sandy and Tige took their places on either side of Rufus. They lay on the ground and looked into the distance. Ari realized that this posture signaled obedience to the Sunchaser's will.

"You have been absent too long, Your Majesty." There was regret — and something else — in Rufus's speech. He was worried. That was it, Ari decided. The pack leader was concerned.

"I *have* been away too long," Chase agreed.

"And I may be absent yet awhile, wolf. My full powers have not been returned to me. There is . . ." He turned his dark eye on Ari. Atalanta was right. Chase knew about the Valley of Fear. He knew what Atalanta needed her to do. He knew about the quest. ". . . a task before me that will take me once again away from Balinor."

"For how long, sire?"

"A month. From Shifter's Moon to Shifter's Moon."

Sandy and Tige howled softly. Rufus lowered his head, panted, and then looked up. "We have trouble, Your Majesty. In the forest."

Chase waited patiently.

"You know that we were losing our way of speech with the humans of Balinor. More than speech left us, Your Majesty. We — that is, many of us — became wordless. And with the loss of words came something else. The loss of our selves. We held fewer and fewer Councils. Those that we did hold became places of great danger. Some of us — some of my own pack, Your Majesty — began to prey on others."

The wrinkles over Chase's eyes deepened.

"Yes, sire. We eat insects, grubs, nuts, berries, and fruits. But as our words left us, so did our appetite for eating these safe things."

"And?"

Rufus dropped his head to his paws, then

raised it. "There is now a hunt. For rabbit. Deer. For small creatures, such as mice."

A shudder passed through Chase's frame. His mind screamed, but no audible sound passed from him, so only Ari heard. She bit her lip to keep from screaming herself.

"The wolves only?" Chase asked, after a long moment.

"Ah. I thought perhaps the others would tell you of their crimes, sire. I only speak for my pack. I do not bear tales of others' crimes."

"My good wolf," Chase commanded. "Who commits the hunt? And when? Tell me!"

Tell me, Ari echoed silently.

Rufus turned around several times in agitation, following his tail with a fierce intensity. At last he settled on his haunches, facing his King. "The big cats, as well as my pack. The bears. The ferrets. The great birds. Thank the One Who Rules that dragons have all but disappeared from Balinor."

"Be still," Chase said, cutting him off. "Enough." He lowered his head. He scraped one foreleg across the earth. "And now? The animals of Balinor have had their words restored to them, Rufus, with the return of my horn. Her Royal Highness and I do not have command of our full magic, but speech between animal and human, at least, has been saved. There is no excuse to break the law. Does the hunt continue?"

307

"It does, Your Majesty. To my sorrow. There are those who now have a taste for . . . for blood."

"Those who hunt," Ari asked, "have they renounced their King? Have they turned to the Shifter as their monarch?"

Rufus turned his head to Sandy. He touched the other wolf with his forepaw, then nodded to him. "Tell them," he said. "Tell the King."

Sandy threw back his head and howled, a long, agonizing cry that took Ari's breath away. "Yes, Your Highness," Sandy said. "And my own brother Fig is among them."

All three wolves howled in grief. Ari felt the back of her neck prickle.

"Well, honestly," Lori said. "This is stupid. It's the way things are. I mean, I'm sorry, but that's what the world's like. Big fish eat little fish. Little fish eat teeny fish."

"Not here," Chase said.

"But —"

He whirled, then reared, his horn piercing the night. "NOT HERE IN BALINOR!" He came to all fours with a crash. Lori, her face pale, sat down with a thump.

Rufus broke the long silence. "There is a Council of the Animals called for the last night of the crescent moon, Your Majesty. Will you come?"

Chase turned to Ari. "I must," he said. "It will add two days to our journey home. But I must be there."

308

Ari nodded. "We will come to the Council, Rufus. Where shall we meet?"

The wolf looked at her with his yellow eyes, then squeezed them open and shut, open and shut. "Thank you, Your Highness. Thank you. We meet at the red oak, by Staines Waterfall."

"We shall see you there, then, pack leader." Chase blew out with a long, angry whistle. "And take this message to all who live in the forest. The law has been broken. Those who broke the law will be judged. And sentence will be passed."

The wolves dropped to their bellies to signify obedience. Then they melted off into the night.

Dr. Bohnes cleared her throat, then began to feed the fire with the wood she'd brought back. Ari opened the sack of provisions that Dr. Bohnes had dropped on the ground, and methodically laid out wheat cakes, apples, and cheese. She set aside a canister of oats meant for Toby and Chase.

"Hel-*lo-oh*," Lori said in a very sarcastic way. "Isn't anybody going to say anything?"

"What is there to say?" Ari set half of the oats in front of Toby, and took the other half to Chase. She handed Dr. Bohnes a thick slice of bread, an apple, and a ball of goat cheese.

"So we're going to add two extra days to this stupid trip."

"We must," Ari said.

"We *must*," Lori mimicked furiously. "What we *must* do is start figuring out a way to get back to

Glacier River. Let these guys figure out for themselves what to do."

"We can't, and that's final, missy," Toby said.
"Eat your cheese. And if you're not going to eat that
apple, give it to me."

"Get your own apple, Toby," Lori said. She bit
into her apple with a loud crunch. "Ari, this hunt is
not our problem."

Toby shook his head violently. "It most certainly is our problem." He began to eat his oats.
Grain spilled out of the sides of his muzzle. "Animals
who hunt deer and rabbit aren't going to stop at that
for dinner." He paused, head up, listening. The howls
of the departing wolf pack floated across the crescent moon. "I want to be sure those howls are
friendly. That they aren't the sound of the Shifter's
pack hunting . . ." He swallowed his oats with a gulp.

"Hunting what?" Lori asked.

Toby blinked at her. "Hunting us."

5

"Of course I'm going with you to the Council," Dr. Bohnes said. "Don't be ridiculous. You need me."

Ari had spent a restless night, lying back-to-back with Chase near the fire. She had dreamed fitfully. Not the sort of dreams sent by Atalanta, but horror-filled nightmares. Eagles darted at her out of a flaming sky, beaks wide and hungry. Sly foxes nipped at her ankles as she struggled through nightmarish swamps. Something cold and slimy slipped after her, just out of sight.

She woke early, unrested. Her breakfast went down like a cold lump. Her legs ached.

Ari stretched now, trying to loosen the tight muscles in her calves and thighs. She put her arms over her head and bent from the waist, touching her toes. "Chase and I should be able to handle the Council, Dr. Bohnes. And the extra two days is

311

through a rough part of the forest. It will —" She bit her words off. The tough little vet was sensitive about her age. Ari didn't want to say what she was thinking. That the trip would prove too hard for her old nurse.

"The more of us there are, the safer we'll be," Dr. Bohnes said. "And with some of the animals of the forest on the Shifter's side, we're going to have to take extra measures for safety."

"You mean, sentries at night? That kind of thing?"

"That kind of thing. We don't have to worry here near Atalanta's Grove." She caught Ari's surprised glance. "Oh, yes, I know she came to you and spoke of the quest. I know what you and Chase have to do, and I'm going with you on that trip, too. We all need to stay together. We've been lucky so far but as soon as we leave the better-traveled highways, we're going to have to look sharp. My magic — such that it is — will let us know if any of the Shifter's army is around, but I can't count on it to tell us when an animal that's usually safe isn't."

Ari looked at Dr. Bohnes shyly. She knew the old lady had been her nurse in the days when her mother and father sat on the thrones of Balinor, but she still didn't recall her very well. She knew her better as the crusty vet who had taken care of the horses at Glacier River Farm. "What sort of magic do you do?" she asked. "I mean, if it's okay for you to tell me."

"Oh. A little bit of this. A little bit of that."

312

"Can you send someone through the Gap?"

"I? Certainly not! That takes a one-hundred-percent-committed wizard. I can cure warts. Make a few love potions. Help a cow give better milk." She gave Ari's cheek a cheerful rub. "Not anything like yours will be, when you retrieve the Royal Scepter. Certainly not like the Dreamspeaker's magic."

"And even she has limits," Ari echoed thoughtfully. "What about . . . the Old Mare of the Mountain?"

Dr. Bohnes straightened up with a jerk. Her fierce blue eyes held Ari's. "Oh, yes. There is that. There's a deep magic beyond the Celestial Valley. And the Old Mare is part of it. But none of us knows much about her. Now, Your Highness. Let's get packed up and rolling. It's a bit of a jaunt to Staines Falls, and the sun's almost over the hilltop."

"And we'll part company at Balinor Ford," Ari said firmly. "You and Lori and Toby will go to Balinor Village, and Chase and I to the Council."

"No, Your Highness."

"Yes, Dr. Bohnes." Ari took a deep breath, lowered her chin, and said in her most impressive imperial voice. "I command it."

Dr. Bohnes's bright blue eyes opened wide. She worked her jaw back and forth, as if chewing a bit of gum. Then she nodded and said without any expression at all: "So be it."

Ari let her breath out. "You don't mind?" she said anxiously. "I just feel it's for the best. Poor Lori is

313

so homesick, I feel sorry for her. We're going to have to find some way to get her back to Glacier River. If you can't do it, we'll have to find someone who can. In the meantime, I know she'll feel more at home in the village. She's afraid of the forest, afraid of the animals, afraid of everything here."

Dr. Bohnes wrapped Ari's blanket into a neat roll and tucked it into Chase's saddlebags.

"Dr. Bohnes?"

"Let me know when you wish to leave, Your Royal Highness." She bowed. It hurt Ari to see her sturdy form bent over in front of her. She took Dr. Bohnes gently by the shoulders, but the old lady lowered her head and walked away without a word. Ari felt Chase's presence behind. She turned and buried her face in his flank. "She's angry with me. But Chase, it's for the best."

"Perhaps," he said gravely. "There is a price that Royals pay, Ari. You have just seen part of it now. Your subjects must obey you. But they may not like you for it."

Ari watched Dr. Bohnes adjust the bridle on Toby's head. She buckled the throat latch, then the noseband, talking angrily all the while. Ari was too far away to hear, but she could guess they were talking about:

How bossy she was.
How ignorant of the realities of life.
How stubborn.

Ari ran her fingers through Chase's forelock. "I *knew* I wasn't going to like this Princess stuff," she said.

She liked it even less when the party split up, and they said their good-byes at Balinor Ford. Balinor Village lay less than a day's ride directly south across the river. To the south were clean clothes, baths, hot food, and Lincoln. Ari couldn't believe how much she missed her dog. To the north lay a swell of forbidding mountains, Staines Waterfall, and the giant red oak where the animals of the forest held Council. Farther north — she wasn't sure. Danger. Maybe even mortal danger.

She and Chase watched until Dr. Bohnes, Lori, and Toby had safely forded the river. Then they turned to their own task.

She walked Chase the first part of the way. The sun was pleasantly warm, and the sky was blue. They saw few animals: a pair of squirrels, a covey of guinea hens, an occasional glimpse of white-tailed deer in the scattered groves of trees. Toward afternoon, the sky began to darken with rain clouds. Ari flexed lightly to bring Chase to a halt. "How much farther, do you think?"

He raised his head, sensitive nostrils probing the air. "At this pace, we should reach it an hour or so after sunset."

"When does the Council meet?

"As soon as the sun goes down, on the last night of the crescent moon."

"I think I'd like to be there, to greet them as they arrive. Do you feel up to a canter?"

She felt him dance underneath her on the tips of his hooves. The muscles in his back rippled in anticipation. "I would welcome a canter, milady."

She cued him — tapped her left heel against his side, raised the right rein slightly, and he sprang into a steady, joyful canter that made the miles speed away. The road was straight and free of holes. When the rain started, the water ran off the road and into muddy ditches. Over the thundering sound of Chase's hooves, Ari called, "Who made this road?"

"I do not know, milady. It is called the Mountain Road, for that is where it leads. There are no villages or towns here, this far from Balinor itself. Perhaps the magic of the Forest Folk has created and maintained it."

In a little less than an hour, the rain increased to a downpour. Ari felt Chase check beneath her. "Do you want to stop?"

"No, but you do," he called back. "Your left leg is cramping, isn't it?"

It was, but Ari refused to give in to it. "It's fine. We'll go on. We're getting soaked enough as it is. I'd like to reach the cover of the trees as quickly as possible."

He said nothing more, but forged steadily on. Ari wondered if the day would come when Chase would refuse her. The laws governing a Bonded Pair were strict, that much she recalled of her life before the accident in the Gap. The human partner in a Bonded Pair was to be obeyed, as all riders should be obeyed by the steeds they ride, whether they are unicorns, horses, or even — as Ari had once seen at Glacier River — farm cows. A rider's cues were made with hands, feet, legs, and body balance. Communication about the animal's physical movements was limited.

As the road moved upward toward the mountains, Ari heard Chase's breathing change from its deep, easy rhythm to shorter, harder breaths. Only then did she allow herself the ease of a trot. She flexed him down and stretched her left leg in the stirrup.

Suddenly, Chase halted. His entire body quivered under her. He moved forward just as suddenly. Ari knew immediately that something was wrong.

"What is it, Chase?"

He said nothing, merely snorted. Then in her mind she heard, *There is something trailing us.*

"Following us?" Ari asked aloud.

Chase jerked impatiently.

What do you mean, trailing us? she thought at him.

Tracking us. Hunting us.

The hunt! Was it one of his own animals, turned traitor? Or was it some awful thing from the Shifter's army of demons and monsters?

Fear flooded her. Outwardly, she remained

calm, back straight, one hand casually laid on her knee — but near the scabbard that carried her father's knife. She held Chase's reins in the other hand, guiding him with her knees. Rain dripped down her back and plastered her hair across her cheeks. She cast a quick look at the surrounding forest. There. A large pine tree — perhaps a quarter of a mile ahead. If they could reach the tree before their stalker sprang — they might have a chance.

She felt it — a large, sinuous shadow gliding on the ground behind them.

She rode casually, afraid to make a sudden move. Afraid to force whatever it was into battle.

They reached the large pine tree. Out of the corner of her eye, she saw a metallic flash of scales. She dismounted quietly, her back to the trunk of the tree. She pulled her knife from its sheath and passed it in a slow half-circle. Beside her, Chase lowered his horn.

I hope it's not a snake, she thought at Chase. *Anything except a —*

It dropped from the tree, winding around Chase's neck with the terrible certainty of a hangman's noose. Chase reared, trumpeting his battle cry. Ari shrieked with rage. She sprang up, knife poised to slash, but her great stallion was too tall. The serpent — at least two feet thick and fifteen feet long, wound its scaly length tighter and tighter

318

around the unicorn's neck. Chase's eyes bulged. His war cry was cut off. Ari leaped and leaped again. Her left leg gave way. She fell hard against the tree, her breath knocked from her lungs.

The snake's head was diamond-shaped, its eyes flat, black, and evil. A long red tongue flicked from its mouth, a sinister whip with poison at the tip.

Ari scrambled up the tree, skinning her hands raw on the bark. She reached the lowest branch and swung her leg over it. Below her, Chase plunged and reared, his struggle silent now.

Closer, Chase! Come closer!

He rolled his eyes, dark with agony, then whirled and smashed his body against the tree trunk. Ari bent far out from the branch, her father's knife in her right hand, her left clutching the punishing bark. She slashed at the flat black eyes, knowing that this was the most vulnerable part of the snake, that she had no hope of slashing that ropy scaliness free from Chase.

"Ariiii-aaaa-nnnnaaaa!" it hissed.

"You get OFF him!" she panted. "You leave him alone!" She reached out with the knife again, too far this time, and fell.

Instinctively, she rolled herself into a ball, protecting her already scarred legs from further hurt. She landed with a thump at the base of the tree, slamming her head against a gnarled root. Above her, Chase whirled and spun, ducked and

319

kicked. With a sudden, ferocious burst of power, he swung his neck against the tree. The snake's head connected with the trunk with an audible thud.

"It's stunned! Chase! It's stunned!" She pushed herself to her feet and fell into Chase's flank. His side was slippery with sweat. Gasping, she pulled at the suddenly inert length of scales, tugging the snake's body free from Chase's neck. The reptile landed in the grass, mouth open, thin red tongue lolling from its jaws.

"Is it dead?" Ari asked in a half-whisper.

Chase's head was low. He breathed in great gulps of air. Grasping her knife firmly, Ari crept closer. She held her breath.

The flat black eyes snapped open. The snake struggled weakly, then fell back. It looked at her. The look was as cold and as venomous as Ari had ever seen. "Come closssser," it whispered. "Closssser."

Ari held her knife up, so that the snake could see it. "I'll use this," she threatened. She edged nearer carefully. Above her, Chase gasped and coughed. "Who are you?" she demanded. "Who sent you? Where do you come from?"

"Princessss," it hissed. "Oh, Princessss. My masssster would have ssspeech with you. Ssssometime. Ssssometime. Perhapsss. In the Valley. Come to the Valley."

The black eyes looked inward for a long,

long moment. Then, with a flick of its red tongue, a last, ugly hiss, it slid from view into the forest. Ari covered her face with her hands. She was shaking so hard her teeth were chattering. Chase buried his muzzle in her hair.

"We fought it off," he said.

"What about the next time?" Ari said. "And the time after that? Oh, Chase. I don't think I can do this. I'm so afraid!"

He didn't speak for a moment. The rain dripped from the trees. It grew colder. Ari leaned against the warmth of Chase's body. Finally, her shivering stopped.

"Are you ready?" Chase asked. His voice was deep and kind.

"No, I'm not ready," Ari said bitterly. "I'll never be ready. I didn't ask for this, Chase. I didn't want to be the Princess!"

"But you are," Chase said. "And the Council waits for us. If you decide, Arianna, that we cannot do this, then I will go with you wherever you wish. Back to Glacier River Farm, to teach young humans to ride. Or back to Balinor or some small village where we can live in peace. Where no one will know who we are."

Ari wiped her face. She took a long shuddering breath. "No," she said. "I'm not letting a miserable snake stand in the way of peace in Balinor."

He blew out a soft sound, the way a unicorn

mare comforts a foal. "Perhaps there will be peace," he said. "If we don't give up."

Ari nodded. She remounted. They climbed the last rocky path to Staines Falls and the giant red oak tree.

They had reached the Council.

6

It was very peaceful and lonesome. A brisk wind blew in the treetops. But the trees were so old and so tall, the air around the Council place was still. The waterfall was slow and quiet. It slipped into a rock pool with the gentlest of sounds. The red oak was gnarly, twisted, full of strange and wonderful whorls in the bark. Beneath it was a large piece of granite rock, polished to a flat smoothness on top, ringed round with fossil stones at the base. The area around the red oak tree and the granite rock was covered in grass as smooth and short as if someone had scythed it.

She followed Chase's lead. He walked majestically to the foot of the oak. He bent his head and dipped his horn in the water: once, twice, three times. The water sparkled and shone.

A memory came to Ari, a story about the magic of a unicorn's horn. The touch of the horn made foul water sweet, turned muddy streams to clear pools. All of a sudden, Ari was thirsty. As thirsty as she'd ever been before. She knelt at the pool, cupped her hands, and drank. The taste was sweet, cold, like drinking rain clouds. Her tiredness and fear ebbed away. She felt strong, clearheaded. More, she told herself, like a Princess than she had felt before.

Chase settled himself at the base of the tree, hind legs tucked under his belly, his forelegs knuckled under his chest. Ari sat down a little way from him, her back against the granite rock.

They waited.

The animals came slowly to the Council. First was a pair of foxes: the male fox, a vibrant red with a black mask and golden eyes, and the vixen, a multicolored swirl of brown, cream, and gray. They sat quietly at the edge of the meadow. Then came the deer, timid and graceful. A raccoon, with a clever, merry face. *Three bears — just like the fairy tale!* Ari thought. A huge black male, a smaller dun-colored female, and a cub, who chattered and giggled until his mother pushed him gently down onto his father's back. He clung there, button eyes bright, and hummed a tiny song to himself.

The meadow was full by the time the sun went down. The pool was filled with otter and beaver. The crescent moon was thin, pale, and shed no light. The Sunchaser was a vivid spot of bronze in the gloom. The ruby jewel glowed crimson at the

324

base of his horn. The animals faded into shadow, and all Ari could see was the occasional flash of a yellow eye. She thought she saw Sandy and Rufus and Tige in the gathering pack of wolves, but she wasn't certain.

There was a murmur and a shifting. The pad of heavy feet.

A lion came into the clearing.

He was big, heavy with muscle, and slow with the confidence of the strong and powerful. He came very near Ari on his way to the base of the tree. She caught a heavy, musky scent as the lion passed by.

He stopped in front of Chase. The unicorn looked full into the lion's wild eyes. Then he rose to his full height, towering over the lion, his ebony horn a vivid black against the dusky twilight.

"My lord," the lion said. He braced himself with his heavy forepaws. Slowly, deliberately, he settled onto his side, then rolled over on his back, exposing his belly to the Sunchaser's sharp horn. Ari blinked. Even the lion showed obedience to the Sunchaser! She tried not to laugh at the thought of Balinor villagers rolling over like that to show their loyalty; it was a good thing people and animals were different.

"Vanax. My friend and adviser," Chase answered. "It is good to see you again."

Vanax rolled to his feet. "And it is good to see you again, Sunchaser, Lord of the Animals. Bonded to the Royal House of Balinor. The animals of the forest welcome you." A chorus of growls, yips, bleats, and snuffles from the others followed.

Chase waited gravely until the salutations died away. "I have been gone too long. I have returned to disappointment and despair. There are fewer of our brothers and sisters here than there have ever been before. I do not see the cougars. The ferrets are absent. And others. Too many. They have joined the hunt?"

The tip of Vanax's tail twitched back and forth. He growled, low in his throat. "Yes, Your Majesty."

Chase's eye darkened in anger. "There are laws against the hunt. Since humans and animals first celebrated the Bond. It is so."

"It is so," the forest creatures responded.

"The punishment is the breaking of the Bond. Those animals who hunt will be forever mute. Before judgment is passed, are there those who would speak for the traitors?"

An uneasy silence fell over the Council. Finally, a voice from the back hissed out: "They are afraid to sssspeak!"

Ari jumped. She knew that voice! The snake!

"All may speak without fear at Council," the Sunchaser said gravely. "This is neutral ground. Any may come and go at will."

"Proof!" the snake called out. "Proof of aaaamnesssssty." Ari narrowed her eyes and searched the dimness of the meadow. Was it there, the creature? In that hedge of sumac?

"My word is proof enough," Chase said angrily.

An undulating hiss came from the sumac. The snake laughed. "Fool!" it murmured. Then, with barely a ripple of the leaves, it glided into the center of the grounds. Yellow-green scales glittered poisonously in the low light. The snake regarded Chase with lidless eyes. "Sssssunchaser!" it mocked. "Lord of the Animalsssss. Phhhha!" The red tongue flicked the air. The snake rose on its tail like a cobra and began to sway back and forth. "My massster callssss you all to the hunt! You, Vanax!" The lion's tail twitched faster and faster. "Do you not dream of the hunt at night? And you, Basil. Dill." The pair of foxes jumped and snarled at the snake. "Do not your eyessss and nossssessss enticccce you to follow the tracks of a nice juicy *rabbit*?" The snake stood still. Its lipless mouth stretched into a grin. "Thissss is the right way. The way of prey. My massster will give thissss to all who wish to join him."

"It is not the way of Balinor," Chase said gravely. "Is this all you have in the way of defense, Snake? That the evil ways of the Shifter are just?"

"It issss all the defensssse we need," the snake said. "It is jusssst becausssse the hunt issss in our nature. Come! Bear! Fox! Cougar! Join ussss and be free!"

"Join the Shifter and become mute forever,"

327

Chase said. "The bonds with humans will be broken past retrieving. That is the punishment."

"Oh?" The snake swiveled suddenly. Its eyes glowed red. "And how will you accomplissssh *that*, great one? Mighty unicorn. *Powerful* one!" It laughed again. Ari's skin crawled. "You have no magic! Thissss one," it hissed, ducking its head toward Ari. "Thissss one is only the sssshell of a Princesssss. Sssshe hassss no power!"

"Not yet," Ari said. She stood up. Her knees were shaking, but her voice was clear and firm. "But I shall retrieve the Scepter, snake. And when I do, all will be right in Balinor."

"Sssso you sssseek my masssster? You — and that four-legged fool! We await you, Princessss. We look forward to it. We will welcome you, Arianna, to the Valley of Fear!" To Ari's terrified eyes, the snake grew larger and larger. Its scaly body seemed to fill the grove. Then with a last, thin laugh, it slid away into the brush.

Vanax growled. His haunches clenched and his powerful claws dug into the grass.

"No," Chase said. "Do not pursue the snake. All are guaranteed safety here, Vanax. This is not a place for battle." Vanax half-closed his eyes and opened them again. He sank unhappily to the ground.

"Sire?" The red fox — Basil, the snake had called him — came forward. "Is it true? You and Her

Highness Arianna are not in possession of your full powers?"

"Not yet," Chase said. "And the snake is right. We need the Royal Scepter."

Ari took a deep breath. "And we will find it," she said.

"You are going to the Valley of Fear?" Basil asked.

"We must." Ari hoped she didn't sound as scared as she felt.

"Oh, my." The fox rubbed his pointed nose with his paw. "Oh, *my!*" The vixen darted up beside him, and gave him a sharp nudge. "For goodness' sake, Basil, get a grip."

"Don't *shove* me, Dill," the fox said crossly.

"I'll shove you when I please," Dill shot back. "I'll shove you whenever I like. I say, if Her Royal Highness and His Majesty are going on a quest to the Valley of Fear, then, of course they'll get the Scepter back. Just because the place is filled with shadow unicorns and ghouls . . ."

"Monsters," Basil said gloomily.

"Hideous mutants!" Dill added. "That doesn't mean that one unicorn and one Princess won't be able to find the lair of the Shifter, battle the shadow herd, find their way out again, and bring the Scepter to safety."

"When you put it like that, Dill —"

"I'll put it any way I like, Basil."

"—it doesn't seem safe for them to go alone."

Dill nodded in satisfaction. "Right!" She turned to Ari, ducked her head in a short bow, and said, "You need an army, Your Royal Highness."

Ari blinked. At the moment, her mind filled with the visions of shadow unicorns, ghouls, mutants, and monsters, an army seemed like a very good idea.

"There *is* the question of how," Basil said fussily. "I mean, an army is all very well and good, Dill. But who's going to join up? Where are the weapons going to come from?"

Dill yawned casually, showing her pointed teeth.

"Us?" Basil yelped. "You want us to be the army?"

"Just think for a minute, Basil." She turned and addressed Ari with a casual flip of her tail. "We might even see if we can coax Noki the dragon out of her cave for once. . . ."

"She's gained a lot of weight," Basil said doubtfully.

"But she's a dragon," Dill said, "and everyone's afraid of dragons, even those in the Valley of Fear. Honestly, Basil, can't you agree with me just *once* without some stupid argument?"

"Stop," a voice behind Chase said. "There will be no army."

"No army!" Dill narrowed her eyes at Chase. It

330

was clear she thought the voice came from him. Her thick gray fur bristled. "Huh! You *need* an army. You can't *do* this without an army. You'll get mashed, crushed, smooshed, and obliterated without an army!" Abruptly, she noticed the scowl in Chase's eyes. "Sorry, Your Majesty," she added hastily. She sank to the ground in confusion.

"Now you've done it, Dill," Basil muttered.

"Listen to me!"

Ari and Chase turned around, looking for who had spoken, but no one was there. Ari leaned back against the granite rock. Then she leaped forward. The rock was alive!

Ari backed into Chase. The granite rock swelled with the heavy breathing of an animal. Slowly . . . slowly, the rock softened and took shape in the summer dark.

It was a unicorn. An old gray unicorn. The hair in her ears was stiff and white. Her back was swayed. Her horn was short and chipped in places. Whiskers covered her chin. But her eyes! Her eyes were youthful, clear, and as transparent as water.

Beside her, Chase sank to his knees and touched his horn to the ground. Ari looked around the clearing. Vanax covered his eyes with his paws. Dill's head was buried in Basil's flank. Basil himself stared at the old unicorn in awe.

"The Old Mare of the Mountain!" someone whispered.

"Well!" the Old Mare said. She coughed, a deep, hollow cough. She stretched her neck forward. "Armies! Never heard such nonsense in all my life!"

Ari wasn't sure where it came from — or even why she felt it, but the Old Mare of the Mountain radiated power and strength. Ari felt very small in the presence of this being. The ancient body, the scraggly coat, the stiff, whiskery hair, all cloaked a magnificent power.

Ari held her breath, then asked softly, "Milady? The Dreamspeaker said you might come. If it is you."

The unicorn stopped scratching her ear, put her hind leg down, and peered at Ari.

"But . . . are you the Old Mare of —" Ari started to ask.

"Be still." The voice was thunder. It filled the Council grove. The animals moaned.

Ari swallowed hard. The old unicorn swung her head slowly back and forth. She settled onto the ground and curled up like a unicorn foal. She began to turn back into rock. The granite crept up her sides, across her flanks, moved up her neck. But her eyes remained locked on Ari's: clear, young, vibrant eyes.

She said, "Now that I think about it. Yes. I am the Old Mare." She yawned, showing yellow teeth, worn by years of grazing. "And I have a word for you. Or two."

Ari, hypnotized, gazed into those clear, clear eyes.

"Pay attention, human child!"

Ari jumped. The Old Mare's voice was suddenly booming, shaking the trees.

> *"Six shall find the Scepter Royal,*
> *The quick, the smart, the brave, the loyal.*
> *Of humans there shall be but two,*
> *One young and one whose past is new.*
> *Of Six who go, two wait to learn,*
> *Three of Six shall not return."*

The gigantic booming voice stopped. And then the Old Mare was gone, or her physical body was. Turned back into rock. Ari walked up to the boulder and touched it. Stone. Cold stone.

Chase rose to his feet.

"Oh!" Ari said. "Did you see that? She just . . . just . . . showed up and then, poof!" Ari snapped her fingers. "What do you suppose . . . why, Chase! You're trembling." Concerned, she put her hands on his neck. He was sweating.

"The deep magic," Dill said in a hushed voice. She trotted briskly up to them, her face alive with excitement. "The deep magic! I saw it!"

"Do not speak of it, Dill," Basil whispered. He'd been deeply affected by the Old Mare. Ari looked around the clearing. All the animals were shocked, stunned. Some of them sat and stared, others talked quietly among themselves.

"It was a message for you, Your Royal Highness," Dill said respectfully. "Ah, to think I lived to see this. Most of us would not expect to see the deep magic once in a lifetime. Not once in *three* lifetimes."

"I see," Ari said, although she didn't, not really. What was she supposed to do with this message? She would think about it later, she decided. Right now, she needed the assistance of the forest animals. "Now, what about this army, Chase? I think it's a pretty good idea, myself."

"'Six shall find the Scepter Royal,'" Dill quoted. "No armies for us, Your Royal Highness. She said six. And she meant six."

"The Valley of Fear sounds like a terrible place," Ari said frankly. "But we *have* to get that Scepter. Our odds will be better if we have an army behind us."

Dill stared at her. Rather rudely, Ari thought. "It's the deep magic," she repeated loudly, as if to a child. "'Six shall find . . .'"

"Yes, yes," Ari said, "I heard."

"Her Highness does not have all of her memory," Chase said. He'd recovered from the shock of the Old Mare's visitation. "We are hoping — that is, the Dreamspeaker has said that the Princess will recall everything of her former life when the Scepter is in her hands." He bent his head. His dark eyes looked directly into Ari's. "We have no choice, milady. The Old Mare has told us the way. She has told us what must be."

"Oh." Ari rubbed her forehead. "Then we go into the Valley of Fear with just six? Which six?"

"'The quick, the smart, the brave —'" Dill said. "That's pretty obvious to me. The quick is Basil, here. I'm the smart one."

"Excuse me, Dill," Basil said. "But it's the other way around. I'm the smart one."

"No, you aren't."

"Yes, I am!"

"No, you're not!"

"Excuse me," Ari said. "But I think it's safe to say that we're all pretty smart here."

"Not as smart as I am," Dill said smugly. "*I've* been to the Valley of Fear!"

There was a short, impressed silence from everyone.

"I'm smart because I can show you the way after we get there. And because I got out alive, which is more than I can say for some." Her gold eyes darkened. She was in the grip of some unpleasant memory. She shook herself briskly, and Ari noticed for the first time a thin red scar around Dill's neck.

"We need to take apart the message and figure out what it means," Dill said. "His Majesty, the

Sunchaser, is the *brave* one. And you, Your Royal Highness, are the one whose *past is new* — because you don't have all your memory yet. Now, as far as *loyal* goes, well, that could be any one of us here — we're all loyal to the Crown. And the young one."She frowned. "I don't like the idea of having a youngster with us. I don't even know which youngster it would be. I'm sure that the Old Mare would not send a cub into danger without a good reason."

"It will not be a cub," Chase said. "It will be a human. She prophesied two humans. And as for loyalty — there is one other who is loyal to the Princess unto death, besides myself. But he is not with us."

"Do you mean Lincoln?" Ari asked. She so wanted to see her collie again! "Of course. And the young human — oh, Chase! Lori absolutely will not go. She'll think we're out of our minds!"

7

❦

"Y ou're out of your mind!" Lori yelled. "Go with you to this Valley of Fear place? Are you *crazy?*" She stamped up and down the length of her room at the Inn of the Unicorn. Lincoln the collie, with only a shaved patch on his forehead to show he'd been deeply wounded after fighting off an attack on Arianna, yawned deeply and snuggled against Ari's side. Ari stroked his ears, and tried to explain for the third time why they needed Lori with them.

The trip to Balinor Village had taken Chase and Ari less than a day at a canter. They had left the forest early in the morning following the Council of the Animals, bidding farewell to those who had remained to discuss the events of the meeting. At the outskirts of the village, they took care to be as inconspicuous as possible. They had gone straight to the Inn of the Unicorn, where Dr. Bohnes, Lincoln, and Mr. Samlett, the Innkeeper, had greeted them with joy. Lori wasn't particularly happy to see them again — and was really *un*happy when Ari told her of the Old Mare's Prophecy: that they had to pack up and leave for the Valley of Fear. Right now.

"No!" she shouted for what seemed to be the thousandth time. "No! No! NO!"

Dr. Bohnes, her lips compressed in a tight line, kept on packing the bedrolls. She heard Chase and Ari's news. Then she heaved a sigh straight from the bottom of her leather boots. "If it was the Old Mare — and, oh, I wish I'd seen her myself! — you don't have a choice. You're right. You have to leave, and leave right away. Samlett will drive. Toby will take you in the cart to the shore of the Sixth Sea, and from there you can get a ship to take you to Demonview, gateway to the Valley of Fear. I'll help you pack."

"Lori. Please try to understand." Ari leaned forward in yet another attempt to make the blond girl understand. "If we go with five, it doesn't fulfill the Prophecy. Six of us must go. I told you there's a total of five who have agreed to go. You're the sixth."

"Tough!" Lori kicked at the wooden bench in front of the fireplace. "Who cares? You want to go roaming around in a place like this Valley of Fear, you go right ahead. But count me out!" She gave the bench a final kick, whirled around, and slammed out the door.

Ari wrapped her arms around her knees and stared into the fire.

What were they going to do now?

8

Atalanta lifted her head from the scene in the Watching Pool, a thoughtful expression clouding her violet eyes. At her forefeet, the clear waters of the pool swirled briefly and the image of the Princess, the collie, and Eliane Bohnes faded into the depths. Beside her, Tobiano sniffed disapprovingly. "I knew Lori wouldn't go," he said with glum satisfaction. "Now we are in trouble."

"Perhaps." Then Atalanta quoted softly, "'Three of Six shall not return.' What do you think the Old Mare meant by that?"

Toby shook his head.

"We have questions," Atalanta said to herself. "Questions with answers as hidden as the sun during storms. There is the Shifter himself, Tobiano. He knows that the Six will come, but he doesn't know when. And he can only guess at who the Six will be. Then there is that dog, Lincoln. Who gave the collie the ruby jewel to take to Arianna back at Glacier River Farm, Toby? I have not yet found an answer to that. The dog bothers me."

"If you don't know," Toby said with perfect truth, "who would?"

"The Old Mare. Some of this is part of the deep magic. Perhaps the dog is part of the deep magic. Perhaps not."

"Pretty amazing," Toby said. "That the Old Mare showed up like that. If she hadn't intervened, we would have had a whole army of animals storming the Valley of Fear. And no one's anywhere near ready to fight."

"Not so amazing," Atalanta said with a slight smile. "Toby? You behaved with great courage down below in Balinor. You were quite heroic."

The stout little unicorn puffed out his chest. The Celestial unicorns were at risk in the world of humans — vulnerable to hurt, to illness, and worst of all, to death. Celestials who spent too much time below in Balinor could lose the unicorn's most precious gift: immortality. But Toby had bravely agreed when Atalanta had asked him to accompany the Princess and the Sunchaser, despite the risk to himself.

"May I send you back to Balinor? Just one more time?"

Toby didn't hesitate, a testament to his courage. "To go into the Valley of Fear? To be one of the Six! Yes, Dreamspeaker!"

"No. Not to the Valley of Fear. Arianna is right. Lori must go with them to the Valley of Fear, and no one else. I want you to go below to help Princess Arianna get to the Sixth Sea. And you must be alert to danger."

"What kind of danger?" he asked suspiciously.

Atalanta gazed at him. The black-and-white unicorn was the rudest herdmate they had ever had. But Atalanta was convinced he had the bravest, most loyal heart of them all. "Danger of the worst kind."

9

ori stamped into the stable yard at the back of the Inn of the Unicorn. She was furious, confused, and homesick.

She sat on the edge of the watering trough and tossed bits of straw into the water. Mr. Samlett bustled by, trundling a wheelbarrow filled with manure from the stalls. "Now, milady, quit that, I say quit that," he exclaimed. "The trough will just have to be cleaned up again. Her Highness will not like that at all, I say not at all."

"Fine!" Lori said crossly. She got up. "That's just fine!" She crossed the cobblestones with the air of knowing where she was headed, just in case Samlett asked her to clean the trough herself.

"Milady?" he called after her. Lori turned around. His round, red face had an apologetic frown on it. "I'm sorry to bring this up, milady, but about your bill for room and board . . ."

"Ask Her Royal Highness!" Lori shouted furiously.

Samlett dropped the handles of the wheelbarrow with a thump. Straw scattered all over the footpath. "Ssssh!" he whispered. "No one is to know she's here!"

"That *who's* here?" asked a smooth, caressing voice. Lady Kylie rounded the corner of the Inn. She was dressed in chocolate-colored velvet, beaded with pearls. Her black hair was caught up in an elaborate gold-mesh net. She looked rich. She looked as if no one had ever bugged *her* about a bill for a crummy, sagging bed and a few bowls of lousy vegetable stew.

"Hey," Lori said, by way of greeting. She had become friends with the smooth-voiced woman while Ari and her pals had been off on one of their busybody trips trying to regain power over this so-called kingdom. She'd been to Lady Kylie's mansion — well, it was her brother's manor — for lunch a few times. She kept hoping that Lady Kylie would ask her to stay. Lord Lexan's manor was a lot nicer than this crummy Inn.

Lady Kylie had been very interested in Ari's adventures on the other side of the Gap. Lori had told her that Ari was just a stable hand at Glacier River Farm. And that *there*, she, Lori, was the important one. Her father, Lori said, was as rich as Lady Kylie's brother. Maybe even richer. And he wouldn't

343

have stood for the way Lori was being treated around *here* for one little second.

"We aren't supposed to know that *who* is here?" Lady Kylie asked in her creamy-voiced way.

"Well, don't tell anybody," Lori said, "but —"

"Lori!" Toby trotted into the stable yard. His withers were damp with sweat. It looked as if he had run long and hard to get there. Lori made a face at him. He'd left her and Dr. Bohnes at the edge of the village two days ago, and she'd thought she'd seen the last of him.

"Ah! Tobiano!" Kylie purred. "How good to see you again."

"The last time I saw you, you were having a bit of trouble getting your unicorns to take you home," Toby said. "Things a bit different now?"

"Yes," she said shortly.

"They're talking again, those two. Must be a lot easier to go from place to place, now that your animals can talk to you again," Toby said with a grin.

"He may have his *horn*," Kylie hissed furiously, "but my masssster has the power!" Her flat black eyes glittered with malevolence.

"Are you talking about Chase?" Lori said, mainly to avoid being ignored.

"Your master is going to lose. And lose big," Toby said shortly. "I'd get back home if I were you."

Lady Kylie raised one thin black eyebrow. "You would?" she asked softly. "And then what? Prepare for a journey, perhaps?"

"Stay home, is my advice," Toby said. "If you know what's good for you."

Lady Kylie fingered the elaborate knife at her belt. "Ah, now, Tobiano. Why would I want to remain at home? When I and my fellows can hunt?"

"What *are* you two talking about?!" Lori demanded.

"Unicorn stew?" Kylie said. "Perhaps. Perhaps not. Good day to you, Tobiano." She turned to Lori. She placed a hand on the blond girl's sleeve. Her nails were long and painted bloodred. "Stop by," she hissed. "Before you leave. Yes?"

"Um, I guess so," Lori said uncomfortably. "But I'm not going anywhere." She glared at Toby. "Not anywhere."

"Beat it, Kylie," Toby said. "If you know what's good for you."

Lady Kylie looked around, as if to gauge her chances. Mr. Samlett stared at her from the door of the stables. Two draft unicorns, their heavy necks thick with muscle, gazed at her from the open doors of their stalls. She nodded to herself, gave them all a nasty smile, then glided away.

"That's a gorgeous dress she's wearing," Lori said.

Toby snorted. "Now, miss," he said sternly. "I have a message for you. You are going on that trip. And you're not going to tell anyone but Ari and Chase why."

10

"**I**'m glad you've decided to go with us," Ari said gravely. They were in the great room downstairs at the Inn. Lori had been out all afternoon. When she came back, she seemed in good spirits. And she told Ari that she would be one of the Six.

The light was failing and night was coming on. It was the first night of the Shifter's Moon — which meant, of course, no moon.

"I don't want to go, thank you very much. But Toby says I can go back through the Gap — he's not sure how. He thinks some old unicorn is going to take care of it. All he would say is 'it's part of the deep magic' — and stuff like that. Anyway, I'm going. And I'm telling you, I'm not doing anything but riding along. No getting wood for the fire, no cooking. Nothing. Got it?"

Ari nodded. "Toby said that three of the Six will be sent through the Gap?"

"That's what this Prophecy means, suppos-edly." Lori picked up a peach from the wooden bowl on the sideboard. She bit into it. Peach juice ran down her chin.

Ari said, " 'Of Six who go, two wait to learn, Three of Six shall not return.' "

"Toby said the other one who gets to go home is Lincoln." Lori tossed the peach pit back into the wooden bowl. "He's not supposed to be here, either."

I do not wish to go back! Lincoln gazed up at Ari with worried eyes. *I want to stay with you.* His bronze-and-black coat was ruffled.

Ari bent over and smoothed Lincoln's fur with her hands. She swallowed hard. She bit her lip, then whispered into one tulip ear, "Being Princess is so *hard*, Linc." She grabbed his white ruff with both hands and shook it gently. Then without looking at Lori, she said evenly, "Did Toby think that there was another meaning to the Prophecy?"

"Like what?"

Ari got up and faced her. "It's dangerous. What we're about to do. The future of the Kingdom hangs in the balance." Then, seeing that Lori still didn't get it, she said, "Lives are at stake. We may be killed."

"Yeah. He said that. But I'm telling you, I'll travel with you, but I'm not doing more than that. I won't fight. I won't lift a finger against that guy, the Shifter."

347

"That may not matter to him."

Lori looked smug, but didn't say anything more.

Ari shrugged. "Okay. I've warned you. Are you ready to go?"

Lori widened her eyes. "Now? We can't go now. I told . . . I mean, I thought we should wait until after this Shifter's Moon thing is over."

"We'll go now."

"I can't go right this minute," Lori said sulkily. "I have to say good-bye to . . . to . . . my friends. And I have to pack my stuff."

"There's no need to wait any longer," Ari said patiently. "The foxes Dill and Basil have been waiting by Balinor Ford since this afternoon. We'll stop and pick them up. I won't sleep tonight, anyway, and we'll be less conspicuous in the dark."

"I'm *not* going now." Lori folded her arms across her chest. "I'm spending the night in a real bed. I'll think about leaving in the morning."

Ari marched over to her. She grabbed Lori's shoulders in both hands and stared directly into her face. Ari dropped her voice to a fierce whisper. "You. Will. Do. What. I. Say." She punctuated each word with a little shake of Lori's shoulders. Lori's mouth dropped open. "I've agreed to your terms, Lori. Now listen to mine. If you want to survive this journey, you will do exactly what I say exactly when I say it. You got that?"

Lori nodded, too shocked to speak.

"Good," Ari chirruped softly. "Linc? Let's go." She turned on her heel. "You've got five minutes, Lori. Then the cart leaves without you."

Ari went back to her room to collect her saddlebags and say good-bye to Dr. Bohnes. The little old vet kissed her firmly on both cheeks, then pressed a small bag into her hand. "My magic is for small things," she said. She chuckled, her face breaking into a thousand wrinkles. "A little bit of this. A little bit of that."

"Magic," Ari said. "Thank you." She had two talismans now. The Star Bottle with Atalanta's water, and this little bag. She started to open it. Bohnesy's strong hand closed over her arm. "Use it when there's no way out! Get going now, Princess." If there were tears, she didn't let Ari see them. "And *you*," she scolded the collie. "Keep watch over her!"

Lincoln barked. Ari picked up her saddlebags, then left her room to tap on Lori's door. When the blond girl came out, she was dressed in a brown velvet dress.

"Wow," Ari said. "That's an amazing outfit. Did Samlett give that to you?"

Lori avoided a direct answer. "He said we had to travel in disguise, at least until we reach the Sixth Sea. So I said the best disguise would be if you were my maid. Remember how we first came to

Balinor? You were my maid then." She smoothed the dark velvet with a complacent air. "So you can be my maid now."

Ari didn't bother to correct her. When they had first arrived in Balinor Village, Mr. Samlett had assumed Ari was Lori's maid because Lori had refused to walk and was riding Chase. Ari led the way downstairs, carrying Lori's sack of clothes — as well as her own saddlebags — to avoid further argument. Mr. Samlett was waiting outside in the cart. Toby was in the harness. He nodded to them as the two girls and the dog came out the back door.

Chase stood a short distance away. He was haltered, but had no saddle or bridle. They were traveling light, and the tack would be an encumbrance. If Ari had to ride, she'd ride bareback.

Ari had been worried that Chase would be recognized on their journey to Sixton, the village that lay on the shore of the Sixth Sea. So she had rubbed kitchen grease all over his beautiful bronze coat, dulling his brilliant glow to a muddy brown. She'd covered the glowing ruby jewel at the base of his horn with a couple of dabs of black paint. But there wasn't much she could do about his size — larger than any other unicorn in Balinor — or his magnificent walk.

Mr. Samlett glanced anxiously at the sky. The moon was dark — the first night of the four days of the Shifter's Moon. "You sure you want to start out *now*, Your Royal Highness? No *good* magic works in these hours."

"It's best," Ari said. "Our enemies won't expect us to leave at this time. We'll increase our chances of traveling unnoticed."

"It'll take two days to reach the Sixth Sea, milady," Mr. Samlett said. "Depends on the state of the roads. We're to leave you there, according to Toby. You know where you're goin' from there? I say, you know where you're goin'?"

"Best not to ask, Samlett," Chase said.

"That's right, Your Majesty. I won't. Only Sixton is somewhat a rough town from all accounts."

Chase lifted his ebony horn. The sharp end glinted in the starlight. "We are well-protected," he said.

Lincoln stationed himself at Chase's left. Lori and Ari climbed into the cart. Mr. Samlett had covered the bottom with thick quilts, and it was actually quite comfortable. There was a roof over the cart, held up by four sturdy posts at the corners. Two lanterns hung at the rear. They were so bright, Ari could have read a book — if she had anything to read — which she didn't. She sighed. She hadn't read anything for weeks. And she missed it. A long, narrow chest was tucked under the driver's perch. Ari leaned over and opened it: provisions! Thick sandwiches, peaches, flasks of lemonade, several pies. They had enough for a week's journey!

"Are you ready, Your Royal Highness?"

"Ready."

Mr. Samlett slapped the reins against Toby's rump and said "Gee-yup!" Toby moved out at a rapid walk. The cart rumbled on the cobblestones.

They were off.

Ari sat with her knees up, back braced against a cushion propped against the side of the cart. She was wearing her breeches underneath the red skirt. She fingered the skirt material and sighed to herself. It was so nice to have some clean clothes and something different to wear. Like Lori's brown velvet dress. If she ever regained the throne — no, she told herself firmly, she *was* going to regain the throne, it was best to take a positive attitude — the one Royal privilege she was going to allow herself was new clothes. She wriggled her toes inside her riding boots. They were worn and cracked after all her adventures. And new shoes. She hoped there was a Royal Shoemaker. If not, one of her first Royal acts was going to be hiring one.

"Why are we stopping?" Lori asked nervously.

Ari jerked herself out of her musings. Samlett had pulled the cart over. They must be at Balinor Ford already. "We're picking up two more passengers," she said. "Basil and Dill."

Lori sniffed disapprovingly. "This cart is already too small —" She interrupted herself, and said with interest, "Did you say Basil? We're picking up a guy? Is he cute?"

"Well, he's male," Ari said, choking back a laugh. "And he's got gorgeous red hair. But he's — um — committed already, you might say." She stood up and peered into the darkness. Balinor River rippled softly under the starlight. The area around the ford was broad and flat. Ari didn't see any sign of the fox and vixen. Then she heard a splash from the riverbank, and a pair of familiar voices.

"I told you, didn't I? Let *me* catch the fish, I said. Honestly, Basil. You are so *lame*! I told you what would happen if you leaned over too far."

"You *pushed* me, Dill."

"I did not."

"You did too."

"I did —"

"Dill?" Ari called softly. "Basil? We're here!"

"NOT!" Dill concluded triumphantly. "We'll be right there, Your Royal Highness."

Ari heard the sound of energetic swimming, the sound of little bodies splooshing out of the mud, a short, furious squabble, and both foxes leaped into the wagon.

Lori jumped up and screamed. Ari grabbed her forearm and said sternly, "*Be quiet!*" She released Lori's arm. "Dill? Basil? This is Lori Carmichael."

Dill sat on her haunches and looked Lori up

353

and down. "Hmm," she said. "You know who she reminds me of, Basil? That little brat of a ferret that lived one meadow over when we had our den in Luckon. Same shifty look to her."

"Hey!" Lori said indignantly.

Basil, whose dark red fur was wet and muddy, put his paws on Lori's riding habit so that he could stretch up and see her face more clearly. Lori opened her mouth to scream, cast a hasty look at Ari, then settled for pushing Basil away with her toe. "Ugh!" she muttered.

"She doesn't look at all like that ferret. That ferret had dark brown fur and beady brown eyes."

"She's got beady *blue* eyes," Dill said. "Don't argue with me, Basil."

"I'm not arguing with you, Dill."

"You are *too*!"

"Stop, please," Ari said pleasantly. "It's a long journey to Sixton and the shore of the Sixth Sea, Dill. We have plans to make on the way. First, I want to know everything there is to know about the Valley of Fear. The best defense is to be prepared. I'd like to create a map, so that we can all see where we're headed."

Dill, for once, was completely quiet. She looked up at the night sky. The moon was dark — the Shifter's Moon. The stars seemed faded and far away. "I'll tell you what I know, Your Royal Highness," she said. "But not now. Not now. Tomorrow, when the sun is bright, and we won't imagine things coming after us in the dark."

"Tomorrow, then," Ari said. "Tonight, we may as well sleep while we can." She raised her voice, "Mr. Samlett? Shall we find a place to pull over for the night? You don't want to exhaust yourself driving all the way to Sixton without any rest. And Toby, you'll need to rest, as well."

"Don't worry about me, Princess," Toby said.

Mr. Samlett shook his head vigorously. "No, no, no, Your Royal Highness. We're not tired. No, we're not tired at all. We'll ride until the dawn comes up. And then we'll eat a little something and ride some more."

"If you're sure," Ari said. She settled back on her heels. "Basil? Dill? Find a comfortable spot. Lori? You can cover yourself with that quilt."

"And you, Your Royal Highness, you get some sleep, too," Basil said in a kindly way. "I'll sit up front with Samlett, for a while."

Ari settled into a corner of the cart and pulled the extra quilt over her shoulders. She fell asleep.

And as she slept, she dreamed.

Arrrr-iiii-aaaannnna, a cold voice breathed in her ear.

Princessss, hissed another.

She woke with a start. The lanterns were out.

Up front, Toby jogged steadily on. Mr. Samlett held the reins in one hand, but his head was slumped forward on his chest. Ari heard the faint echo of a snore. Basil and Dill were intertwined on her lap. Sometime during the night, Lincoln had jumped into the cart. He slept at her side.

Lori slept with her mouth open.

Ari pushed herself upright and looked over the edge of the cart. Chase walked steadily beside it, his head low, his eyes abstracted. He looked into Ari's eyes as her head appeared over the side.

Do not speak, he thought at her.

What is it? Ari thought.

Do you hear it? Do you feel it?

Ari listened. Yes. There it was.

The cold sound of the snake. Ari shuddered. Chase arched his great neck over her and blew softly on her cheek. *Sleep, milady. It will not approach us this night. I will see to that.*

Ari slumped back into the cart and put her face in her hands. The last line of the Prophecy echoed in her brain.

Three of Six shall not return.

Linc, Chase, Basil, Dill, Lori. And she, Ari, herself. Six of them set out on an impossible journey. The Six referred to in the Old Mare's Prophecy.

Three of Six shall not return.

She was so tired! The way seemed so long! The task ahead of her was so hard!

Three of Six shall not return.

356

Linc and Lori were to pass through the Valley of Fear and go home, to Glacier River Farm.

Three of Six . . .

What if the Old Mare of the Mountain was wrong?

What if death lay ahead for all of them?

. . . shall not return.

11

"**I** will show you what I saw in the Valley of Fear," Dill said. They had stopped for a breakfast of wheat cakes, honey, and fruit, near a tiny roadside market about thirty miles outside of Sixton. It was early; dew was still on the grass and the morning haze had not yet been burned from the sky. Cultivated fields of oats and sweet alfalfa spread to the east and west. A few of the neighboring farmers were already in the fields, hoeing the weeds and clearing the cropland of those rocks and branches that had escaped the spring harrowing. Two women sat under a gaily striped canopy at the side of the road, selling sweet milk, butter, cheese, and early summer berries. A third sold bread and muffins from a rough shed. They glanced at the cart once or twice, and raised their hands in greeting. Ari wished she had money to buy baked goods. The smell of the muffins was delicious, even at a distance.

Dill sat on her haunches in the middle of the cart, bushy tail curled around her feet. Her pointed nose quivered with tension. "So you want to know about the Valley of Fear, Your Royal Highness," she said. "If you could spread some fine dirt on the floor, I can draw a map for you."

Ari jumped out of the cart and scooped up a handful of grit from the side of the road. She got back in and spread it in a thin layer in front of the vixen. She sat down with Lincoln on one side and Lori on the other. Toby, Mr. Samlett, and Chase stood outside the cart and peered over the side.

"The Valley lies on the northernmost shore of the Sixth Sea." Dill placed her paw carefully at the edge of the dirt, making a round spot. "From the shore, you take the Trail of Tears to the top of De-monview — a mountainous hill where it never stops snowing." She drew a thin line from the round spot to the middle of the dirt patch. "Then, it's down, down, down. The lower you go, the hotter it gets. You reach the Fiery Field. This is a terrible place, worse than the snows of Demonview. And there is . . ." Her voice dropped away. She shuddered. "The Fiery Field is patrolled by the shadow herd."

"The shadow herd?" Lori cleared her throat. "What is that?"

"Black unicorns. Black." Dill's voice was a mere thread. "With fiery eyes and horns like molten spears. The sand where they walk is black and hot. All around them, there are holes with fire."

"Lava bed," Lori said unexpectedly. At Ari's startled look she explained, "Sounds like there's a volcano around there somewhere."

"There is a waterfall of fire," Dill said. As soon as they were past the subject of the shadow unicorns, her courage seemed to have returned. "I don't know what a vol-can-oh is. Anyhow, you humans will have to walk this path without shoes."

"Without shoes?!" Lori said.

"There's a cooler path through the middle. Not much cooler, but cool enough so that you won't burn up if you step on it. You won't be able to feel the difference unless you have bare feet."

"You'll burn up if you step on the hotter part!" Lori said.

Dill nodded. Like Basil's, her mask surrounded her eyes and covered the top of her forehead. It made it harder to read her expression. "You get past the Fiery Field and you have to travel carefully around the Pit."

"The Pit?" Ari asked. "What's in the Pit?"

Dill didn't say anything for a moment. Basil, who was curled next to her, put a protective paw on her back. "She'll tell you what she can tell you."

"We go around the Pit," Ari said in an encouraging way. "And then?"

"You'll see it then. Castle Entia. And we just . . ." Dill took a deep breath. "We just walk in the front door."

"We just walk in?" Ari said. "Aren't there guards?"

"There's plenty of guards — if you can call those evil, twisted beings guards — to sneak past when we're in the Valley itself. But no, not at Castle Entia itself." Dill shook her head. "*He* doesn't need them at the Castle. Why should he? No one goes to Castle Entia unless they're summoned. It's not the kind of place that you hang around for fun. Half the time, the Shifter himself isn't even there."

"Atalanta said she and the Celestial Valley unicorns would create a diversion," Ari said. "So the Shifter won't be there, I hope."

Nobody said anything for a moment. Everyone was wondering what would happen if the diversion didn't work.

Dill broke the silence. "So. The Dreamspeaker is supposed to create a diversion, so that the Shifter and most of his army are going to be off chasing the Celestial unicorns. So *he* won't even be at home. And the Shifter won't leave guards when he's not there because it's worth your life to take anything that belongs to him." Dill shuddered. "You'll see what happens to thieves when we pass by the Pit. Who'd be crazy enough to ask for that kind of punishment?"

"We are," Lincoln said wryly. "If you ask me, it's hopeless. We're supposed to sneak past the monsters, ghouls, and shadow unicorns that live in the Valley of Fear, walk into the Castle Entia as nice as you please, and walk out again with the Royal Scepter? I can believe that the Shifter's subjects are so afraid of him that he doesn't need guards. But I can't believe that there isn't some hidden trap, just waiting for us."

"We'll be disguised as soldiers," Ari said, her voice much more hopeful than she felt. "And we don't really have a choice about how to get in. Maybe there's a back way."

Lori stood up, rocking the cart back and forth. She put her foot on the dirt map and rubbed it into nothingness. "Come on. Let's get this over with."

They left the peace and quiet of the roadside market and rode on into Sixton. They came to the outskirts of the town in the late afternoon. Great white seabirds soared high in the sky. Before they saw the houses and shops of the village, they smelled the sea. The salty air was soft and warm.

Sixton was a bustling, thriving town. "Every-one here's a fisherman," Toby said over his shoulder as he pulled the cart down the cobblestone streets. "They pretty much stayed out of the Shifter's war last year. They're too far from the Palace at Luckon to care much about government affairs one way or the other. But they're mostly loyal to the Crown."

He trotted briskly through the busy streets, and said no more.

Ari couldn't remember if she'd ever been in Sixton, and she looked around curiously. The whole town smelled of fresh fish. There seemed to be a fish shop on every corner — servants of the great houses brought carts and wagons from all over to buy Sixton's produce. Ari saw a wagon with the blue-and-yellow crest of the House of Harton and servants wearing the red livery of the House of Finglass. Her heart beat a little faster. If she could remember two of the seven Great Houses of Balinor, perhaps her memory was finally returning!

Chase drew attention, even though his coat had been dulled with grease and the ruby at the base of his horn painted over. It was the way he carried himself, Ari noticed with a sense of pride. Head held high, neck arched, there was majesty in every stride he took. Chase crowded close to Samlett's cart, and bent his great head to her. "You're smiling, milady."

"Do you see those men in the blue-and-yellow vests? And the two women in red? I remember which Houses they're from, Chase. And I don't even have the Scepter yet. Do you think I'll remember more and more as time goes on — without the Scepter?"

"Perhaps."

"It's just . . ." She was quiet for a moment, thinking. "What if we fail? What if we don't get the Scepter back? What if something goes wrong? I'm not afraid of the danger, you know," she said softly. "Well, maybe a little. But I am afraid to come back without the Scepter. If I could remember everything about my past all on my own, maybe there'd be a different way to find my parents and my brothers. If only so much didn't depend on me!"

Chase's muzzle briefly brushed her hair. "We are in this together, milady. If we fail — and I do not think we shall, not while I have breath in my body — we will find another way."

"Heads up," Toby called. "We're headed down to the wharf!" He made a sharp right, and they descended into the port of Sixton itself.

Sixton was located at the shore of a natural harbor. The sea took Ari's breath away. It stretched before her — calm, deep, an intense turquoise. Sea-gulls swooped and cried, their calls thin and cheerful in the late afternoon sun. The harbor itself formed an almost perfect semicircle, as if some giant long ago had chomped a large bite out of the land's flank.

More than a dozen wooden piers poked into the waters of the harbor. And the boats! There were all kinds of boats! Dinghies packed with nets and poles for deep-sea fishing, pleasure boats with silken sails, a racing sloop or two, and three large frigates. High-masted sails furled, they rocked in the gentle swell of the Sixth Sea.

"There it is," Toby said. "The *Dawnwalker.* She's the middle frigate. See it? The one painted deep green with the figurehead of the Dawn Princess on the prow."

364

Ari squinted. She could read the name on the ship's side. The letters were painted in gold: DAWNWALKER.

Toby came to a halt. "We'll leave you now, Your Royal Highness." He took a breath, as if to say something more. But then he merely nodded.

Ari, Lori, and Linc got out of the cart. Dill and Basil, after some minor squabbling about who should get out first, jumped out together and stood near Chase's hocks. Ari went up to Mr. Samlett on his perch and took his hand. "Thank you, Mr. Samlett." She raised herself on tiptoe and kissed his cheek. "We will see you soon, I hope."

The chubby landlord flushed bright pink. He bit his mustache to hide his pleasure in Ari's kiss. "We'll be waiting right here, Your Royal Highness, I say, right here. I have a cousin who's a lobsterman, lives a few miles up the village. Toby and I'll stay with him. We'll come to the wharf every morning to check for you."

"We shouldn't be gone too long," Ari said.

"And you won't see me again at all, Samlett," Lori said. "So, here's some pay for my room and board." She dug into the pocket of her velvet dress and pulled out a few small gold coins. Samlett accepted them with a nod of thanks.

"Where did you get the money, Lori?" Linc asked. A worried frown appeared between his dark brown eyes.

"Oh, I've got friends, same as you two," Lori said airily. " And Carmichaels always pay their bills."

"Thank you, miss," Mr. Samlett said. "I can't say as it's been a pleasure having you, I say, having you stay at the Inn. But I'm glad to get the bill settled."

Lori said, "Humph."

Ari took a deep breath. "Well!" She forced a smile. "We're off! See you in a few days, Mr. Samlett." She went to Toby and threw her arms around his neck.

"Stay safe," he grumbled, "and good luck."

With Lincoln on one side and Chase on the other, Ari set off for the *Dawnwalker.* She didn't look back. Lori mooched along behind, holding up the velvet skirt of her riding habit to avoid soiling it on the damp quay. Basil and Dill scurried ahead. They walked straight toward the deep green ship.

Behind them, a long, dark length slithered over the wooden walk.

12

Ari liked Captain Tredwell. He was tall, as broad as a barrel, and the part of his face visible over his chocolate-colored beard was tanned to leather. His eyes were gray; they looked as if they were used to staring into broad horizons. He was waiting to greet them as they walked up the gangplank to the *Dawnwalker*.

"Captain Nick Tredwell, at your service . . . milady." He swept off his captain's hat with a flourish and winked at Ari. "You'd be wishin' passage aboard the *Dawnwalker* for yourself and your companions?" He addressed Lori. Clearly, he had been warned of the group's need for disguise. Lori loved being treated like a wealthy lady. She stuck her chin in the air and nodded in an arrogant way. "Yes, Captain. I'd like the best cabin for myself. And my maid, too, I guess."

"And your destination, milady?"

Lori opened her mouth and then shut it.

"The north shore," Chase said quietly. "Near Demonview."

"Ah. Going to check on the ice-gatherers?" His voice slid easily over Lori's bewildered look. "I take it, milady, that you have sent members of your House ahead to gather ice to store the fish you'll be taking back home."

"Um. Well. Yes."

"Good! Good! A good mistress always checks on her servants. And Demonview is the only place in Balinor where you can obtain ice year-round."

"And thank goodness for that," Ari said, before Lori could jeopardize their disguise with questions. "Milady, I think you mentioned how tired you were after our trip. Wouldn't you like the captain to take us to our cabin?" She put her hand on Lori's back and gave her an unobtrusive shove. "Here! Let me help you cross the deck."

Lori shook Ari's hand off. "I can get there myself, thank you very much." She scowled at Ari. "Oh, Captain. The dog will need a place to sleep. I don't want him with us. I have . . . allergies. Maybe you can find a nice place for him in the open air. Like on that pile of rope over there."

Ari gave Lincoln a rueful look. He wagged his tail at her and grinned. "I'll stay with Chase, milady."

"Yes, we have a fine cabin for the unicorn," Captain Tredwell said. "Now, if you ladies will settle in, I have the sails to set. We want to catch the tide."

Ari didn't see much of the sailors' activity setting sail. She stayed in the cabin with Lori and unpacked their few belongings, "Because," as Lori pointed out, "it'll seem weird if I unpack for myself. I could get used to having a maid. Hah!" With a smirk, she settled into one of the hammocks that served as their beds.

Ari ignored her, and shook out the few clothes they'd brought with them. Her mind was full of the dangers ahead. She went over and over her mental map of the Valley of Fear. Demonview. The Fiery Field. The Pit. Castle Entia.

Three of Six shall not return.

Ari curled herself into a corner of the cabin and dozed. Nightmarish images floated in her mind.

Princess. She didn't want to be a Princess. Oh, if only things had been different!

She shook herself fully awake when one of the crew tapped on the cabin door and told them dinner was ready. She followed Lori outside. The sails were full and the wind brisk. The air had a clean, cold scent. The *Dawnwalker* forged steadily across the sea.

Ari looked up. Clouds rode high over the

water, obscuring the stars, hiding the fact that there was no moon.

Perhaps the Dreamspeaker was watching them from the pool in the Celestial Valley! Ari raised her hand and waved, then crossed the deck to the captain's cabin, where dinner waited.

13

Atalanta stood motionless at the edge of the Watching Pool. She was alone. Some distance away, the unicorns of the Celestial Valley waited for her. The image of Arianna on the deck of the *Dawnwalker* faded into the waters of the pool.

It was almost time. Tomorrow, as the sun rose over Demonview, the Dreamspeaker would lead an army of Celestial unicorns to Balinor, where they would challenge the Palace where the Shifter reigned. They wouldn't fight. They would race through the Forest of Ardit, the Shifter in hot pursuit.

"Are you sure that he will only follow us?" Numinor had asked. "May we not be prepared to fight?"

Atalanta had agreed. They would fight if they had to. She raised her crystal horn. She closed her eyes. Her silvery mane flowed over her withers.

"I call on the deep magic," she said, so softly

that only the One Who Rules could hear. "Transform me. Change me. For the sake of us all."

The waters of the pool churned. The waves sprayed high. A fine mist floated in the air. The mist whirled, took shape, then settled over the Dreamspeaker like a bridal veil, as fine as a spiderweb.

The net floated onto her horn, passed over her violet eyes, hid her completely. She grew in size. Her body darkened to a fiery purple. Her silver mane grew longer, thicker, swinging from her neck with a metallic clang. Her eyes burned with a fierce indigo flame.

The waters in the Watching Pool calmed. The mist drifted away. The unicorn called the Dreamspeaker no longer stood at the edge of the pool. A warrior unicorn stood there instead, chest and withers gleaming with chain mail, hindquarters covered with hammered silver shields. Her crystal horn was a diamond sword, flaming at the tip.

Atalanta took two steps and reared. She trumpeted a war cry to the sky. In the distance, Numinor answered, and with him, the call of the stallions of the Celestial herd. Atalanta leaned over and gazed at herself in the water. She shuddered at the sight of her own warlike image.

She *would* maintain it. If it took all of her strength and personal magic to do it!

"Oh, yes, Numinor," she said. "We are ready for the Shifter now!"

14

Arianna slept heavily that night. She woke up early and lay in her hammock, listening to the slap of waves against the hull of the ship. Lori was sound asleep in the other hammock. Ari swung herself onto the floor and pulled on her boots. She was, she decided, tired of sleeping in her clothes. She wanted a hot bath, to wash her hair, to ride Chase — anything rather than face what was coming.

She packed up her few belongings in her saddlebags. The Star Bottle with the water from Atalanta's Grove was at the top. She held it in her hand. It made her feel safer, closer to the Dreamspeaker and the faraway meadows of the Celestial Valley. On impulse, she tucked it into her leather vest. And Dr. Bohnes's red leather bag: She'd carry that with her, too. The old vet's words came back to her: *Use it when there's no way out!*

Ari let herself quietly out of the cabin. The dawn was misty and the whole world seemed veiled in low gray clouds. The sailors on deck looked at her, but didn't speak. Chase was standing at the prow of the *Dawnwalker*, his long mane blowing in the ocean spray. Lincoln stood next to him. Ari went to Chase and leaned against his warmth. Linc wagged his tail at them, and she caressed the white snip on his nose.

"Demonview," the unicorn said. He nodded, pointing his horn. "Off to starboard."

"There's snow on the top of the mountain," Lincoln said.

Ari forced herself to look. Demonview reared its jagged peak in front of them. It was close. The mountain's icy peak was a sullen white, now visible, now hidden as the wind pushed the clouds along.

Everything seemed frozen in this early light — all but the figure of a giant blackbird, riding the currents of air high above the ship. Ari glanced up at it. The bird circled the ship. She could just see its curved beak. She caught a glimpse of its dull black eye. There was something about that eye. Had she seen it somewhere before?

Suddenly, the bird swiveled its head around, as if receiving a far-off call. It screeched, a long, dying cry that made the hair on the back of Ari's neck prickle. Then it turned around and headed south, its powerful wings thrusting it forward at an amazing speed.

The unicorns of the Celestial Valley are advancing on Castle Entia, said a voice in Ari's mind. *The Shifter has already seen us. Soon the diversion will begin. It is time for you to go forward. Move swiftly through the Fiery Field, my child. But be careful. If you fail, all is lost.*

Atalanta! Somehow the Dreamspeaker talked to Ari the same way Chase talked to her — through her mind. But it was more than talk. It was a vision.

Ari could see the Celestial unicorns — hundreds and hundreds of them — marching on Castle Entia under the white banner of peace.

Numinor led the march. Rednal of the red band trotted beside him. Cinched to Rednal's flank was the tall white banner of peace. Numinor stopped on the hill overlooking the castle, and the Celestial unicorns gathered behind him.

"We come in peace, under a white flag!" Numinor called. "I, Numinor, the Golden One, Herd Leader of the Celestial Valley unicorns, shall speak to Lord Entia!"

A black unicorn trotted out of the castle, his red eyes shining with hatred. "What is your business here?" he sneered.

Behind him, more coal-black unicorns slipped silently out of the castle and into the dismal

375

forest. Soon Numinor and his gallant band would be surrounded.

"My business is with your lord," Numinor stated proudly. "It is time we talked of peace, not war."

Ari cried out to Atalanta, *The Shifter has sent out his legions to surround Numinor and the Celestial unicorns. You must warn him before it's too late!*

Atalanta answered, *We expected this, Arianna. We knew the Shifter would not allow us to come and go in peace. Although we are not ready to fight a war, we can lead a merry chase. And we will fight if we have to!*

The evil unicorns leaped upon the rainbow herd. Numinor and the Celestial unicorns split up and galloped north, south, east, and west. The shadow unicorns were momentarily confused. It was the delay that Numinor and his troops had hoped would occur.

The shadow unicorns gave chase, but Ari could see that they were divided, running this way and that. They no longer held the advantage of surprise or superior position. The Celestial unicorns were faster, stronger, smarter. Evil and the lust for power had a way of corrupting the body and the mind.

Then, out of the castle flew the Shifter himself — this time transformed into the shape of a black dragon. His body was thick with muscle. His long wings sprang from his shoulders, stretched out like those of a gigantic wasp. His iron hooves grew grossly large. He had not one horn on his head but two, one behind each ear, curling up above his head in a huge ram's arc.

Where the Shifter's eyes and mouth should have been, there were exploding pockets of fire. Buried in the flames were black stars reaching out from the depths of dying galaxies.

Ari buckled at the knees. Was this what the Shifter truly looked like? Was it another terrible disguise? The vision faded. Ari felt Sunchaser lean against her body to support her.

"What is it, Princess?" he demanded. "What's wrong?"

"Nothing, Chase, I'm fine. Atalanta sent me a vision. Numinor and the Celestial unicorns have cleared the way for us."

You must go now, Arianna! said Atalanta. *We don't know how long we will be able to keep the Shifter and his legions away from the castle. We're all counting on you. Good luck!*

Yes, everyone was counting on her, Arianna, the Royal Princess. She trembled with fear.

"Your Royal Highness?" Captain Tredwell's voice was close behind her.

Ari jumped, then turned to him. "I'm sorry, I'm just the lady's servant."

The captain smiled kindly. "I'm no fool, Princess. I know Royalty when I see it. You'll be going ashore in about half an hour. I'll have to anchor the ship beyond the reef. We'll take you in with the dinghy."

"Thank you, Captain," Ari said.

"Do you have something for my companion?" Chase asked. "And for the four others who travel with us?"

"I almost forgot!" Captain Tredwell exclaimed. "Yes, I do. Your old nurse, Eliane Bohnes, sent it to me some days ago. She asked me to keep it safe for you." He looked doubtful. "It's a large package, Your Royal Highness. Will you be able to carry it?"

The disguises! Ari had almost forgotten them herself.

"We'll take it from here, Captain," Chase said. "Lincoln, would you please call the others — Dill, Basil, and Lori?"

Lincoln trotted off. In short time, the Six assembled on deck, and Demonview loomed in front of them. Ari stared up at its icy peak and shivered, rubbing her arms.

To Ari, the next half hour sped by in seconds. The cabin boy brought them hot tea and wheat cakes. The *Dawnwalker's* anchor was lowered, and the dinghy put into the water. One of the deckhands attached a short plank to a network of ropes to make a seat. He winched the plank into position, then stood at attention, waiting for orders.

Lori, her hair uncombed and a frown on her face, looked crossly at the captain. "We're going to sit on that thing?"

Captain Tredwell nodded.

"How's he going to get into that little boat?" She jerked her thumb at Chase.

Chase's eyes narrowed in amusement. "I'll see you ashore," he said. And before Ari could stop him, he leaped into the air and over the *Dawnwalker*'s side into the ocean. He landed with a tremendous splash, then struck out for the shoreline, swimming strongly. The black paint covering his ruby jewel washed away, and the jewel shone in the gray air like a beacon.

Captain Tredwell's eyes widened. "I have heard that the Sunchaser had returned with you, Your Royal Highness. Is that . . ." He stopped himself midsentence. "I am forbidden to ask more. Forgive me." He bowed in front of Ari, his gray eyes lively. "We will wait here three days. Then I must return to Sixton."

Ari nodded. Suddenly, she felt very tired. The words of the Old Mare's Prophecy haunted her: *Three of Six shall not return.* "Very good, Captain. We will meet you here sooner than that, I hope. It will take a day to reach our destination, and a day to come back."

Captain Tredwell's clear gray eyes darkened. "Milady, you know what lies on the other side of Demonview."

"Yes, Captain."

"I do not know your quest, Princess Arianna. But I wish you well. Did they warn you? Do you know where the Shifter's territory begins? It is not safe to go past the line of ice-gatherers."

"I know all about it," Dill said bossily. "Just get us into that boat, Captain. Chase is practically on land, and we're standing here gabbing the time away."

Ari, Lori, and Linc took their places on the plank. Basil and Dill sat in Ari's lap. One of the sailors winched the plank to a position just over the dinghy. The sailor manning the oars reached up, and the five of them scrambled into the boat. He shipped the oars expertly and turned the boat in the water. He rowed steadily, not speaking. Ari watched the north shore come closer and closer.

The sailor beached the dinghy. He hopped out into the water and pulled the little boat up onto the sand. Chase stood there waiting for them, sea-water dripping from his bronze coat. He glowed like a lantern in the gray light. Ari helped Basil and Dill onto the sand. Then she and Lincoln got out. Lori sat huddled on her seat, her face pinched with fear.

"Are you coming?" Ari asked.

Lori looked at the sky. It was empty, except for the clouds. She bit her lip, nodded, and got out. The sailor tugged at his cap in farewell, then rowed the dinghy away.

Ari looked up at the forbidding mountain of Demonview.

They were on their way to the Fiery Field and the dark home of the Shifter.

15

❧

"This is a disguise?" Lori shrieked. "This is *dis-gusting!*" She looked down at herself. She and Ari were dressed as soldiers in the Shifter's army, and Ari had to admit Lori was right. They looked creepy. But it was almost impossible to tell who they really were. Humans in the Shifter's army dressed in black leather from head to foot. The uniform consisted of leather pants with metal knee and shin guards and a close-fitted leather jacket. A breastplate worked in leather and metal was wrapped over the front of the jacket. The weapons belts were heavy; both Lori and Ari had a mace, a short sword, and a wooden implement that looked a little like a slingshot.

"Catapult," Chase said. "There should be small iron balls to go with it."

Ari dug in the bag. There were a dozen iron balls, with places in the weapons belt to hold six each. But it was the helmet that provided the most protection. The leather skullcap fit tightly over the skull. A faceplate attached to it completely hid the wearer's face. Ari's chief problem was her hair. She coiled it on top of her head, and pulled the leather collar of the jacket over the back of her neck. She put the helmet on and presented herself to Chase. "What do you think?"

The great unicorn nodded his approval.

"Grim," Lincoln offered. "You look grim."

Dr. Bohnes had also provided helmets for Chase, Linc, and the two foxes. There was a container filled with a sticky, tarlike substance. Ari rubbed this over Chase's horn and the ruby jewel. Then she rubbed it over the rest of him. She'd dulled his coat with grease for the trip to Sixton, but it had been nothing like this. When she finished her work, Chase was completely black. His horn was an iron spear. His eyes glittered at her through the eye holes in the mask. A shiver went up Ari's spine.

She and Lori covered the foxes and the dog with sticky dye, then fitted them with helmets. They looked at one another. The disguises were perfect. Ari had a cover story ready if they were stopped by any of the Shifter's subjects: They were a scouting party, out to search for deserters.

"Well," Lori said, "I guess we're ready."

"Wait." Ari took the Star Bottle and Dr. Bohnes's leather bag out of her vest and tucked them in her weapons belt. Then Lincoln dug a hole

in the sandy shore, and Ari put their discarded belongings in it.

"Okay." Ari took a deep breath. "Now."

They marched across the sandy beach to the
foot of Demonview and began to climb. The path
was rocky, with an almost vertical slope. The dog
and foxes had the easiest time of it, scrambling over
stones with their feet splayed, using their claws to
grip the rocky terrain. Chase took the mountain in
great leaps, launching himself into the air and landing with delicate precision in just the right spots.

Ari and Lori sweated their way up, crawling
along on all fours.

The higher they went, the colder it got.
Clouds swirled about them, obscuring the way. They
passed an occasional party of ice-gatherers, chip-
ping away at chunks of ice, loading it in baskets to
carry on down the mountain to be shipped back
to Balinor. The ice-gatherers straightened up and
turned their backs when the Six passed them. Lincoln put his muzzle to the air and sniffed. "They are
afraid," he said. "There is nothing quite like the smell
of fear."

"The disguises are working well," Dill said.
"Let's hope the folks on the other side of this ratty
mountain believe it, too."

The last yards to the top were the worst.
Snow swirled around them, a cold dense blanket. It
was hard to see more than a few feet in front of

them. Ari organized her companions into a line and ran a rope among them, Chase at the head, Lori after him, with herself at the end. If they lost sight of one another in this thick blizzard, they might never find one another again.

They struggled on. The cold numbed their feet and bit fiercely at their cheeks and ears. Lincoln's fur was matted with snow. Dill was white with it. Only Chase appeared unaffected, his great body steaming in the frigid air.

Ari slipped, slid, and crawled her way up, up, up. Her fingers reached out, clutching the rope, and she stumbled to her feet.

They were at the top!

Chase stood next to her, looking down. Dill and Basil sat down in the snow and bit the ice balls from their paws. Lincoln pressed close to Ari's side. Lori stood off by herself, arms wrapped around her body, shivering.

Ari gazed down at the Valley of Fear.

There was no snow on this, the Shifter's side of Demonview. The mountain's barren sides plunged to a vast, black expanse of sand. Steam drifted up from fire-filled holes pocking the landscape. A faint odor of rotten eggs reached Ari. *Sulfur,* she thought.

The Fiery Field was swollen with hummocks of sand and black granite. Black dots moved in clusters on it, like maggots on a log. Work parties? Soldiers? There weren't many. Ari thought about the message Atalanta had sent her: Even now, the bulk of the Shifter's army was chasing the Celestial unicorns through the Forest of Ardit.

She hoped.

The horizon of the Valley of Fear was filled with dense, oily smoke. It coiled around itself like a huge, undulating snake. Through the coils, Ari could just glimpse a sprawling building. Two turrets stood on either end. The middle had a steep roof. It was hard to tell in the shifting smoke, but it seemed that an iron fence circled the massive castle.

Castle Entia. At least a day's walk away.

Take no food or water, Atalanta had said.

It was going to be a thirsty hike.

Without a word to one another, they began the trek down the desolate sides of Demonview. The cold air grew warm, then hot. Sweat trickled down Ari's back and made great patches on Chase's sides. They scrambled through thorny brush that sliced through Ari's leather jacket. She bit her lip and kept on.

They reached the bottom of the mountain after a nightmare of harsh gravel and painful scratches.

"Stop here," Dill said in a low voice.

Ari halted and stretched her aching muscles. She had an urgent desire to rip off her helmet and take in great gulps of air. A low sobbing made her rigid with fear; she turned. Lori sat on a rough piece of lava rock, her helmet on her knee. Her blond hair tumbled over her shoulders. Her face was streaked with dirt.

"Put your helmet back on, Lori," Ari said softly.

"I can't! I'm so *hot!*"

"It's going to get hotter," Dill said. "Put your helmet back on and take off your boots."

"I can't!"

"Then," Dill said brutally, "we'll leave you here."

"You wouldn't! You couldn't!"

Dill looked at Ari, a question in her golden eyes. Ari shook her head. "We're all in this together. I won't leave any of you. But we have to go on, Lori. We can't stop now. This is the only way you'll get home to see your father."

"All right!" Lori jammed her helmet on her head and tore off her boots. Ari pulled her own boots off and tucked them under her arm.

"Follow me!" Dill said. "Walk carefully. The fire shifts, so a spot where I'm able to step can be cool one minute and boiling the next. Whatever you do — *don't stop!*"

Ari placed one foot lightly in front of the other, drawing back instantly when she came close to the searing heat. Lori's screams, muffled by the helmet, told her Lori wasn't as careful. Ari made them all stop, while she explained again how to get through the terrible ashes.

"I can't do it!" Lori cried. "I can't!"

"Then I will carry you," Chase said.

"Not a good idea." Dill squeezed her eyes shut and opened them wide. "You can't be as agile with someone on your back. The weight will slow you down. You'll burn your hooves, Chase."

"Give her a leg up," Chase commanded.

"Your Royal Highness!" Dill said indignantly. "Are you going to allow this?"

"We have to," Ari said. "I'll say it as many times as I have to say it: We're all in this together. Here, Lori. Put your foot in my hands." Ari positioned herself carefully next to Chase. This near to the great unicorn, she could smell singed hair and hooves. She swallowed her own tears. Lori put her right foot clumsily in Ari's cupped hands and scrambled on top of Chase. She clung there, crying.

They started again. Ari followed the tip of Dill's tail, stepping where the fox stepped. The stench of burning lava seemed to choke and gag everyone.

The path wound on and on. Ari's movements grew automatic: touch; draw back; touch again; step. She imagined hideous faces in the coals beneath her feet — faces with slitted eyes and protruding tongues. She tried to breath shallowly.

"Princess!"

Dill's voice, close to her ear.

"Your Royal Princess!"

Ari snapped awake.

"We're out!" The little vixen hissed triumphantly. "Now all we have to do is get by the Pit!"

Ari pulled herself together. She breathed deeply. The Fiery Field was behind them. Ahead was sand and gravel. No trees. No shade. No water. But at least no burning heat. Ari ran her hands carefully over Chase, checking for burns and singe marks. He refused to lift his hooves for her inspection. She bit her lip. She knew he was burned. She made Lori get down and put her boots back on. She pulled her own boots over her seared feet, biting back a shout of pain. She checked Lincoln over, who suffered more from smoke inhalation than burns, and looked at the foxes' paws. Everyone had suffered burns, but none of the burns looked worse than blisters.

"Okay." Ari nodded to Dill. "Now the Pit."

"Form a single file. Don't stop," Dill warned. "Keep on going. No matter what you see."

They heard the Pit before they saw it. The tramp of iron hooves on stone, shouts, groans, the crack of a whip. It lay to the right of the stony path. Ari kept her eyes lowered. Dill led the way, Chase right behind her. Ari was behind Chase. She saw Chase's hindquarters bunch, as if he were going to leap. She saw his horn lower, as if he were going to fight. She heard Dill's cautionary hiss, and thought at him, *Steady, Chase, steady!*

And then she saw it — the Pit. Her own hand

darted toward the knife in her weapons belt. She must free them! The poor slaves!

The Pit was a great hole gouged in the middle of the Valley of Fear. A narrow roadway spiraled to its smoldering depths. Dozens of animals worked the Pit, harnessed by the neck to stone collars. The shadow unicorns, those that Ari had seen when she first came to Balinor, surrounded the lip of the Pit, iron horns ready to spear any of the animals who tried to run away. Their red eyes gleamed, and their black coats shone.

The Six walked past in silence. Ari saw the wounds and scars the cruel collars made in the necks of the animals trapped there.

And suddenly, she remembered. The thin red scar around Dill's neck! The vixen had been here, a slave in the Valley of Fear, and had somehow escaped! So *that's* why she knew how to draw the map.

Ari made a vow. She would come back. She would get the Scepter and come back. One day she would free the poor slaves here!

"Brother!" A unicorn, larger than the others, shouted at Chase. "Where are you bound?"

Chase came to a halt. Ari went to his side, laid a calming hand on his neck. She watched the shadow unicorn gallop toward them, her heart in her throat. Close up, he would see through Chase's disguise.

"Come no nearer, brother," she said loudly. "We carry disease."

The shadow unicorn came to a halt. He squinted his red eyes at them. "You what?"

"A vomiting illness," Ari said, inventing as she went along. "With fever. It will go through the herd like a man with a scythe in a wheat field."

"Huh," the shadow unicorn said. He walked two strides toward them, head cocked to one side. His iron horn gleamed wickedly sharp. Two other shadow unicorns eyed the Six suspiciously. "I've never heard of such a thing," the first one said. "Who are you, anyway? I don't recognize the horn markings." The two other shadow unicorns started to argue about the horn markings. Horn markings? From the argument, Ari gathered that the squads of shadow unicorns were marked differently. There were no markings at all on Chase's horn. Ari bit her lip. Her hand went to her weapons belt. She fumbled for her catapult. That was the weapon to use. It might give them time to run.

Instead, her hand fell on the bit of soap she carried for washing her face.

Soap! She almost screamed with frustration. What was she supposed to do with soap? Wash the arguing unicorn's mouth out with soap?

Soap!

"Chase! Chew on this!" she hissed. She slipped the soap into his mouth. He worked it around with his lips. Foam dripped down his muzzle.

"You see, brothers!" Ari called. She pointed at Chase. "We think he has the summer madness! Rabies!"

Even the shadow unicorns were afraid of rabies. The summer madness struck without warning, sending its victims mad with fear and thirst.

"Go on!" the biggest one shouted. "Get out of here!"

Chase nudged Ari forward. She forced herself to walk slowly, slowly, until the Pit was far behind them all.

They stopped. The sun beat down mercilessly. Ari was so thirsty her tongue was swollen. Lincoln panted dreadfully in the heat.

"I can't go on," Lori panted. "I've got to have water!"

"Atalanta said not to carry anything into the Valley," Ari said. Her tongue was so thick with thirst she could hardly speak. "Everything here is poison, I guess."

"Well, I can't go on," Lori said. Her voice was so faint Ari could hardly hear her. "I can't."

"When there's no way out," Dr. Bohnes had said. "Use it when there's no way out!" And — "My magic is for small things."

Ari fumbled for the leather bag. She drew it from her tunic and opened it with shaking fingers. She looked inside.

There was only a small dish and a rock. Ari could have screamed with disappointment. Instead, she shook the little dish onto the ground and laid the pebble beside it. She stared at the dish — then, the half-forgotten legend of the unicorn's horn came back to her. "Chase," she croaked, water-starved. "Chase . . ." She waved one hand at the dish.

Chase nodded. Slowly, he walked up to her and slowly lowered his horn until the tip touched the small dish. For a moment, nothing happened. Then, with a pale blue shimmer, a pool of water formed at the bottom of the bowl!

Lori leaped on it with a shriek and gulped it down.

"There, now!" Dill hissed angrily. "How dare you, you little rat! That should have been for Her Royal Highness."

"It doesn't matter," Ari said softly. "She had the most need."

"We all have need," Chase said gravely. "Put the bowl back on the ground, Lori."

Sullenly, Lori set the dish back on the hot ash. Chase touched it again: The dish filled up. Ari picked the bowl up and offered it to Dill. To her relief, Dr. Bohnes's magic worked every time Chase touched his horn to the bowl, and at last, everyone had a cooling drink. Then Chase cocked his eye at the pebble with a mischievous look. "Shall I?" Without waiting for an answer, he lowered his horn. The rock transformed itself into bread! Ari divided the pieces carefully, making sure that everyone got an equal share, saving her own hunger for last.

Finally, they were all fed. They sat on the ground for a moment, silent, feeling their strength return.

"How far now?" Ari asked.

"Not far at all." Dill pointed with her slim muzzle. "Look ahead. Look ahead."

Ari raised her eyes. There it was, dark and forbidding. The two turrets on either side. The high, pointed roof in the middle.

Castle Entia. The home of the Shifter.

16

They walked right through the front gates and into the castle. They saw no one and heard nothing. The interior was dark, huge, and quiet. The floor was dark polished stone. The walls soared to unimaginable heights. Ari couldn't see the ceiling. She would not have guessed the ceiling was that high. Perhaps it was some dark magic, which made the inside seem greater than the outside.

Lincoln's claws went tick-tick on the stone floor. Chase stood like a statue, ears forward, head up.

"Where do we look?" Lori's voice echoed eerily in the huge space.

"Be *quiet*!" Dill hissed.

"I'm taking this *helmet* off," Lori said crossly. "I'm so hot, I can't stand it! And I'm thirsty again." She pulled it off her head.

Lincoln rounded on her ferociously. "If you don't shut up, I will bite you!" he snarled. "The place looks empty, but the last thing we need is to be discovered by any of those black unicorns."

"Well, you don't have to worry," Lori said confidently. "We're supposed to meet someone here."

"What?" Ari pulled her own helmet off. It was hard enough to see in the dark; it was even harder with the helmet on. "Meet who?"

"I didn't think much of this plan, you know." Lori set her helmet on the floor and ran her hands through her hair. "Gosh, I'm sweaty. Anyway, I heard that after you got into this place, it wasn't so bad. Especially since this Shifter guy isn't here."

"Who told you that?" Chase demanded sharply.

"I did." Lady Kylie glided toward them. Ari looked at her, bewildered. Where did she come from?

"You must be so tired. And so thirsty!" Lady Kylie said. She smiled smoothly. "Come and have something cold to drink. And a bit of food."

"I don't think so," Lincoln muttered. "Besides, we're full."

"Lori's right, you know. It's safe here, at least for now. *He* is gone. Away from . . ." Kylie bit her words off. She strained forward, peering into the gloom. Lady Kylie's flat black eyes glittered, elongated. The pupils narrowed into a snakelike slit. She slithered up to Ari and grabbed her chin in one cold, scaly hand. "So you are here for a reason, Princess?"

"I am on a journey," Ari said calmly. "And your master is not at home, is he, Lady Kylie?"

"Lori betrayed us!" Dill cried. "I told you she looks like that ferret!"

"You shut up!" Lori screeched furiously. "I haven't betrayed anybody. Lady Kylie said this would be a hard trip and it was. She said if we made it to the castle safely, she'd be here to help us get that stupid Scepter so I can go home! I haven't betrayed anyone!"

"You fool!" Chase roared. "Don't you know who Kylie is?!"

Lori looked uncomfortable. "She's the sister of Lord Lexan," she said. "And she's my friend."

Dill snorted. "Hah! She's a lot of things, Lori. Like the Shifter, she changes herself to suit the occasion. In Balinor, sure, she's Lord Lexan's sister. And she was the Queen's best friend. But she sold out, didn't you, Kylie? Sold out for power. She betrayed the Queen and the King. And in return, the Shifter gave her the Power of the Snake!"

Kylie laughed. A low, ugly, snakelike laugh. Her tongue flicked in and out of her mouth. It was red and forked—a serpent's tongue.

"The Power of the Snake?" Lori sounded scared.

Dill squeezed her yellow eyes open and shut.

"Nasty kind of magic, if you ask me. She can change into a snake as quick as you please. And she has all the nastiness of those reptiles, too. Sneaky, crawly, lethal things. And all so she could swank around to be Second-in-Command of the Shifter's army."

"Bite your tongue," Kylie purred. She writhed, and the dim light played across her thin lips. She smiled evilly at Chase. "This what you're after, isn't it, my pet? My Sunchaser." She held up her right hand. She was holding a short, beautifully carved staff. It glimmered briefly with a warm, rosy color. Rosewood inlaid with lapis lazuli.

The Royal Scepter.

So Atalanta had been right. They would find the Royal Scepter near one of the Shifter's greatest victories. And this victory had been to make Kylie turn traitor!

Kylie laid it with great care at her feet. Its glimmering light went out.

"Well!" Lady Kylie began to sway back and forth. Her body grew slimmer, longer. Her robes merged with her body and turned into scales. She writhed there, the snake. The Shifter's counselor.

Lori screamed.

"And I have you now, don't I? He will be so pleassssed. My massssster!" She stretched to an enormous height. Darkness swirled around her. Chase reared and trumpeted a challenge, then lowered his horn, prepared to charge. With a shriek, the snake writhed and dropped, coiling around Lori, who was so terrified she couldn't even scream. Ari reached for her knife, determined to hack away at those lethal coils.

"Don't move," Kylie hissed. She tightened her coils. Lori gasped, a faint, pitiful sound that went straight to Ari's heart. She put her sword back into her weapons belt.

The bottle, Chase thought at Ari. *Princess. The Star Bottle!*

Ari remembered the Dreamspeaker's words: *"Use it only when all is dark and there seems no hope."* Ari fumbled at her belt for the Star Bottle.

Kylie laughed. "Now you will come with me! I will imprissson you until my masssster returnssss! And then, *then* we sssshallll sssseeee!"

Ari held the Star Bottle up. It flickered, dimmed in the huge hall. "Atalanta," Ari said.

"Atalanta!" Chase cried.

"Atalanta!" Dill, Lincoln, and Basil shouted until the roof rang with their calls. The Star Bottle burst into light, brighter than the moon, more glorious than the stars. The snake shrieked in agony, flinging herself away from the brilliance. The light seemed to blind only the snake.

Lori fell free, scrambled to her feet, and ran to Ari. Lincoln sprang forward and grabbed the Scepter in his jaws. Dill and Basil rushed at the snake, one on each side, jaws snapping furiously. Chase reared and struck the stone floor with a mighty clanging sound that made the walls shiver and the air shake.

The snake hissed, spat, and twisted, trying to hide her eyes. But at each frantic turn the foxes were there, needlelike teeth flashing.

"I am not your slave anymore!" Dill cried. She ducked and bit and darted in again.

"For my mate!" Basil shouted. He sprang forward and sank his teeth into the snake's tail. They drove the snake before them, like dogs herding sheep, snapping and snarling. The snake hissed, whipping her tail, fangs bared.

But the foxes were quick and clever. They drove the snake down the hall and out of sight.

When they returned, Dill's eyes were peaceful. "Well," she said. She sat down and scratched herself heartily. Ari could see the thin scar around her neck. "Well," she said again. Basil sat beside her and licked her ears.

Lincoln trotted up to Ari, the Scepter in his jaws. He crouched down carefully and dropped it at her feet.

Ari tucked the Star Bottle in her weapons belt, bent over slowly, and picked up the Scepter. It felt — right — in her hands, like something she'd been born to carry. It belonged to her. She held it carefully, feeling the warmth of the wood as if it were a living thing.

Chase came up to her. Ari stroked his nose

with one hand. Then, she grabbed his mane in her left hand, and held the Scepter in her left. She sprang up from the floor and mounted his back.

This, too, felt right. She belonged here. She held the Scepter up. There was a unicorn's head at the top, carved in wood, traced with precious blue stone. The eyes gleamed at her with something of the clear wisdom of the Old Mare of the Mountain. The rosy glow around the Scepter deepened, engulfed both Chase and Ari in a cleansing wash of light.

The unicorn head spoke in a deep yet distant voice. *"Arianna. Arianna. You shall remember now."*

And Ari remembered.

Slowly, as if a sun flooded her being with the light of dawn. Dinner with her father and mother after a day by the seashore. Her brothers, Bren and Stally, playing a complicated game of hide-and-seek in the Palace gardens.

Chase and the magic they could do together. The healing touch of Sunchaser's horn, when they worked to heal sickness in the village. The long conversations with the animals in the Forest of Ardit, and the settlement of small arguments among them. And Lincoln, there was something about Lincoln that she needed to learn. And only the Scepter could help her. The Scepter could help her with all these things. There was much more to learn from the Scepter! She and Chase had been in training with it — a training which had been interrupted by the Great Betrayal. Yes, she could use the Scepter to rule — but she would need time to learn about its powers.

"Time," the unicorn's head said. "There is no time. The Shifter's army approaches. And you must leave this place."

The Sunchaser's coat became bronze again. The ruby jewel at the base of his horn glowed in answer to the Scepter's own color.

Ari jerked herself out of the dream. She looked at Chase, his face alight, her heart singing. She flung her arm around his neck. "Well," she said into his glossy neck. "I guess this was worth it, after all."

"Milady!" Dill's tones were urgent. "I think we'd better get out of here. Now!"

"I agree," Lincoln said. "We've been lucky so far. And I want our luck to hold."

Ari tapped Chase lightly with her heels. Holding the Scepter before her, the two proceeded out of Castle Entia. Lincoln, Basil, and Dill followed. Lori ran after them, her face still pale with shock.

Princess Arianna and the Sunchaser rode into the Valley of Fear.

"I remember," Arianna said aloud, with gladness. "I remember everything." Her mother, blond and slim. Her father, the King. Her beloved nurse, Bohnes, and the Palace they lived in before the Great Betrayal.

Where Chase and Ari walked, the dirt and

gravel of the Valley of Fear turned to healthy green grass. Thorn bushes burst into bloom. They walked, the six of them back to the Pit, the Royal Scepter held like a beacon before them.

Ari rode Chase to the edge of the Pit, and scribed a circle in the air with the Scepter. Wherever its light fell, the chains and shackles fell away from the prisoners, and the air was filled with shouts of joy. The shadow unicorns fled deeper into the Pit. The prisoners ran for freedom, crying their thanks to the Royal Princess.

Tears of joy came to Ari's eyes. She had promised to free the slaves from the Pit, and she had kept that promise. Perhaps there were some good things about being Princess, after all.

"Ari!" shouted Lincoln. "There's something wrong — it's Lori!"

"What has she done now?" asked Ari.

"She's gone into the Pit."

"Oh, no. She *couldn't* have."

Ari dismounted Chase and followed Lincoln.

"This way." Lincoln paced down to the Pit. Ari clutched the Scepter — she wasn't about to let it out of her hands now, after all that trouble! — and walked with Chase to the head of the road that wound down into the bowels of the huge hole.

"She went down there." Lincoln nodded. Ari leaned over the edge. She saw a small figure with a faint gleam of blond hair. She braced herself against

Chase and leaned further. "Lori? Lori! Come back! I —"

She heard the rasp of scales on rock too late. She whirled, one hand on Chase's mane.

The snake loomed, huge, menacing, jaws open wide to bite. Ari jerked back without thinking.

She fell. She fell over the edge of the Pit, and with a shout, Chase leaped after her. She fell endlessly into the black, Scepter in her hand, its light bobbing wildly. She hit something soft, bounced, rolled, and then — for a moment — all was a confused whirl of bronze unicorn, blond hair, her own feet, and a dizzying blinding light.

She fell on her back with a thump that knocked the breath from her and made her head swim. She lay still, remembering what her nurse Bohnesy had said: "Don't get up right after a fall, Your Royal Highness. Make sure all your bones are in place."

She wiggled her right hand. Yes, that was okay. Then her left. Then her toes. She sat up carefully. Blinked. She was in a familiar meadow. It was surrounded by white three-board fencing. A herd of horses grazed nearby.

Horses? There weren't any horses in Balinor!

Ari got to her feet. Chase was next to her, a confused expression in his eyes. Lori was sitting down, her head in her hands.

Milady! Chase thought at her. *Where are we?*

"Oh, dear," Ari said. She held the Scepter tightly. "Oh, *dear!*" She looked around. "We're back, Chase! We're right back where we started! Glacier River Farm! We've crossed the Gap!" She went over to Lori and helped her to her feet. "Well, Lori," she said. "You're home! Just as the Dreamspeaker promised."

Lori looked around in a dazed way. A huge smile spread across her face. "You're right!" she said, astonished. "I'm home! Oh, thank you, Ari. Thank you! After I was so awful about Lady Kylie. The thing is . . . she promised . . . I'm . . ."

"It's okay," Ari said quickly. Lori being apologetic was almost worse than Lori whining. "Let's not talk about it anymore, okay?"

Lori dusted the seat of her leather pants. "Gosh," she said. "I don't suppose you counted on being here, too?"

"No," Ari said ruefully. "But that's what the Prophecy said, come to think of it. Three shall not return to Balinor. At least, not right now." She looked at the Scepter. "Although I'm pretty sure I remember now how to get us back. I'll figure it out if I have enough time."

Lori nodded. "Well, that's good," she said. "But if you're going to be at Glacier River Farm for a bit, you're going to have to do something about his horn."

They stood and looked at Chase. He stood tall and proud among the horses, his horn black and gorgeous and very, very obvious.

"I mean," Lori said, "people will wonder!"

"So they will." Ari threw her arms around her unicorn. "But I'll figure that out, too. First, we're going to say hello to Ann and Frank. And then, Chase, it's back home to Balinor!"